# THE LAUGHING HANGMAN

ALSO BY EDWARD MARSTON

In the Nicholas Bracewell series:

*The Roaring Boy*
*The Silent Woman*
*The Mad Courtesan*
*The Nine Giants*
*The Trip to Jerusalem*
*The Merry Devils*
*The Queen's Head*

In the Domesday Books series:

*The Dragons of Archenfield*
*The Ravens of Blackwater*
*The Wolves of Savernake*

# *The* Laughing Hangman

[A NOVEL]

*Edward Marston*

ST. MARTIN'S PRESS NEW YORK

Library of Congress Cataloging-in-Publication Data

Marston, Edward.
The laughing hangman : a novel / by Edward Marston.
p. cm.
ISBN 0-312-14305-2
1. Bracewell, Nicholas (Fictitious character)—Fiction.
I. Title.
PR6063.A695L38 1996
823'.914—dc20 96-6990
CIP

First Edition: August 1996

10 9 8 7 6 5 4 3 2 1

*To*
*VISCOUNT KRICHEVSKY*
*Laird of Dobbs Ferry*
*Lone survivor of the Stuart dynasty*

Plays will never be suppressed, while her Majesty's unfledged minions flaunt it in silks and satins. . . . Even in her Majesty's chapel do these pretty upstart youths profane the Lord's day by the lascivious writhing of their tender limbs and gorgeous decking of their apparel, in feigning bawdy fables gathered from the idolatrous heathen poets.

—ANONYMOUS, *The Children of the Chapel Stripped and Whipped* (1569)

# [ CHAPTER ONE ]

He missed her. Nicholas Bracewell felt a pang of regret so sharp and so unexpected that it made him catch his breath. He looked down involuntarily to see if the point of a knife had pricked his chest and drawn blood. Nicholas had not even been thinking about Anne Hendrik, still less talking about her, yet she was suddenly filling his mind, standing before his eyes and stroking his cheek with wistful fingers. It was at once reassuring and tantalising.

For several minutes, Nicholas was so enveloped by a flurry of wonderful memories that he paid no heed to the argument that was raging in front of him. Anne Hendrik whispered softly in his ear and kept out the violent discord. The book holder did not even hear the fist that banged the table like the blast of a cannon.

'I'll not be thwarted!' roared Lawrence Firethorn.

'Then leave off this madness!' argued Barnaby Gill.

'I put the good of the company first and foremost.'

'You have never done so before, Lawrence.'

'I have *always* done so! It is you who believe that Westfield's

Men exists for the greater glory of one paltry individual.'

'And who might that be?'

'Look in any mirror, Barnaby. He will leer back at you.'

'That is a gross slander!'

'I speak but the truth.'

'Calumny!' said Gill, rising to his feet and inflating his chest to its full extent. 'But for me, there would *be* no company. I have oftentimes saved it from extinction and I am trying to do so again.'

'You are obstructing the path to triumph.'

'Yes, Lawrence. Triumph for our rivals. If we follow your lunatic advice, we hand the advantage to them.'

'My plan puts Westfield's Men in the seat of power.'

'It is a cucking-stool and we shall be drowned by ridicule if we place our buttocks anywhere near it.'

Firethorn gave a mock bow. 'I defer to your superior knowledge on the subject of buttocks.'

Barnaby Gill turned purple and slapped his thigh with a petulant palm. Turning on his heel, he tried to make a dramatic exit, but Edmund Hoode jumped up to restrain him.

'Hold, Barnaby. This is no way to settle a quarrel.'

'I'll not stay to be insulted.'

'Then scurry off,' said Firethorn, 'for the very sight of you calls up a hundred insults. We'll make the decision without you and inform you in due course.'

Gill stamped a foot. 'I demand to be part of that decision.'

'Take your seat once more and you will be,' soothed Hoode. 'Your voice is needed at this table, Barnaby, and you shall be heard. Is that not so, Nick?'

A nudge brought Nicholas out of his reverie and he adjusted quickly to the familiar scene. Lawrence Firethorn and Barnaby Gill were at each other's throats again. Two men who could combine brilliantly to lift the performance of any play were sworn enemies the moment that they quit the stage. Their mutual antagonism went deeper than mere professional jealousy.

Firethorn, the company's actor-manager, felt that his remarkable talents were not properly acknowledged by his colleague; Gill, the resident clown with Westfield's Men, saw himself as the true leader of the troupe and resented any reminder that he occupied second place behind Firethorn.

Nicholas Bracewell helped to calm the quivering Gill and the latter eventually agreed to resume his seat. The four men were in the parlour of Firethorn's house in Old Street. Everyone in Shoreditch was aware of the fact because it intruded stridently on their eardrums and they were not sure if they found Firethorn's deep bellow or Gill's high-pitched wail the more tiresome. Regular acrimony in the parlour had one domestic compensation. It dusted the room so thoroughly that the servant did not need to brush the cobwebs from the beams or sweep the beetles out of corners. Every creature that could walk, crawl or fly vacated the premises at once. Even the mice in the thatch fled to a quieter refuge.

'I thought it might be a moment for more refreshment.'

Margery Firethorn came sailing into the room with a wooden tray in her hands and a benign smile on her handsome face. Her entry was perfectly timed to break the tension and allow the combatants to cool off. As she set a plate of warm cakes and a fresh pitcher of wine in front of them, she caught Nicholas's eye and gave him an affectionate wink. He replied with a quiet grin of thanks. Not for the first time, a woman who could rant and rail as loud as her husband on occasion had imposed a welcome stillness with a show of gentle hospitality.

While Gill reached for the wine, Firethorn grabbed a cake to pop into his mouth. He munched it happily and the crumbs found a temporary lodging in his black beard.

'Thank you, my dove,' he cooed.

'We are most grateful,' added Edmund Hoode, replenishing his own cup and taking a deep sip. 'Nectar!'

'Do you have need of anything else?' she said.

'No,' grunted Gill.

'We will call if we do, my angel,' said her husband, blowing her a fond kiss.

'I'll stay within earshot, Lawrence.'

Hoode nodded ruefully. 'All of London does that!'

Margery let out a rich cackle and went back into the kitchen. Her intervention had taken the sting out of the discussion. Anger subsided and reason slowly returned. Firethorn was soon ready to draw the others into the debate.

'What is your opinion, Nick?' he asked.

'It matters not,' said Gill, testily. 'This is a question to be decided by we three sharers, not by one of the hired men. Nicholas is a competent book holder, I grant you, but he does not rank with us.'

'No,' said Hoode, coming to the defence. 'He ranks far higher. His wisdom and loyalty have rescued us from damnation more times than I can count. Lawrence seeks his counsel and so do I. Speak up, Nick.'

'Yours is the more important voice here, Edmund.'

'Mine?'

'Yes,' observed Nicholas. 'This touches you more directly than any of us. The argument thus far has simply been about a new play.'

'A masterpiece!' affirmed Firethorn.

'A monstrosity!' countered Gill.

'It is only right that players should dispute the merits of a drama,' continued Nicholas tactfully, 'but you may be more concerned with the character of the dramatist.'

Edmund Hoode winced slightly. He had been doing his best to separate the play from the playwright because the very name of Jonas Applegarth could set his teeth on edge. It was not a case of naked envy. Hood admired the other's work immensely and was the first to admit that Applegarth was the superior poet. In terms of literary talent, the latter could outshine anyone in London, but there were other aspects of Jonas Applegarth that were far less appealing. Edmund Hoode made an effort to draw a veil over them.

'*The Misfortunes of Marriage* is a fine play,' he said with unfeigned enthusiasm. 'It is comedy with a satirical edge and far exceeds anything that my wilting pen could produce. The Queen's Head will not have seen a more riotous afternoon than Applegarth's play will offer.' He swallowed hard. 'I believe that we should put personal considerations aside and stage the play. There is pure genius in *The Misfortunes of Marriage.*'

'I love the piece,' said Firethorn.

'I hate it,' said Gill, 'yet I applaud the title. The misfortunes of marriage are far too many and varied to attract me into the connubial state.'

Margery Firethorn snorted with derision in the kitchen. Her husband chuckled and Nicholas traded an amused glance with him. Edmund Hoode tried hard to convince himself that it was in his own best interests to accept the new play for performance by Westfield's Men.

'Jonas Applegarth has his vices, I know,' he said with masterly understatement, 'but they are outweighed by his virtues. We must always embrace rare talent where we find it. For my own part, I will be happy to work alongside Master Applegarth. I look to learn much from him.'

Firethorn beamed. 'Nobly spoken, Edmund!'

'Indeed,' said Gill, 'but I would urge a little less nobility and a little more caution on your behalf. You are our poet, Edmund, and your art has served us well. Do you want to be eclipsed by this freak of nature? Do you wish to have your livelihood squashed flat beneath the hideous bulk of Jonas Applegarth?'

Hoode shifted uneasily on his chair. 'I must recognise a good play when I see one.'

'That is more than Applegarth does,' retorted Gill. 'He pours scorn over everything you have written.'

'Only in his cups,' said Firethorn airily. 'What poet does not abuse his fellows when too much drink is taken?'

'Edmund Hoode does not,' noted Nicholas.

'He is far too trusting,' said Gill. 'Applegarth will tread all over him and unsettle the entire company.'

'That will not be tolerated!' said Firethorn firmly. 'You have my word on that. He works here on our terms or not at all. Nick will make him understand that.' He slipped another cake into his mouth and looked around contentedly. 'Well, Edmund and I agree that *The Misfortunes of Marriage* is a worthy addition to our repertoire.'

'I refuse to countenance the idea,' said Gill.

'Our two votes tip the scales against your one.'

'We have not heard Nick's opinion yet,' said Hoode.

'Nor need we,' muttered Gill.

'Unless it chimes with your own, Barnaby,' teased Firethorn. 'You'd elevate Nick Bracewell to sharer on the spot for that.' He turned to the book holder. 'Well? Cast your vote, Nick. Speak freely among friends.'

Hoode leant forward. 'How do you like *The Misfortunes of Marriage?*'

Nicholas sat up with a start, realising that it was the title and matter of the play which had conjured up Anne Hendrik's memory. When he had finally come to see how dearly he loved her, he proposed marriage on the confident assumption that she would accept his hand. Misfortune had struck. Anne Hendrik refused him and his emotional life had been adrift ever since.

'How do you like it?' pressed Firethorn. 'Tell us!'

'I like it well,' said Nicholas, shaking his head to evict its female ghost. 'The play will offer Westfield's Men a challenge but I am certain that we can rise to it. My only reservations concern the author.'

Firethorn flicked a dismissive hand. 'Jonas Applegarth cannot help being so ugly and ill-favoured.'

'I speak not of his appearance,' said Nicholas. 'It is his behaviour that troubles me. Quarrels, fights, drunkenness. Some companies refuse to let him near them.'

'So should we!' hissed Gill.

'Strict conditions need to be laid down at the outset. That is my advice. If he joins Westfield's Men, let Master Applegarth know that he must abide by our rules. We want no upheaval in the company.' Nicholas gave a shrug. 'In short, present the play for its sheer delight but keep a tight rein on the playwright.'

Barnaby Gill blustered but all to no avail. The die had been cast. *The Misfortunes of Marriage* would receive its first performance the following week. It would be left to Nicholas Bracewell to break the news to Jonas Applegarth and to make him aware of his contractual obligations. Edmund Hoode was sad and pensive. Honesty compelled him to praise the play but he sensed that he would suffer humiliation as a result. When Gill stalked out, therefore, Hoode also took his leave. Both men had grave misgivings, albeit of different kinds.

Lawrence Firethorn watched them through the window before turning to clap the book holder on the shoulder.

'Nick, dear heart!' he predicted. 'We have made one of the most momentous decisions in the history of Westfield's Men. I dote on Edmund and on his plays, but Jonas Applegarth puts his work in the shade. My only complaint is that *The Misfortunes of Marriage* will spring to life in the mean surroundings of the innyard at the Queen's Head under the gaze of that death's-head of a landlord. It calls for a truer playhouse. It deserves to be staged at The Curtain or at The Theatre.'

'The Rose would bc a fitter place,' said Nicholas.

As the words came out of his mouth, Anne Hendrik stepped back into his thoughts. The Rose was a recently built theatre in Bankside. When the book holder lodged with Anne, sharing her life and basking in her love, he had been within easy walking distance of the playhouse. He would always associate The Rose with the happier times he spent on the south bank of the Thames.

Firethorn saw the faraway look on his friend's face. He knew the book holder well enough to guess at its meaning.

'Still brooding on her, Nick?'

'I must away. There is much work to do.'

'Go to her, man. Plead your case.'

'That is all past,' said Nicholas briskly. 'Pray excuse me. I must seek out Jonas Applegarth. He will be eager to know the fate of his play and I must explain clearly the conditions on which we accept it.'

Firethorn caught his arm. 'How long has it been?'

There was a brief pause. The pang of remorse was even sharper this time, the sense of loss more extreme.

'A year,' said Nicholas, as the truth dawned on him. 'A year to the day.'

He at last understood why he was missing Anne Hendrik so much. It was the first anniversary of their parting.

Jonas Applegarth lay back in the oak settle and rocked with mirth. Delighted that his play had been accepted by Westfield's Men, he was celebrating in the taproom of the Queen's Head with some of his new fellows. Applegarth was barely thirty but his vast girth, his thinning hair, his grey beard and his pock-marked skin added a decade and more. Whenever he moved, the hooks on his doublet threatened to snap and his huge thighs seemed on the point of bursting the banks of his breeches and flooding the settle.

The colossal body was matched by a colossal appetite and a seemingly insatiable thirst. Jonas Applegarth drank tankards of beer as fast as they could be filled, but it was no solitary indulgence. Generous with his money, he invited four of his new friends to join him in his revelry and they were soon cracking merry jests together.

Owen Elias laughed loudest of all. An ebullient Welsh actor with a love of life, he discerned a soulmate in Jonas Applegarth. The dramatist had not only provided Elias with an excellent role in his play, he was showing that he could roister with the wildest of them. In the short time he'd been with the troupe, Applegarth had taken the measure of Westfield's Men.

'What think you of Barnaby Gill?' asked Elias.

'Far less than he thinks of himself,' said Applegarth as he

preened himself in an invisible mirror. 'Not a pretty boy in London is safe when Master Gill is strutting about the town in his finery. 'Tis well that he is not employed at Blackfriars or the Chapel Children would fear for their virtue every time they bent in prayer.'

Owen Elias led the crude laughter once again and two of his fellows joined in. The one exception was James Ingram, a tall, slender young man with the dashing good looks of an actor allied to the poise of courtier. As the others enlarged upon their theme, Ingram remained detached and watchful. The target of the general amusement was now fixed on the Children of Her Majesty's Chapel Royal, a theatre company of boys who performed at the reconstructed playhouse in Blackfriars. Westfield's Men competed for an audience with the Chapel Children so they had good reason to mock their rivals. James Ingram had equally good reason to stand apart from the ribaldry.

Jonas Applegarth told of his Blackfriars experience.

'He had the gall to ask me for a play.'

'Who?' said Elias.

'Cyril Fulbeck, the Master of the Chapel.' Applegarth emptied another tankard. 'He and his partner in the enterprise, Raphael Parsons, expected a full-grown poet like me to devise a drama for his dribbling pygmies. As if I'd turn punk and sell my art at so cheap a price!'

'What was its subject?'

'The stalest of all. Antony and Cleopatra.'

'Can a ten-year-old chorister with a piping voice wield power over the Roman Empire?'

'No, Owen. And think of my martial verse in the sweet mouths of those little eunuchs. I told Master Fulbeck as much. "Let me write another play for you," I suggested. "It is called *The Plague of Blackfriars* and tells of a verminous swarm of locusts, who devour the bread that belongs to their elders and betters. A wily beekeeper tricks them and every last parasite is drowned in the River Thames." When he realised that I was talking about his young charges, Cyril Fulbeck walked off in disgust and Raphael Parsons, Lord Foulmouth himself, used language that would have turned the black friars blue and set their cowls alight. In the whole history of Christianity, there cannot have been such irreligious cursing on consecrated ground. It was wondrous sport! I have not been so joyously abused by a vile tongue since my wedding night!'

Once again, James Ingram offered only a token smile.

Jonas Applegarth was in his element, carousing with his new-found companions as if they were his oldest friends and drawing from an apparently inexaustible well of anecdote and jest. Seeing him in such a benevolent mood, it was difficult to believe that he had such a reputation for violence and wild behaviour. He seemed the epitome of amiability. Words gushed out of him in a happy torrent. Arresting phrases and clever conceits bubbled on the surface of the water. He positively exuded goodwill.

It vanished in a flash. When a figure came into the taproom and signalled with his hand, Jonas Applegarth stopped in mid-flow. The massive frame stiffened, the flabby cheeks shed their smile, and the teeth began to grind audibly. But it was his eyes which underwent the greatest change. Set close together beneath the bristling eyebrows, they had sparkled with such merriment that they almost redeemed his unsightly features. They now became black coals, glowing with a hatred which ignited the whole body and turned the face itself into a grotesque mask.

He grabbed the side of the settle to haul himself upright. His companions were shocked by the transformation.

'What ails you, Jonas?' said Owen.

'Spend this for me,' rumbled Applegarth, taking coins from his purse and tossing them onto the table. 'I'll return anon to share in your pleasure.'

Leaving the others still bemused, he waddled purposefully across the room and went out with the newcomer. Owen Elias was the first to recover. Scooping up the money, he called for more beer and grinned at his fellows.

'Let's raise our tankards to Jonas Applegarth!'

'Which one?' murmured Ingram. 'There are two of them.'

The genial dramatist from the Queen's Head was now a furious avenger with murder in his heart. As he swept along Gracechurch Street with his friend at his heels, Jonas Applegarth was cursing volubly and buffeting anyone foolish enough to stand in his way. He swung into a side street, then turned off that into a narrow lane. It was late evening and shadows were striping the buildings. When he reached a small courtyard, however, there was still enough light for him to recognise the two figures who lurked in a corner.

Applegarth glared at the bigger of the two men. Hugh Naismith was a stocky individual, in his twenties, with a handsome face set now in a scowl. His hand went straight to the hilt of his sword, but his companion, a much older and thinner man, held his wrist.

'Viper!' snarled Applegarth.

'Pig-face!' retorted Naismith.

'Rascal!'

'Knave!'

'Gentlemen, gentlemen,' said the older man, coming to stand between the two of them. 'There is no call for bloodshed here. Tempers were too hot when this tryst was arranged.' He turned to Naismith. 'Make but a simple apology and the matter is ended. You make shake hands again and part as friends.'

'He'll get no apology from me,' sneered Naismith.

'Nor would I hear one,' exclaimed Applegarth. 'I've come to separate this slave from his miserable existence. That is the only parting which will take place here.'

'Send for six horses!' yelled Naismith. 'You will need at least that number to drag away his fat carcass when I have cut the villainy out of it.'

'Gentlemen, gentlemen,' implored the peacemaker.

'Stand aside, old sir,' warned Applegarth, 'or I'll run you through as well. Honour must be satisfied.'

'Then let us not delay,' said Naismith.

Handing his cap to the old man, he drew his sword and took up his position. Jonas Applegarth reached for the rapier that his companion offered him and swished the blade through the air a few times. Duelling was illegal and both parties would be imprisoned if they were caught by the watch. The seconds were not there merely to ensure that the rules of fair combat were observed. They would also keep one eye out for any patrolling officers and be on hand to summon a surgeon in the event of a wounding. Jonas Applegarth and Hugh Naismith were both resolved that any wound they inflicted on their opponent would be fatal.

'I am ready for you, sir,' invited Applegarth.

Naismith smirked. 'Bid farewell to London.'

Steel touched steel in a brief greeting and the duel began. Jonas Applegarth held his ground while his opponent circled him. The seconds stood out of harm's way in the lane. Hugh Naismith sounded much more confident than he felt. Challenged to a duel during a fierce row, he had been forced to accept. Calm reflection had made him regret his decision and several cups of wine had been needed to lubricate his courage for the event itself. He still loathed Applegarth enough to want him dead but he was also aware of his adversary's strength and determination.

In theory, Applegarth's bulk made him an easy target. In practice, however, he was supremely well defended by a flashing rapier and a powerful wrist. When Naismith launched the first attack, it was parried with ease. A second assault was beaten away and a third met with such resistance that Naismith's sword arm was jarred. It was the younger and fitter man who was now breathing hard and perspiring freely. Jonas Applegarth moved in for the kill.

Swords clashed again. Thrust, parry and counter-thrust sent Naismith reeling back against a wall. Applegarth used his weight to imprison his opponent and his strength to finish the contest.

Their rapiers were now locked together below the hilt and Applegarth was forcing the blade of Naismith's sword slowly but inexorably towards the man's unguarded throat. Naismith's eyes filmed over with fear and his sweat dripped onto the weapon. Chuckling with triumph, Applegarth applied more pressure and the keen edge drew its first trickle of blood from the white neck.

Panic gave Naismith a fresh burst of energy and he contrived to push his adversary away, but he gained only momentary relief. Applegarth slashed the man's wrist and made him drop his sword with a howl of anguish. A second thrust opened up a wound in Naismith's other arm and sent him down on one knee in agony. Applegarth stepped back and drew back his arm for a final thrust, but the old man flung himself in front of his wounded friend.

'Hold there, sir!' he begged. 'You have won the day. Honour is satisfied and needs no more blood to assuage its thirst. Hugh kneels before you as a penitent. Show mercy!'

Applegarth was about to brush the old man aside when the other second saw someone coming along the lane.

'Officers of the watch!' he called.

The duel was over. Sighing with relief, the old man bent over his stricken friend. Jonas Applegarth was not yet done with Hugh Naismith. Kicking him to the ground, he used the toe of his shoe to flick offal into the man's face. He stood astride the body and hovered menacingly over it.

'Thus perish all actors who mangle my plays!' he said.

Then he fled nimbly into the shadows with his friend.

# [ CHAPTER TWO ]

Thames Street was his seventh home since leaving Bankside and he knew that he would not stay there long. Anne Hendrik's house had provided a secure mooring for Nicholas Bracewell in every way. Deprived of that, he drifted aimlessly through a succession of lodgings, never settling, never feeling at ease, never using the respective dwellings as anything more than a place to sleep. Loneliness kept him on the move.

Nicholas lived in a room at the top of a house on the corner of Thames Street and Cordwainer Street. Through its tiny window, he could watch the fishing smacks taking their catch into Queenhithe and larger vessels bringing foreign wines to the Vintry. Across the dark back of the river, he got a glimpse of Bankside with its tenements jostling each other for room around a haphazard collection of churches, brothels, taverns and ordinaries. The Rose Theatre blossomed above the smaller buildings surrounding it.

He woke early that morning, as every morning, to the happy clamour of tradespeople below and the plaintive cries of the gulls wheeling hopefully above the wharves. After washing and dressing, Nicholas made his way out into Thames Street and paused to let its pungency strike his nostrils. The smell of fish dominated but the stink of the nearby breweries was also carried on the wind. A dozen other strong odours merged into the distinctive aroma of the riverside.

After throwing a nostalgic glance at Bankside, Nicholas headed east towards the subtler fragrances of the fruit market. He did not get very far.

'Good morrow, Master Bracewell.'

'And to you, sir.'

'Are you bound for that den of iniquity?'

'If you mean the Queen's Head,' said Nicholas with a smile, 'then I fear that I am. It is not the ideal arena for our work but it is all that we may call our own.'

Caleb Hay put his head to one side and studied Nicholas carefully. The old man was short, neat and compact, and he carried his sixty years with surprising lightness. His sober apparel and intelligent face suggested a scholar while the ready grin and the glint in his eye hinted at a more worldly existence. Caleb Hay was one of Nicholas's neighbours and they had struck up a casual friendship. On the former's side, it consisted largely of jovial teasing.

'What made you do it?' said Hay.

'Do what?'

'Sell your soul to such a thankless profession.'

Nicholas shrugged. 'I like the theatre.'

'But how can such a patently good man work at such a manifestly bad trade?' The grin lit up his features. 'The theatre is the haunt of all the sweepings of the city. For every gallant in the gallery, there are three or four trulls and pickpockets and arrant knaves breathing garlic all over your innyard. You play to plebeians, Master Bracewell.'

'Everyone who can buy entrance is welcome.'

'That is where the boys lord it over you,' said Hay. 'The Chapel Children and the Children of St Paul's charge higher prices at their indoor playhouses and keep out the commonalty. Sweeter breaths are met at Blackfriars. And finer plays may be set before a more discerning audience.'

'You'll not find a better comedy than the one that we next stage, Master Hay,' said Nicholas proudly. 'Its author is a scholar of repute with a wit to match any in the city. *The Misfortunes of Marriage* is a feast for groundlings and great minds alike. As for the children's companies,' he added with an indulgent smile, 'there is room for them as well as us. We serve the same Muse.'

Caleb Hay chuckled and patted him affectionately on the shoulder. He was carrying a leather satchel under his arm and Nicholas could see the scrolls of parchment poking out of it. Hay was a retired scrivener, who was devoting every waking hour to the writing of a history of London. Having been born and bred in the city, he knew it intimately and had witnessed extraordinary changes in the course of his long life. Those changes would all be listed scrupulously in his book, but research had first to be done into the earlier times of the capital, and Caleb trotted zealously about his task from dawn till dusk.

Nicholas was intrigued by the old man's obsessive interest in his native city. Caleb Hay was engaged in a labour of love that kept him glowing with contentment. It was impossible not to envy such a man.

'How does your book progress?' Nicholas asked.

'It grows, it grows. Slowly, perhaps, but we antiquarians may not rush. There is so much to sift and to weigh.'

'Then I will not keep you away from your studies.'

'Nor I you from your sinful occupation.'

'You do not fool me, Master Hay,' said Nicholas with a pleasant smile. 'Though you denigrate the theatre, I'll warrant that you have more than once rubbed shoulders with the lower sort in order to cheer a play in an innyard.'

'I do not deny it,' admitted the other, 'but I did not venture there in search of pleasure. I forced myself to go in the spirit of inquiry. To know this city well enough to write about it, one must visit its most noisome quarters. How can a man describe a cesspool unless he has wallowed in it?'

They shared a laugh and exchanged farewells. Nicholas was about to move off when Caleb Hay plucked at his sleeve.

'Your author is a noted scholar, you say?'

'He can speak Greek and Latin like a schoolmaster.'

'What is his name?'

'Jonas Applegarth.'

Hay's cherubic face darkened. He walked abruptly away.

No, no, no!' bellowed Jonas Applegarth. 'Speak the speech as it is set down, you dolt, and not as you half-remember it. If you cannot learn my lines, do not pile insult on incompetence by inventing your own.'

Barnaby Gill spluttered with fury and waved his arms like a windmill out of control.

'I'll not be talked to like this!'

'Then play the part as it is written.'

'My art enhances any role that I undertake.'

'You are certainly proving a vile undertaker here, sir,' said Applegarth with heavy sarcasm. 'You have killed the character that I created and buried him in a wooden casket. Exhume him straight or I'll step up on that stage and aid the resurrection with my dagger.'

Barnaby Gill was so outraged by the criticism of his performance and so mortified by the threat of violence that he was struck dumb. His arms were now revolving with such speed that they seemed about to part company with his body.

'And do not saw the air so!' shouted Applegarth. 'If you wave your arms thus during my play, I'll tie them to your sides with rope and weight you down with an anchor. Gestures must match the verse, not slap it to death!'

Gill had heard enough. Jumping in the air like a startled rabbit, he bolted into the room which was used as a tiring-house.

Torn between amusement and horror, the rest of the company either burst out laughing or slunk away from Jonas Applegarth in fear. Edmund Hoode did both. James Ingram did neither but simply watched Applegarth with a quiet disgust. The dramatist himself continued to berate the absent Gill in the most obscene language.

Nicholas Bracewell and Lawrence Firethorn came running to see what had caused the commotion. When trouble erupted in the yard of the Queen's Head, they had been having one of their regular quarrels with its erratic landlord, Alexander Marwood. A minor irritation was postponed as they raced to confront a major problem.

Nicholas read the situation at a glance. A predictable skirmish between player and playwright had occurred. He blamed himself for not being on hand to stop it and took instant steps to make sure that the skirmish did not turn into a battle, a certain result if Firethorn were drawn into it. Nicholas persuaded the actor-manager to go after Barnaby Gill and mollify him, then he announced a break in the rehearsal and cleared the yard of all but Edmund Hoode and Jonas Applegarth.

Hoode was still swinging to and fro between amusement and apprehension but he was able to give Nicholas a swift account of what had transpired. *The Misfortunes of Marriage* had claimed its first casualty. Unless firm action were taken, there would be many more. Nicholas let his friend join the others before crossing over to the playwright. Jonas Applegarth was sitting in the middle of the yard on an upturned barrel, chortling to himself.

'How now, Nick!' he greeted. 'You missed good sport!'

'Baiting Master Gill is not my idea of pleasure.'

'He asked for it!'

'But has it advantaged your play?'

'He will not be so rash as to forget my lines again. Players are all alike, Nick. Unless you hammer your wishes into their skulls, they will go their own sweet ways and destroy your work.'

'That has not been my experience,' said Nicholas, 'and it is not the way that Westfield's Men conduct their business. Master Gill is a most highly respected member of the company, and his contract as a sharer guarantees him an important role in everything we present.'

'He *has* an important role,' argued Applegarth. 'It is because of his significance in the piece that I taxed him about his shortcomings. Barnaby is one of the foundations of *The Misfortunes of Marriage.* If he falters, the whole edifice will come tumbling down.'

'Understand one thing, Jonas,' said Nicholas with polite reproach. 'Without Master Gill, there will *be* no edifice. Drive him away with your bullying and abuse and the whole enterprise crumbles. Your play will not reach the stage.'

Applegarth bristled and rose from his barrel. 'But you are contracted to present it.'

'Only if certain conditions are met, pertaining to your behaviour. That was made abundantly clear to you at the outset. I explained the terms myself.'

'My play has been advertised for performance tomorrow.'

'*The Misfortunes of Marriage* would not be the first piece to be substituted at the eleventh hour. We have been on tour many times, Jonas, and are used to plucking a play from our repertoire at a moment's notice.'

'Cancel my masterpiece! It's a betrayal.'

'The play will have been betrayed by its author.'

'All I did was to box his ears with my tongue.'

'Then you will have to use that tongue to lick those ears better, Jonas, because Master Gill will not stir in the service of your play until you have apologised.'

'I'd sooner eat my night-soil!'

'I'll convey that message to Master Firethorn.'

Nicholas turned away and headed for the tiring-house. Mastering his anger, Applegarth lumbered after him.

'Wait, Nick! Be not so hasty!'

'I must say the same to you,' said Nicholas, stopping to face him again. 'Hasty words from your mouth are the culprits here. Hasty jibes and hasty threats have put your play in jeopardy.'

'It *must* be staged!'

'Not if you grow quarrelsome.'

'I put my life's blood into that play.'

'Master Gill makes an equal commitment in his acting.'

Jonas Applegarth bit back the stinging retort he was about to make and stared deep into the book holder's eyes to see if he was bluffing. Nicholas met his gaze unwaveringly and the playwright was forced to reconsider his actions. His companion was making no idle threat. *The Misfortunes of Marriage* really did have an axe poised above its neck.

The playwright sounded a note of appeasement.

'Perhaps I was a little overbearing,' he conceded.

'That is patent.'

'It is my way, I fear.'

'Not when you work with Westfield's Men.'

'Barnaby Gill annoys me so!'

'You are not his favourite human being either, Jonas.'

'And must I kneel in supplication to him?'

'A sincere apology is the best balm for his wounds.'

'What about the scars he inflicts on my play?'

'They will not be there during the performance itself,' said Nicholas confidently. 'Master Gill has never let us down in front of an audience. Spectators bring the best out of him and he has a loyal following.'

Applegarth had to hold back another expletive. Heaving a sigh, he spread his arms wide and opened his palms.

'*The Misfortunes of Marriage* is my best play, Nick.'

'Its brilliance has been remarked upon by all of us.'

'Any company should be proud to present it.'

'So shall we be, Jonas, if you but stand aside and let us rehearse without interruption.'

'It was agreed. I have the right to offer advice.'

'Not in the form of abuse.'

'It is my play, Nick. I wish it to be played aright.'

'Then form a company on your own and act all the parts yourself,' said the book holder, 'for that is the only way you'll be satisfied. Give your play to us and you must allow for compromise. Theatre always falls short of perfection. Westfield's Men can simply offer to do their best for you.'

'Under my direction.'

'With your help,' corrected Nicholas.

There was a long pause as Applegarth reflected on the situation. It was not a new one. He had fallen out with other theatre companies in more spectacular ways and had found himself spurned as a result. Westfield's Men were a last resort. If they did not stage *The Misfortunes of Marriage,* it might never be seen by an audience. Applegarth weighed pride against practicality.

'Well,' said Nicholas finally. 'Am I to tell Master Firethorn that you are now ready to eat your own night-soil?'

Applegarth guffawed. 'Tell him I am ready to drink a cesspool and eat every dead dog in Houndsditch if it will put my work upon the scaffold in this yard.'

'And Master Gill?'

'Send him out to me now and I'll cover him with so many kisses that his codpiece will burst with joy.'

'A less extreme demonstration of regret will suffice,' said Nicholas with a smile. He adopted a sterner tone. 'I will not caution you again, Jonas. Unless you mend your ways and give counsel instead of curses, there is no place for you here. Do you accept that?'

Applegarth nodded. 'I give you my word.'

'Hold to it.'

'I will, Nick.'

'Wait here while I see if Master Gill is in a fit state to speak with you.' Nicholas was about to move away when he remembered something. 'Rumour has it that you fought a duel in recent days.'

'That is a downright lie.'

'With an actor from Banbury's Men.'

'I have never crossed swords with anyone.'

'His offence, it seems, was damaging a play of yours.'

'Who is spreading this untruth about me? I am the most

peaceable of men, Nick. I love nothing more than harmony.'

'It is so with us, Jonas. Bear that in mind.'

On that note of admonition, Nicholas went off to the tiring-house and left the playwright alone in the yard. Jonas Applegarth padded back to his barrel, flopped down onto it and stared at the makeshift stage in front of him. It was empty now but his quick imagination peopled it with the characters of his play and set them whirling into action. *The Misfortunes of Marriage* was an overwhelming success and he was soon luxuriating in thunderous applause from an invisible audience.

The lone spectator in the innyard of the Queen's Head did not join in the acclamation. He stayed watching from the upper gallery. One wrist was heavily bandaged and his other arm was supported in a sling.

A long and arduous rehearsal produced a legacy of sore throats, aching limbs and frayed tempers. When their work was finally over, most of the members of the company adjourned to the taproom of the Queen's Head to slake their thirst and to compare notes about an eventful day. Opinion was divided about Jonas Applegarth's verbal assault on Barnaby Gill. Some praised it, some condemned it. Others felt that it was unfortunate but beneficial because, when Gill's ruffled feathers had been smoothed by an abject apology, he gave such an impressive performance of his role that he had the playwright gleaming with approbation.

Owen Elias belonged among Applegarth's supporters. Sharing a table with Edmund Hoode and James Ingram, he confided his feelings about the incident.

'Barnaby deserved it,' he said. 'He has grown lazy at conning lines. Jonas acquainted him with that truth.'

'Truth should have a softer edge,' said Hoode, with evident sympathy for the victim. 'Why belabour Barnaby so when you could request him with kind words?'

'Jonas Applegarth does not *know* any kind words,' said Ingram. 'Threat and insult are his only weapons.'

'You do him wrong,' defended Elias. 'He speaks his mind honestly and I admire any man who does that. Especially when he does so with such wit and humour.'

'I side with James,' said Hoode. 'Wit and humour should surprise and delight as they do in *The Misfortunes of Marriage.* They should not be used as stakes to drive through the heart of a fine actor in front of his fellows. Barnaby will never forgive him.'

'Nor will I,' thought Ingram.

'Jonas is a wizard of language,' asserted Elias. 'When I see a play such as his, I can forgive him everything.'

Hoode nodded. 'It is certainly a rare piece of work.'

Ingram made no comment. Elias nudged his elbow.

'Do you not agree, James?'

The other pondered. 'It has some wonderful scenes in it, Owen,' he declared. 'And the wit you spoke of is used to savage effect. But I do not think it the work of genius that you do. It has too many defects.'

'Not many,' said Hoode, reasonably. 'A few, perhaps, and they mostly concern the construction of the piece. But I find no major faults.'

'There speaks a fellow-writer!' noted Elias. 'Praise from Edmund is praise indeed. What are your objections, James?'

'Master Applegarth is too wild and reckless in his attacks. He puts everything to the sword. Take but the Induction . . .'

He broke off as Nicholas Bracewell came into the taproom to join them. Edmund Hoode moved along the bench to make room for his friend, but the book holder found only the briefest resting place. Alexander Marwood, the cadaverous landlord, came shuffling across to them with the few remaining tufts of his hair dancing like cobwebs in the breeze. The anxious look on Marwood's face made Nicholas ready himself for bad news, but the tidings were a joy.

'A lady awaits you, Master Bracewell.'

'A lady?'

'She has been here this past hour.'

'What is her name?'

'Mistress Anne Hendrik.'

Nicholas was on his feet with excitement. 'Where is she?'

'Follow me and I'll lead you to her.'

'Let's go at once.'

'Give her our love!' called Elias, pleased at his friend's sudden happiness. 'We'll not expect you back before morning.' He winked at Hoode, then turned to Ingram. 'Now, James. What is amiss with the Induction?'

Nicholas heard none of this. The mere fact of Anne's presence in the same building made him walk on air and forget all the irritations of a tiring day. Marwood conducted him along a corridor before indicating the door of a private room. Nicholas knocked and let himself in.

Anne Hendrik was there. When he saw her standing in the middle of the room with such a welcoming smile, he wanted to take her in his arms and kiss away a year's absence. She looked enchanting. Wearing a deep blue bodice with a blue gown of a lighter hue, she was as handsome and shapely as ever. Appropriately, it was the hat which really set off her features. Anne Hendrik was the English widow of a Dutch hatmaker and her late husband had taught her the finer points of headgear. She was now wearing a shallow-brimmed, high-crowned light blue hat with a twist of darker material around the crown.

'Nicholas!' she said with evident pleasure.

'By all, it's good to see you!'

She offered a hand for him to kiss and her fond smile showed just how delighted she was to see him. Nicholas felt an upsurge of love that had been suppressed for twelve long months. Before he could find words to express it, however, she turned to introduce her companion and Nicholas realised with a shudder that they were not, in fact, alone.

'This is Ambrose Robinson,' she said.

'I have heard so much about you, Master Bracewell,' said the visitor with an obsequious smile. 'All of it was complimentary. Anne has the highest regard for you.'

Nicholas gave a polite smile and shook his hand, but there was no warmth in the greeting. He took an immediate dislike to the man, not merely because his presence had turned a reunion of lovers into a more formal meeting, but because there was a faintly proprietary tone in his voice. The way that he dwelt on the name of 'Anne,' rolling it in his mouth to savour its taste, made Nicholas cringe inwardly. He waved his visitors to seats and took a closer look at Ambrose Robinson.

Garbed like a tradesman, he was a plump man of middle height, with a rubicund face so devoid of hair that it had the sheen of a small child. His big red hands were clasped together in his lap and his shoulders hunched deferentially.

'Ambrose is a neighbour and a friend,' said Anne.

'A butcher by trade,' he explained. 'I am honoured to provide food for Anne's table. Only the freshest poultry and finest cuts of meat are saved for her.'

Nicholas lowered himself onto a stool opposite them but found no rest. The joy of seeing Anne again had been vitiated by the annoying presence of an interloper. She gave him an apologetic smile, then took a deep breath.

'We have come to ask for your help, Nick,' she began.

'It is yours to command,' he said gallantly.

'You are so kind, Master Bracewell,' said Robinson with an ingratiating grin. 'You do not even know me and yet you are ready to come to my assistance at Anne's behest.'

'*Your* assistance?'

'Let me explain,' said Anne. 'In brief, the situation is this. Ambrose has a son, barely ten years of age, as bright and gifted a child as you could wish to meet. His name is Philip. He is the apple of his father's eye, and rightly so.' She glanced at her companion, who nodded soulfully. 'Until this month, Philip was a chorister at the Church of St Mary Overy. He has a voice as clear as a bell and was chosen to take solo parts during Evensong.'

'Philip sings like an angel,' said the doting father.

'Wherein lies the problem?' asked Nicholas.

Robinson glowered. 'He has been stolen away from me!'

'Kidnapped?'

'As good as, Master Bracewell.'

'He has been gathered into the Chapel Royal,' said Anne. 'Philip's beautiful voice was his own undoing. A writ of impressment was signed and he was spirited away.'

'Is that not a cause for celebration?' said Nicholas. 'They have a notable choir at the Church of St Mary Overy, but to sing before Her Majesty is the highest honour that any chorister can attain.'

'So it would be,' agreed Robinson, 'if that is all that Philip was enjoined to do. But it is not. The Master of the Chapel has made my son a member of a theatrical troupe that stages plays at Blackfriars. The boy is young and innocent. He should not be so cruelly exposed to wantonness.'

'That will not of necessity happen, Master Robinson,' said Nicholas with slight asperity. 'Playhouses are not the symbols of sin that they are painted. We have apprentices in our own company, little above your son's age, yet they have not been corrupted. The Chapel Children are far less likely to lead your son astray. Their repertoire is chosen with care and their audience more select than ours.'

'Ambrose did not mean to offend you, Nick,' said Anne when she heard the defensive note in his voice. 'He does not want to impugn your profession in any way. This is not a complaint about Westfield's Men or about any of the other companies. It relates only to the Chapel Children.'

'And the villain in charge of them,' said Robinson.

'Cyril Fulbeck?'

'He is the Master there, but the deadly spider who has caught my son in his web is called Raphael Parsons.'

'Why so?'

'Read Philip's letters and you would understand. He makes my son's life a misery. Raphael Parsons is a monster.'

Nicholas was still mystified. 'Why bring this problem to me? I can offer you little beyond sympathy.'

'We came for advice, sir,' said Robinson.

'Then take your story to a shrewd lawyer. Get a hearing for the case in the courts. Pursue it all the way to the Star Chamber, if need be. You have good cause.'

'We hoped there might be a quicker way,' said Anne.

'Quicker?'

'And less costly,' added Robinson. 'Lawyers' fees would eat hungrily through my purse.'

'It might take months to reach the Star Chamber,' said Anne. 'We need someone who can go to the Chapel Royal and speak directly to this ogre called Raphael Parsons.'

'His father is the proper person to do that.'

'I have tried,' said Robinson angrily, 'but they will not even hear me. Besides, I could not trust myself to be in Parsons's company and not throttle the life out of him with my bare hands.' He opened his palms to show thick and powerful fingers. 'That would gladden me but deprive Philip of a father. He has already lost his mother and could not bear to see me hanged upon the gallows.'

Everything about the man unsettled Nicholas and he wanted no part in the affairs of his family, especially now that he realised Robinson was widowed and in need of a stepmother for his hapless child. But Anne Hendrik looked at him with such trust and pleading that the book holder found it hard to refuse. He shrugged his shoulders.

'I have little hope of succeeding where you failed.'

'But you'll go?' begged Robinson.

'I have heard stories about Raphael Parsons, it is true, but I do not know the man.'

'He is the Devil Incarnate!'

'Philip must be rescued from his clutches,' said Anne.

'I will pay all I can,' promised her companion.

'I want no money,' said Nicholas. 'Furnish me with more detail and I will look into it. That is all I can promise. One thing I can assure you, Master Robinson. Chapel Children are not the wayward sinners you imagine. We have a young man in the company, one James Ingram, who learned to sing, dance and act with the Chapel Children in the old Blackfriars playhouse. A more personable fellow you could not hope to encounter. I'll see what James can tell me of Raphael Parsons.'

'Let my son's letters speak their full as well,' insisted Robinson, pulling a bundle from his pocket and handing it over. 'I would like them back when you have done with them.'

'Linger a while and you shall have them anon.'

'Yes,' said Anne, rising to her feet. 'Nick will read and absorb them in no time. Wait for me outside, Ambrose, and I will join you in a moment.'

'I will,' he said, getting up. 'Thank you, sir.'

'Save your gratitude until I have earned it.'

'Listening to my tale was a kindness in itself.'

Ambrose Robinson walked heavily to the door and let himself out. Nicholas relaxed slightly and looked up at Anne. She put a hand on his shoulder and smiled.

'How are you?' he asked.

'Much as ever, Nick. And you?'

'I am kept as busy as usual here.'

'You thrive on work.' Her face puckered. 'I am sorry to burden you with this errand but it means so much to Ambrose. He is quite distracted with worry. You were the only person we could turn to, Nick.'

*'We?'*

'Ambrose has been kind to me. I owe him this favour. Do not blame me too much. Philip Robinson is suffering dreadfully, as you will see from his letters, and my heart goes out to him. But he is not the only reason I came here today.'

'What else brought you here?'

Anne bent over to kiss him softly on the lips.

'You,' she said.

Then she let herself out of the room.

# [ CHAPTER THREE ]

Omens for *The Misfortunes of Marriage* were not propitious. The day began with torrential rain. It soaked the stage, blew into the galleries and turned the yard of the Queen's Head into a quagmire. Emotional tempest soon followed. Barnaby Gill awoke with a blazing headache, announced that he was too ill to move, and refused to appear in the play which he saw as responsible for his condition. Lawrence Firethorn experienced his own marital misfortune. Incautious enough to retain a letter from a female admirer because it flattered his vanity, he opened his eyes that morning to find his wife reading the telltale missive before turning on him like a berserk she-tiger.

Then there was Jonas Applegarth. Quiescent after the stern warning from Nicholas Bracewell, he worked through the night on emendations and additions which he wanted inserted into his play, and compiled a list of notes for individual actors whose performances, he felt on mature reflection, needed radical improvement if his work were to be given any hope of success. When his wife rose from her slumber and found him still poring over the foul papers of his play, Applegarth was like a powder keg in search of an excuse to explode. The sight of the downpour threatened to ignite rather than dampen.

Nicholas Bracewell looked out from his lodging to see Thames Street being turned into a replica of the river whose name it bore. Horses churned up the mud, waggon wheels dispersed it with indiscriminate force, and sodden figures waded to and fro with all the speed that they could muster. Nicholas gave a sigh of resignation. Innyard theatre was at the mercy of the elements. In view of the religious satire which propelled *The Misfortunes of Marriage,* he was bound to wonder if the Almighty was inflicting the storm by way of a criticism of the play.

Though the performance dominated his thoughts, there was another vexation at the back of his mind. Anne Hendrik's request for help left him in a state of ambivalence. Willing to assist her in any way, he felt no such obligation towards Ambrose Robinson and still smarted at the memory of the man's unconcealed affection towards the woman whom Nicholas still loved deeply. It worried him that Anne's relationship with the Southwark butcher was so close that he felt able to entrust such a personal matter to her. Philip Robinson's letters were indeed heartbreaking in their description of the boy's ordeal, but Nicholas could not see why Anne Hendrik should be involved in his rescue, still less he himself.

Concentrating on the afternoon's performance, he braced himself for a tense morning at the Queen's Head and left his lodging. He had splashed his way no more than twenty yards along Thames Street when a small, bustling figure cannoned into him and bounced off. With his head bent forward and his cloak all but hiding him, Caleb Hay had not even seen his approaching neighbour.

'A thousand apologies, Master Bracewell!'

'The fault was as much mine,' said Nicholas.

'A deluge such as this makes the most nimble of us blind and clumsy. By the end of the day, we may need to return to our houses by boat.'

'The storm may yet blow over.'

Caleb Hay grinned. 'I admire your optimism but I do not share it. Nor can I offer you any sympathy with a clear conscience. If you serve such a filthy profession, you must expect the heavens to wash it for you out of sheer disgust.'

'We must agree to differ,' said Nicholas tolerantly.

'You are too honest a man for the world you serve.'

'It has brought me true friends and good fellowship.'

'Then I will leave you to join them so that you may all get down on your knees together and pray for a miracle. Without a couple of hours of sunshine, you will have to watch your play float off down the river.'

Adjusting his hat and pulling his cloak more tightly around him, Caleb Hay bade farewell and moved away. Nicholas detained him by touching his shoulder.

'One thing puzzles me, Master Hay.'

'What might that be?'

'The way you behaved at our last encounter.'

'Was I rude or uncivil?' said Hay with genuine concern. 'Was I full of self-affairs? Pray, do not take offence, Master Bracewell. An antiquarian lives in the past. We sometimes forget the good manners we should display in the present.'

'You were not uncivil,' said Nicholas. 'We talked quite amicably. But you departed in a fit of anger.'

Hay's face clouded. 'I remember now. Jonas Applegarth.'

'You know the man?'

'I know of him, sir.'

'Enough to put you to flight in such a way?'

'I saw a play of his once at The Curtain.'

'So you *do* sink to our level from time to time,' teased Nicholas gently. 'What was the piece?'

'A vile concoction set in Ancient Rome.'

'You did not like Master Applegarth's work?'

'I detested it.'

'Too bawdy for your taste?'

'Too bawdy, too brutal and too full of bile. Only a person with a profound hatred of mankind could have penned such a malignant play. Clever, it certainly was. Laden with wit and scholarship of a high order. But, oh so cruel and so unkind. He even made jests in Latin and mocked a beautiful language until its face was covered in ugly sores. That is Jonas Applegarth for you, Master Bracewell. I hope this rain washes his new play into the ditch where it belongs!'

The Queen's Head was a house of mourning. Drenched actors kept vigil around the slimy innyard as if it were a mass grave containing the accumulated bodies of their departed relatives. Edmund Hoode watched a piece of straw being carried on a meandering journey by a tiny rivulet and saw his own life re-enacted in miniature. Peter Digby and his musicians played a dirge. Owen Elias sang in lugubrious Welsh. Lawrence Firethorn could still hear his wife, Margery, hammering nails into the coffin of their marriage as she tore the offending letter to shreds and pronounced a death sentence on their connubial delights. Jonas Applegarth was so grief-stricken that he simply stood in the rain and let it augment the tears that were coursing down his fat cheeks.

Alexander Marwood responded with his usual gleeful misery. Moaning like a wind trapped in a hollow tree, he sought out Nicholas Bracewell and rolled his eyes in despair.

'Your play is drowned,' he said in a hoarse whisper.

'Not yet,' replied Nicholas. 'It is but mid-morning and we have some hours to go.'

'This rain will last a week.'

'I doubt that, Master Marwood.'

'You'll be driven from the stage. No plays, no people to buy my ale. Disaster! How am I to sustain such a loss?'

'The same way as we do, Master Marwood. With patience.'

'But I rely on the income from Westfield's Men.'

'We pay our rent whether we play or no.'

'It is your spectators who give me my profit.'

'And so they will again as soon as the clouds move on. At the first sign of fine weather, they'll flock back to the Queen's Head to fill our seats and your coffers.'

'Causing affrays and damaging my property.'

Alexander Marwood was impossible to please. When a performance was abandoned because of inclement weather, he groaned at the resultant loss of income, yet he complained just as much when Westfield's Men were actually bringing customers into his innyard. His relationship with the company was as joyless as that with his termagant wife. The landlord was the voice of doom in a beer-stained apron.

As Marwood oozed away into the building, James Ingram joined the book holder beneath the thatched roof that overhung the stables. A dozen small waterfalls provided a splashing descant to their conversation.

'What do you think, Nick?' asked Ingram.

'I have not given up hope yet.'

'Our playwright has. He is weeping his own rainstorm.'

'We all suffer in our different ways. But I am glad of a word alone with you, James,' said Nicholas, turning his back on the depressing scene in the innyard. 'I seek advice.'

'On what subject?'

'The Children of the Chapel Royal.'

'I'll tell you all you wish to know about them,' said Ingram affably. 'I joined them as a boy of eleven and spent four happy years there. They so imbued me with a love of theatre that I sought my livelihood in the profession.'

'And you are set to rise swiftly in it, James.'

'Your praise is kind. There is nobody whose judgement I would trust more readily.'

Nicholas liked the young actor immensely and had been instrumental in getting Ingram taken on as a hired man. The latter's talent marked him out at once as a player of high calibre and he was now given more or less regular employment by the company. It was generally accepted that he would, in time, be invited to become a sharer with Westfield's Men and thus have a modicum of security in a wholly insecure trade.

'You must have many fond memories,' said Nicholas.

'I do, Nick. It was hard work, but the joy of performance is like no other. Whether you are thirteen or thirty, it sets fire to your blood. I am forever indebted to the Chapel Children and will never speak harshly of their work.' He flung a hostile glance at Jonas Applegarth. 'Unlike some.'

'Was Cyril Fulbeck the Master in your time?'

'Not at first. He was Master of the Children of the Chapel at Windsor. It was only in my last year that he took charge of the main choir here in London.'

'What manner of man is he?'

'A good and honest fellow. He began as chaplain at Windsor and rose to be choirmaster. He was also a noted composer and later wrote songs for our plays. I cannot speak too warmly of him, Nick. Why do you ask?'

'I have a friend whose son has been impressed by the Chapel Royal. Like you, he is being trained to act in the theatre. The boy does not follow in your footsteps, alas. Where you were happy, he is sorely oppressed and begs his father to release him in every letter he sends home.'

Ingram sighed. 'Things have changed at Blackfriars.'

'Has Cyril Fulbeck grown stricter with his charges?'

'No, Nick,' said the other sadly. 'He has grown older and is much hampered by sickness. It is an effort for him to fulfil his duties as choirmaster. The staging of plays has been handed over to another.'

'Raphael Parsons.'

'He is the manager of the Blackfriars company of boys.'

'A sterner taskmaster, by all account.'

'So I have heard.'

'How long has he been in charge?'

'Since the theatre was rebuilt and re-opened. Raphael Parsons took a lease on it and paid for the new construction. It is a fine indoor playhouse, Nick, much improved since my time there. Blackfriars may not hold as many people as we do here in the Queen's Head but their plays are not plagued by this damnable bad weather of ours. In snow or rain, the Chapel Children can still perform.'

'They hold the whip-hand over us there,' agreed Nicholas with envy. 'You have never met this Master Parsons, then?'

'Only once, and that briefly. It was at their first performance at the new theatre. They played *Mariana's Revels* and did so exceeding well. Raphael Parsons may be a tyrant but he is a true man of the theatre.'

'A tyrant, you say?'

'So it is voiced abroad. He is a martinet. Striving for perfection, he makes the boys work long hours and punishes them severely if they dare fall short.'

'I have seen the letters I spoke of, James. They tell of harsh words and sound beatings.'

'It was never so in Cyril Fulbeck's day.'

'Where might I find this Raphael Parsons?'

'At the Blackfriars Theatre. He rehearses daily.'

'And Master Fulbeck?'

'There, too, as like as not. Master Parsons teaches the boys to be actors, but only Cyril Fulbeck can transform then into real choristers.' Ingram's curiosity was aroused. 'If you need to go there, Nick, I would gladly bear you company.'

'I accept that offer with thanks.'

'Cyril Fulbeck is always delighted to see his old choristers. My presence may open doors that would otherwise be closed to you.'

'It is settled, James. We'll go together.'

A rousing cheer interrupted their discussion. They turned to see that a small miracle had taken place behind them. The rain had stopped. The sun was wrestling with the clouds. Westfield's Men shouted and clapped and stamped their feet with delight. Jonas Applegarth, soaked to the skin, was the happiest man in the yard. *The Misfortunes of Marriage* might after all be performed that afternoon.

The audience that streamed into the innyard a few hours later had no notion of the frenetic activity which had preceded their arrival. Under the supervision of Nicholas Bracewell, the assistant stagekeepers swept the water off the scaffold and strewed it with dry rushes so that an attenuated rehearsal could commence. While that was in progress, the mud was brushed into the corners of the yard and the benches in the galleries were rubbed with dry cloth. George Dart, the lowliest member of the company, was given the job of wringing the damp out of their flag. When it was hoisted at two o'clock to show that a play was being performed, they wanted it to unfurl proudly in the breeze.

Edmund Hoode was despatched to Barnaby Gill's lodging with the fictitious tale that the latter's role in the play had been assigned to Owen Elias instead. Professional pride was a shrewd surgeon. It effected a complete recovery in a matter of seconds and had Gill leaping from his bed of pain with a yell of indignation. Both men were soon taking their places on the stage at the Queen's Head.

Only a double blessing could have made the performance possible. Not only did the storm abate but a second wonder occurred. Jonas Applegarth behaved with impeccable restraint. Instead of cajoling the players, he watched the rehearsal in silence. Instead of unsettling the company with his fearsome presence, he was kept out of their way by Nicholas while the actors snatched refreshment before the performance.

By the time that Lord Westfield and his cronies took their places on the cushioned chairs in their privileged position in the lower gallery, all was in readiness. Bright sunshine turned the thatch into spun gold. Ladies and gallants filled the seating with a veritable riot of colour. The book holder made a final check behind the scenes, then signalled to Peter Digby. Music played and *The Misfortunes of Marriage* began.

The Induction had the spectators laughing within a matter of seconds. Four apprentices—Martin Yeo, John Tallis, Stephen Judd and Richard Honeydew—attired as choirboys, burst onto the stage in the middle of a fierce argument over who should take the leading roles in a play about Samson. They fought over Samson's club, each grabbing it in turns to strike at the others. Since all four of them were far too young and puny to convince in the Herculean role, the audience shook with mirth.

Competition for the part of Samson was matched by four-sided rejection of Delilah. None of the boys wished to don the long red wig of the betrayer, and they threw it at each other continually like a dead cat, hideous to the touch. In the space of a short scene, the stage had been filled with violent action, the audience's attention had been seized and they had been given, as they would later come to realise, the central theme of the comedy.

The interplay between marriage and religion fascinated Jonas Applegarth. It did not matter that Samson and Delilah were lovers rather than man and wife. The Biblical story was ingrained in the minds of all who watched. While the standees in the yard loved the wild antics of the boys, the sharper minds in the galleries also relished the satire on the children's theatre companies. When the scene ended with Richard Honeydew, the youngest of the apprentices, in the guise of Samson, and with lantern-jawed John Tallis, the fattest of them, as Delilah, the deficiencies of the Chapel Children and the Children of St Paul's were writ large. Championing the adult company with whom he worked, Jonas Applegarth mocked their fledgling rivals mercilessly.

*The Misfortunes of Marriage* was a glorious romp with a serious undertone. Its plot revolved around Sir Marcus Coldbed, a wealthy landowner in search of a pretty young wife to satisfy his almost uncontrollable lust. When he marries the beauteous Araminta, he discovers that she is a strict Roman Catholic with a rooted objection to physical contact and an absolute horror of sexual intercourse. To keep her lecherous husband at bay, Araminta employs her Jesuit confessor, Father Monfredo, as a holy bodyguard, allowing him to sleep in the anteroom to her bedchamber in order to protect her virtue. Shuddering with comic frustration, Sir Marcus spends his wedding night in a freezing-cold bed.

Out of sheer desperation, Sir Marcus turns for help to the weird Doctor Epididymis, a notorious mountebank who poses as astrologer, alchemist and necromancer, asking him to provide a potion that will send Father Monfredo to sleep and a powder that will arouse his wife's passion to such a point that she will demand uninhibited consummation. Potion and powder are given to the wrong victims, and it is Araminta who slumbers for twenty-four hours while her aged confessor chases every woman in sight like a mountain goat. Sir Marcus Coldbed returns to a cold bed yet again.

Lawrence Firethorn was at his supreme best as the luckless husband, bemoaning his fate with a range of comic gestures and facial expressions that kept the audience in a state of almost continual mirth.

> *Why, what is marriage if not a licence for a man to take his wife at will? To occupy her body with his largest proof of love and pluck the choicest fruit from out her orchard. To spurn a husband is to geld a stallion in his prime. Do Araminta's Popish thighs not feel the prick of high desire? Is Rome an icy region down below the waist? How, then, will this old religion last if it go*

*forth not and multiply? And how reap a harvest of Jesuitical progeny except by the downright way of creation? Man above a woman is God's law. Man inside a woman is husband's right. Give me the due reward of marriage. Cover this Coldbed with the hottest sheets. Let me wallow in my wife's concupiscence. Throw off your holy garments, Araminta. Be naked in my arms. Be my slave, my mistress, my whore. Be the everlasting bride to my eternal lust. Oh, sweetest Araminta, hear my prayer. Be* mine*!*

As the grotesque Doctor Epididymis, Barnaby Gill was equally brilliant, trotting comically around the stage after his restless client and plying him with all kinds of bogus remedies. When all else fails, the crafty doctor tells Sir Marcus that the only way he will lie beside his wife is to disguise himself as a Cardinal and tell her that it is her solemn duty to serve the Church. The trick succeeds and Araminta submits with grace. In his eagerness, Sir Marcus throws off his disguise in order to ravish her and is left clutching the pillow as she flees in panic.

Abandoning all hope of carnal delight and unable to divorce his first wife, Sir Marcus secretly marries—at the suggestion of Doctor Epididymis—a second beauty, hoping to find a bigamous outlet for his lascivious appetite. Arabella, the new Lady Coldbed, is quite unaware of the existence of his first bride, and all kinds of stratagems are needed to keep the two wives from meeting each other. What Sir Marcus does not realise until his second wedding night approaches is that Arabella is a devout Puritan and will not even share the same bedchamber with him, let alone the same bed.

Sir Marcus spends the rest of the play trying to seduce the second wife while keeping her presence hidden from the first, professing Puritan values to Arabella while promising to convert to Roman Catholicism if Araminta will relent and embrace his manhood. The similarity in their names leads to all kinds of comic confusion. When the bigamy is finally exposed, the two wives join forces to wreak a revenge on their joint husband that deprives him of all wish to lie near a woman ever again.

*The Misfortunes of Marriage* was an uproarious success and the ovation which greeted it lasted several minutes. Lawrence Firethorn led out the troupe to receive the applause. He and Barnaby Gill had been the outstanding performers, playing off each other with dazzling brilliance, but there had been excellent support from Edmund Hoode as the moon-faced Father Monfredo, from Owen Elias as the drunken hedge-priest who was bribed to perform the second marriage, from James Ingram as Arabella's true love, from Martin Yeo as Arabella herself, and from Richard Honeydew as the Roman Catholic spouse.

Jonas Applegarth was suffused with delight. Potentially the sternest critic of the performance, he was completely won over by it, and ignored the minor errors and examples of mistiming which inevitably crept in when such a complex piece was played at such breakneck speed. So thrilled was he with the outrageous Doctor Epididymis that he forgot all his earlier strictures of Barnaby Gill and resolved to make amends by showering him with acclaim. As he clapped his huge hands together, Applegarth was not just applauding his own play. He was expressing his profound gratitude to Westfield's Men. A playwright ousted by every other theatre company in London had finally found a home.

Approbation was still not universal. One spectator had detested every minute of what he saw. The spectre at the feast was in the upper gallery. Hugh Naismith had chosen a vantage point that allowed him to watch the dramatist rather than the drama. It was a painful afternoon for him. His wounded arm and bandaged wrist were constantly jostled by the excited spectators either side of him, but it was his pride which suffered the real agony. A man he loathed was being fêted, a company he despised was being celebrated.

Hugh Naismith was an actor whose occupation had been stolen from him by the sharp sword of Jonas Applegarth. Dismissed from Banbury's Men because of his injuries, he would not rest until he had avenged himself on his enemy. Applegarth had to die.

'I have never known such a day as this,' said Nicholas Bracewell.

'Nor I,' agreed James Ingram.

'This morning, we were like to have our play drowned by rain. This afternoon, it sailed on a tide of triumph. Truly, we serve a profession of extremes.'

'Yes, Nick. Feast or famine, with nothing in between.'

'Today, we had a royal banquet.'

Joyful celebrations at the Queen's Head would go on all evening, but Nicholas and Ingram had only shared in them for an hour before slipping quietly away. It was a long walk to Blackfriars from Gracechurch Street and Nicholas needed a clear head for what he anticipated as a difficult confrontation. Ingram, too, had supped only a moderate amount of ale before quitting the taproom with his friend.

'There is one small consolation,' he said.

'What is that, James?'

'Neither of them will have seen *The Misfortunes of Marriage* today. Cyril Fulbeck is too unwell and Raphael Parsons is too involved in staging his own plays to pay close attention to the work of his rivals.'

'How is that a consolation?' wondered Nicholas.

'They will not have taken offence at the Induction. It pilloried the Chapel Children in particular. Word of the attack will surely reach them soon and my own welcome at Blackfriars will no longer be so cordial. Transact your business with them swiftly, Nick, before they realise that you were party to a scurrilous assault on their work.'

'Jonas merely turned his wit upon them.'

'He traduced them most shamefully.'

'You are bound to feel defensive to the Chapel, but do not

overstate the case that Jonas Applegarth made against them. Mockery there was, certainly, but I hope it will not sour your own name at Blackfriars.'

'They'll hear about that callous Induction soon enough and find a means to answer it in kind.'

They were walking parallel with the river along Thames Street, retracing the steps that Nicholas himself took every night on his way back to his lodging. Even at that time of the evening, it was a busy thoroughfare with the sounds as noisy and the smells as pungent as ever. James Ingram was too fair-minded to let his reservations about the play obscure its finer points.

'Induction apart,' he said, 'it is a remarkable achievement. Only when I saw it performed did I realise how remarkable. How many of those who clapped its antics had any understanding of its true intent?'

'I cannot guess at that, James, but this I do know. The Master of the Revels was blind to its full import. He insisted on but few changes before he granted us a licence. Jonas Applegarth disguised his satire well on the page.'

'But not on the stage.'

'Indeed not. That is where any play is revealed in its true light. Those of discernment must have seen that Sir Marcus Coldbed was kin to our own dear Queen's father, King Henry. Sir Marcus changed the religion of his whole household in order to bed a woman, albeit with no success. Nor was King Henry happy with his change of wives.'

They discussed the deeper meaning of the play all the way along Thames Street. The spiritual upheaval of the reign of Henry VIII had been cunningly transposed into a sexual crisis in the life of a rich landowner. Nicholas was still trying to decide whether the indictment of Roman Catholicism was more searing than that of Puritanism when their destination came in sight.

Blackfriars Monastery had been built over three centuries earlier as the first London home of the Dominican Order. Occupying a prime location near the river, it swiftly grew in size, wealth and influence until it reached the point where major affairs of state were occasionally decided within its walls. The monastery was dissolved and largely demolished in 1538 but it retained its privilege of sanctuary. Its vestigial remains included the Porter's Lodge, the Old Buttery and the Upper Frater, where the monks had taken their meals. Joined together, the resultant building contained the Blackfriars Theatre.

Nicholas had been past the edifice a hundred times but never across its threshold. He was curious to take full stock of the changes to the theatre and irritated that he was there on business which might preclude that. What he was going to say on behalf of Philip Robinson he did not know, but he could at least establish more facts about the boy's alleged ill-treatment. Ingram had warned him that a writ of impressment was rarely revoked and that Nicholas might well leave empty-handed, but he would at least have discharged his promise to Anne Hendrik, and that was paramount. James Ingram took him across the Great Yard.

'Good-even, Geoffrey.'

'What? Who might you be, young sir?'

'Have you so soon forgot your favourite chorister?'

'By the Lord! 'Tis never Master Ingram.'

'The same.'

'Welcome, good sir. My old eyes delight to see you.'

The ancient porter was dozing when they rang the bell at his door. He clearly had a great affection for James Ingram, and Nicholas had to wait some minutes while the two men exchanged reminiscences.

'But what brings you here?' croaked Geoffrey.

'We have come to see Master Parsons about one of the choristers and hope to speak to the lad himself.'

'Then your journey has been wasted. Master Parsons is not here and the choir sing in a special service at the Chapel Royal.' He saw their disappointment and tried to lessen it. 'Master Fulbeck may still be here.'

Ingram was surprised. 'Not conducting the choir?'

'No, alas. Too old and too infirm, like me.'

'You seem as well as ever, Geoffrey.'

'I shall not look on seventy again, master.'

After more pleasantries between porter and former chorister, the visitors set off in search of the Master of the Chapel. They went up the stairs and into the playhouse. Nicholas paused to stare with admiration. It was an inspiring little auditorium with features that made the Queen's Head seem primitive. James Ingram was also struck by the major improvements made to the theatre he had known, but neither man was allowed to take a full inventory.

As soon as their eyes moved to the stage itself, they abandoned their appraisal of the building immediately for they were looking at the most dramatic event ever to take place upon its boards. Cyril Fulbeck was indeed there, but he was in no position to talk to either of them. Hanged by the neck, he was swaying slowly to and fro, his spindly legs some five feet above the stage.

The stunned silence was broken by the sound of eerie laughter that seemed to come from somewhere in the tiring-house. The Master of the Chapel was dead and someone was enjoying his demise to the full. Rising in volume, the laughter echoed around the theatre and took on a note of savage celebration.

# [ CHAPTER FOUR ]

Nicholas Bracewell reacted with speed. Running to the edge of the chest-high stage, he put a hand on it and vaulted up in one easy movement. His first concern was for the victim and he checked to see if the man were still alive, but Cyril Fulbeck was palpably beyond help. James Ingram joined him to look up at the swollen tongue, the contorted expression on the face and the slack body. The last remaining ounces of life had been wrung out of the old man's emaciated frame. Having served his Maker with gentleness and dedication, he had gone to meet Him in the most excruciating way.

The weird laughter stopped, a door banged in the tiring-house and a key could be heard turning in a lock. Nicholas dashed through one of the exits at the rear of the stage and found himself in the tiring-house, which was divided into three main bays. Costumes were hanging from racks and an array of properties was piled up on a low table. A quick search of the whole area revealed a door in one corner, but when Nicholas tried to open it, he found it locked. There seemed to be no other rear exit from the tiring-house.

Leaping off the stage, he sprinted back down the auditorium and descended the winding staircase to the Porter's Lodge. Geoffrey had dozed off to sleep again but he came awake as the book holder went haring past him and out into the Great Yard. Nicholas dashed up to the southern end of the building and scoured it carefully, but he could see nobody. When he tried the door in the room immediately below the tiring-house, it was also locked, as were the doors on the side of the building which gave access to the parlour and the lower hall.

Nicholas called off the search. To reach the exterior of the tiring-house, he had run well over a hundred yards, giving his quarry far too much time to escape. He returned quickly to the theatre itself via the Porter's Lodge. Curious to know what was happening, Geoffrey had staggered up the stairs and gone into the auditorium. The hideous sight halted him in his tracks. Nicholas was just in time to catch him as the porter's legs buckled beneath him. Ingram, who had been peering through one of the arched windows that looked out on Water Lane, hurried across to help him. They carried the porter to a bench and lowered him onto it, taking care to stand between him and the stage in order to block out the sight of the hanged man.

Geoffrey was wheezing heavily and trembling all over. One hand clutched at his breast. Tears flowed freely. It was minutes before he was able to utter a word.

'Not Master Fulbeck!' he groaned.

'That is how we found him,' said Ingram softly.

'He was my dear friend.'

'Mine, too, Geoffrey.'

The porter tried to rise. 'Let me cut him down!'

'Rest,' said Nicholas, easing him back onto the bench.

'Cut him down!' insisted the old man. 'I'll not leave Master Fulbeck up there like that.'

'I'll do it straight,' agreed the book holder.

While Ingram remained to soothe the porter, Nicholas clambered back up onto the stage. The rope from which the Master of the Chapel was dangling went up through a trap-door in the ceiling. Nicholas could see the elaborate winding-gear above that enabled scenic devices and even actors themselves to be lowered onto the stage during the performance of a play. A facility of which Cyril Fulbeck would have been very proud had been used to engineer his death.

Nicholas ran into the tiring-house, went up the ladder to the storey above and found the windlass that controlled the apparatus. Slowly and with reverence, he lowered the dead body to the stage, then returned swiftly in order to examine it. Cyril Fulbeck's bulbous eyes seemed to be on the point of popping out of their sockets. His skin was a ghastly white, his neck encircled by an ugly red weal. But it was the trickle of blood on his shoulder which interested Nicholas. When he rolled the corpse gently onto its side, he saw an open wound in the man's scalp.

As he lay the man on his back again, Nicholas observed that the hem of his cassock was torn, that his black stockings were badly wrinkled and that one of his shoes had come off. He released the noose and lifted the rope clear of its victim. Slipping back into the tiring-house, he chose a large cloak from among the costumes and used it to cover the entire body.

'Let me see him!' sobbed Geoffrey. 'Let me see him!'

'Stay here, old friend,' advised Ingram, putting a hand on his shoulder. 'You have seen enough.'

'He was driven to it, Master Ingram.'

'Driven?'

'To take his own life. 'Tis shameful!'

'Suicide?' asked Nicholas, joining them again. 'Who or what might have driven him to that?'

'It is not my place to say, sir,' said Geoffrey, 'but this I can tell you. Master Fulbeck was very unhappy. It broke his heart, some of the things that went on here. He told me once that his spirits were so low that he was even thinking of putting an end to his misery.' He pointed to the prostrate figure on the stage. 'And now he has!'

'Calm down, calm down!' said Ingram, patting him on the back. 'Master Fulbeck may not have died by his own hand.'

'He did not,' confirmed Nicholas.

The porter flinched from this new intelligence.

'Murdered!' he gasped. 'Never! Who would lay a finger on Master Fulbeck? He was the gentlest soul alive.'

Nicholas sighed. 'Gentle but weak. Unable to defend himself against attack. Who else has been in the building today?'

'None but Master Parsons and the choristers. The boys all left this afternoon.'

'And Raphael Parsons?' said Nicholas.

'He stayed for a while with Master Fulbeck, then left.'

'You saw him go?'

'Not with my own eyes. He left by the other exit.'

'Through the door in the tiring-house?'

'He always comes and goes that way.'

'How, then, can you be certain that he quit the building? That door is a long way from the Porter's Lodge.'

'I spoke with Master Fulbeck not an hour since,' explained Geoffrey. 'He came to the Lodge to draw some water for refreshment. 'Twas he told me that Master Parsons had gone. I think that words had passed between them again. Master Fulbeck was very upset.'

'Did he say why?' probed Nicholas.

'No, sir. Nor was it my place to ask.'

'Did anyone else visit the theatre this evening?'

'Not a soul.'

'Is there no chance that somebody may have come here and escaped your notice?'

The porter was affronted. 'Nobody came, sir. I can vouch for that. Old I may be, but blind and deaf I am not. No man alive could sneak past Geoffrey Bless. Even when my eyes close in sleep, my ears stay wide open. Nobody passed me.'

'But they might have entered by another means.'

'Not into the theatre, sir. The main entrance is up the winding staircase. The only other way to reach the stage is by the back stairs and the back door is kept locked.'

'Who has a key to that door?'

'Only three of us, sir. Myself, Master Parsons and Master Fulbeck. We are very careful to keep the building locked and guarded at all times. Thieves would else come in.'

'Or murderers,' thought Nicholas. 'I saw no keys upon Master Fulbeck. Where did he carry them?'

'Always at his belt.'

'Habitually?'

'He was never without them.'

'The keys are not at his belt now.'

'Then they have been stolen!' cried Geoffrey.

'And used to make an escape through the back door,' said Ingram, trying to think it through. 'That would explain how someone got out, but how did he get into the theatre in the first place?'

'Perhaps he was hiding in here all along,' suggested Nicholas, scanning the galleries. 'There are places where a patient assassin might lie in wait. The rooms above the stage itself would be an ideal refuge.'

'Nobody was here!' insisted the old man, defending himself against what he saw as a slur on his competence. 'I walk around the whole building first thing in the morning and I do the same at night when I secure it. A mouse could not sneak in without my knowing it.'

Indignation had helped to rally the porter and he had stopped wheezing. He was soon well enough to get up and walk. After a few last questions, Nicholas sent him off to fetch constables in order that he could have a word alone with James Ingram.

They knelt by the body in the middle of the stage. Nicholas drew back the cloak to reveal the staring eyes. Ingram blenched and lowered his own lids in a moment of silent prayer. Nicholas then indicated the bloodstains.

'He has a wound on the back of his head. I believe he was struck from behind by his assailant so that he was unconscious when the rope was placed around his neck. He may only have revived when it was too late.'

'Could he not have called out for help?'

'To whom?' said Nicholas. 'The porter was too far away and there was nobody else in the building. The murderer knew that. In case of interruption, he killed his prey sooner than the rope alone could have done.'

'How do you mean?'

'He grabbed Master Fulbeck by the legs and swung on him with his full weight.' He lifted the other end of the cloak. 'You see the tear in his cassock and the wrinkles in his stockings? A buckle snapped and one shoe was pulled off.'

Ingram was aghast. 'He helped to throttle him?'

'No question. It might otherwise have been a lingering death. Our only comfort is that it speeded up a dreadful execution and shortened the agony.'

'Who could *do* such a thing to sweet Master Fulbeck?'

'Someone who did not think him quite so sweet, James. I mean to track the villain down, however long it takes me. This is heinous work and the killer must answer for it.'

'How will you find him, Nick? Where will you start to look? You have no clues to guide you. The murderer vanished into thin air. I caught no glimpse of him when I ran to the window.' He shrugged his shoulders in despair. 'It is hopeless. You have no notion whom you seek.'

'Yes, I do. A Laughing Hangman.'

Anne Hendrik was not expecting any visitors to her Bankside house that evening, and she was consequently surprised when there was a knock on the front door. Her servant answered it and the sound of Nicholas Bracewell's voice filtered into the parlour. Putting her embroidery aside, Anne rose to greet him with spontaneous pleasure.

'Nick!'

'I am sorry to disturb you so late.'

'You are more than welcome.'

'Thank you, Anne.'

She offered both hands and he squeezed them gently. That moment alone redeemed in his mind an otherwise grim evening. For the first time in a year, he was back in the house he had shared with her, and it was both exciting and unnerving. Thrilled to be within those walls again, he was painfully aware of the parting that had taken place between the two of them in that same parlour. Nostalgia touched them both deeply and bathed their mutual wounds.

The silence and the mood were shattered by an urgent banging on the door. The servant opened it to admit an eager Ambrose Robinson. Blundering straight into the parlour, he grabbed Nicholas by the arm.

'Have you brought news of Philip?'

'Master Ambrose—'

'I saw you as you walked past my shop,' explained the butcher. 'Even in the shadows, I could not mistake you. Those broad shoulders and that long stride could belong only to our Nicholas Bracewell. Have you been to Blackfriars?'

'Yes.'

'I knew it! What transpired?'

'If you will calm down, I will tell you.'

'Did you see Philip? Have they agreed to release him?'

'Stop badgering him, Ambrose,' said Anne. 'Take a seat and let Nick explain in his own time.'

Robinson accepted the rebuke with his ingratiating smile and moved to a stool. Anne resumed her own seat and Nicholas remained standing to pass on his tidings. The note of oily familiarity in 'our Nicholas Bracewell' still grated on his ear. After one short meeting, Robinson was presuming a bond of friendship that would never exist between them. The book holder was brief.

'I went to Blackfriars this evening in the hope of speaking with Cyril Fulbeck, but that is no longer possible. Master Fulbeck is dead.'

'Dead?' repeated Anne. 'Was his illness that severe?'

'He was murdered.'

'God in Heaven!'

She was utterly shocked, but Ambrose Robinson took an almost perverse delight in the news. As Nicholas gave the two of them full details of what had happened, the butcher came close to smirking. Anne Hendrik offered wholehearted sympathy to the victim, but her neighbour saw it only as a form of crude justice.

'Fulbeck deserved it,' he grunted.

'Ambrose!' exclaimed Anne in reproach.

'No man deserves such an end,' said Nicholas.

'He stole Philip away from me.'

'Cyril Fulbeck's death may make it far more difficult to gain your son's release. By common report, he was a gentle and well-loved Master of the Chapel. His assistant will now take over his duties, but the theatre will be entirely in the hands of Raphael Parsons. *He* is the one from whom we must wrest your son, and he will be far less amenable than the man whose murder brings you such cruel pleasure. Your joyful response is both premature and in poor taste.'

Robinson was far less abashed by Nicholas's strictures than by the glances of disapproval from Anne Hendrik. For her sake, he mumbled an apology, but his eye still had some truculence in it when it met the book holder's. Every time the name of Cyril Fulbeck was mentioned, the butcher sat there in quiet exaltation.

'What will happen next?' asked Anne.

'The law will take its course,' said Nicholas, 'though not with any great speed, I fear. Constables were summoned to the scene and they made examination of the corpse. James Ingram and I helped all we could, then gave sworn statements to the magistrate. The search for the killer has started.'

'I hope and pray that they catch him,' said Anne.

'We will,' vowed Nicholas.

'Are there sufficient clues that point to a murderer?'

'Not as yet, but they will emerge.'

'Poor man!' sighed Anne. 'Did he have a family?'

'Only the choir. All twenty of them will mourn him. Eight vicars choral and twelve choirboys.'

'Philip will not shed a tear,' promised Robinson.

'He may have more compassion than his father.'

'And more tact, Ambrose,' chided Anne. 'Show a proper respect for the deceased. Your attitude is unseemly.'

'Then you are right to tax me with it,' said the butcher with a surge of regret. 'I do not mean to upset you in any way, Anne, but you know my situation. If someone takes your son away, it is difficult to feel anything but hostility towards him. That is only natural but it is also unworthy, as you point out. I accept your correction. Forgive me.'

'It is Nick's forgiveness you should seek, Ambrose. Not mine. He would never have ventured into Blackfriars except on an errand from you.'

'True, true. I spoke out of turn. I crave his pardon.'

There was a bungling politeness about the man which made Nicholas wonder yet again how he had wormed his way into Anne's affections, but the book holder had given his word in front of her and could not go back on that now.

'This is bound to force a delay,' he explained, 'and it may be some time before I can secure an interview with Master Fulbeck's assistant or with Raphael Parsons. When they have a murder on their hands, we cannot expect them to put the future of one chorister to the forefront of their minds.'

'Philip is at the forefront of my mind always!' said the father proudly. 'We must rescue him. If there is a killer stalking the Blackfriars playhouse, my son must be brought back to the safety of his own home as soon as possible. His own life may be at risk.'

'We must let Nick handle this,' said Anne.

'Of course, of course.'

'He will judge when the time is right to go back.'

'Meanwhile,' said Nicholas to the butcher, 'you must temper your anger with a little patience. Your son may not be as ill-used as you fear. While at Blackfriars Theatre, we took the opportunity to speak with the porter there, one Geoffrey Bless, who has been involved with the choristers for many a year. He knows them all by name and spoke well of young Philip Robinson.'

'What did he say?' demanded the father.

'Little beyond the fact that the lad always had a civil word for him and worked as hard as he was able. Your son is a diligent and talented chorister.'

'That much is not in doubt.'

'One thing still is,' said Nicholas. 'Philip is not the sole victim of Raphael Parsons. All the boys are swinged soundly if they do not attain the high standards which he sets them. Yet none of them is trying to leave the Chapel Children or writing home to entreat some intercession from a parent.'

Robinson's eyes narrowed. 'What are you saying?'

'Your son is the only apostate. Why is that?'

'You read his letters. You could see his terror.'

'His friends do not seem to share it.'

'I do not care a fig for the others!'

'Ambrose!' reprimanded Anne.

'My son is in pain. I must save him.'

'Nicholas is working to that end.'

'Yes,' agreed the book holder, 'and the more facts I have at my disposal, the better am I able to act on his behalf. That is why I would like to know why eleven choristers can tolerate a situation that one finds quite unendurable. I will look into it. Bear this in mind, however. Westfield's Men have first claim on my time and my energy.'

'I explained that,' said Anne.

'I want to hear that Master Robinson understands it.'

The butcher squirmed slightly in his seat before nodding his assent. His face moved slowly into a smile of appeasement, but Nicholas saw the muted resentment in his eyes. Ambrose Robinson was evidently a man who could shift from friendship to enmity with no intervening stages. He was no longer taking such obvious satisfaction from the demise of Cyril Fulbeck. He was dripping with envy. Accustomed to slaughtering animals with brutal efficiency, he felt cheated that the Master of the Chapel had escaped the even more horrific death that he would have inflicted upon him.

Nicholas also sensed danger of another kind, and it touched off his protective instinct again. Anne Hendrik had to be guarded from the man. The butcher would pursue his own ends with single-minded determination. Rescuing his son from the Chapel Children was the normal act of a concerned parent, but Nicholas now realised that it was only the first stage in Robinson's domestic plans. Marriage to Anne Hendrik was his next target. In confiding his problem to her, he had both flattered her by showing such trust and activated all her maternal impulses. Anne was wholly committed to the rescue of Philip Robinson.

Annoyed at first to be inveigled into the situation in which he found himself, Nicholas was now almost grateful. It would not only introduce him to the Chapel Children and give him an insight into the way that his young theatrical rivals operated, it would enable him to keep a watchful eye on the amorous butcher.

'When will you go back to Blackfriars?' asked Robinson.

'When time serves,' said Nicholas.

'Please inform me of everything that happens.'

'I will get in touch with Anne.'

Her smile of gratitude was a rich reward for his pains.

Success was an ephemeral pleasure in the theatre. It soon evaporated and could never be taken for granted. The day after the Queen's Head had reverberated to the cheers for *The Misfortunes of Marriage*, the troupe were back on the same makeshift stage to rehearse *The History of King John*. It was a staple drama from their repertoire and was beginning to look well worn. Edmund Hoode patched it assiduously each time it was played again, but even his art could not turn the piece into anything more than workmanlike chronicle. In the wake of Jonas Applegarth's play, it was bound to look dull and uninspiring. Westfield's Men would have to strive hard in order to lift *King John* to the level of a minor achievement. It could never emulate the triumph that was *The Misfortunes of Marriage.*

Lawrence Firethorn was all too conscious of this fact.

'From a mountain peak,' he said, striking a pose, 'down to the foothills. From cold Sir Marcus to Bad King John.'

'The play has served us well in the past,' reminded Edmund Hoode. 'You have *Magna Carta*-red your way through it fifty times without complaint.'

'That was before we had Jonas Applegarth.'

Hoode recoiled visibly. He was less hurt by the blow to his pride than by the implications of Firethorn's remark. The playwright had gritted his teeth to endure close proximity to Applegarth in the hope that the latter was a bird of passage. Was a more permanent relationship with the company now envisaged? Hoode was bound to wonder where that eventuality would leave its resident playwright.

'No offence meant to you,' said Firethorn hastily, when he saw the dismay on the other's face. 'And it will not affect your position among us in any way, Edmund.'

'I am relieved to hear that.'

'You will always be our leading author. You are the very foundation of Westfield's Men. Take but you away and we all tumble into a bottomless pit.'

He went off for a few minutes into such a fulsome paean of praise that Hoode lowered his guard. They were standing in the innyard after the morning's rehearsal. Five yards away was the stage on which most of Hoode's plays had first come to life before an admiring audience. Firethorn's eulogy bolstered his self-esteem and made him feel deeply heartened. It did not last. Reassurance soon changed to dread.

'On the other hand,' warned Firethorn, 'we would be fools to spurn a dramatic jewel when it falls into our lap, and *The Misfortunes of Marriage* is unquestionably such a jewel. That is why we must stage it again.'

'Again?'

'Again and again and again.'

'It is to be our sole offering, then?'

'Of course not, Edmund. Every jewel needs a setting and we will surround it with baser material.'

'*My* plays!'

'No, not yours,' said Firethorn, trying to placate him. 'Well, not only yours. That does not mean your art is base or merely semi-precious. Far from it, man. You shower the stage with diamonds every time you pick up your pen and dazzle every eye. But Jonas has given us a much larger stone.'

'I feel the weight of it around my neck.'

'He has enriched us all beyond measure. Westfield's Men must respond accordingly.' Firethorn bestowed an affectionate smile on his friend before hitting him with his decision. 'That is why we play *The Misfortunes of Marriage* at The Rose.'

Hoode gulped. 'The Rose?'

'Ten days hence.'

'But my new play was to have graced The Rose!'

'And so it will, Edmund. In time, in time.'

'We so rarely seize upon the chance to work at the theatre. It may be months before *The Faithful Shepherd* travels to Bankside.'

'A good play is like a good wine, old friend. It improves with age. Store it until a fitter time.'

'Why cannot Jonas do that with his play?'

'Because it has already been uncorked. It has already been tasted. You saw that audience yesterday. Drunk with joy at the play and doubly drunk with my performance as Sir Marcus Coldbed. They clamour for more. We must slake their thirst.'

'But not at The Rose, surely?'

'Where better?'

'Lawrence, you *promised.*'

'And I will keep that promise—in due course.'

'*The Faithful Shepherd* stands first in line.'

'Jonas Applegarth leaps over it.'

'That is unjust.'

'Theatre mixes pain with its plaudits.'

'This is cruel in the extreme.'

'Is it not a greater cruelty to deny our patrons what they demand? We serve a fickle public, Edmund. Soon, they may cast *The Misfortunes of Marriage* away as worthless trash. At this moment, however, it is the talk of London. Lord Westfield himself was so entranced with the piece, he'll not rest until everyone at Court has been told about it. He insists that it take pride of place at The Rose.'

'Lord Westfield insists?'

'That was my understanding,' lied Firethorn, using the one argument that Hoode could not defeat. 'Who am I to flout the express wishes of our generous patron?'

Hoode sagged. 'Then am I truly lost.'

'Your day will come again.'

'Will I live to enjoy it, though?'

Firethorn chuckled. 'I knew that you would accept this unwonted check with fortitude. Be not afraid of Jonas Applegarth. He has not come to displace you in any way. Edmund Hoode is what he has always been to Westfield's Men. Our faithful shepherd.'

'Then why let a wolf into the fold?'

'We keep him well muzzled.'

'Look to your lambs. His claws can still kill.'

'It is decided.'

Lawrence Firethorn tossed his cloak over his shoulder and strode off towards the tiring-house, leaving Hoode speechless with indignation. A play over which he had laboured devotedly for months had been pushed contemptuously aside. It was an honour to have any work staged at a fine playhouse like The Rose, and *The Faithful Shepherd* was written specifically for that theatre.

Jonas Applegarth had robbed him of that honour. Hoode had one more reason to resent the obese interloper.

He was distraught. He felt completely estranged from Westfield's Men. It was as if members of his own family had turned him out of the house in favour of a newcomer. Hoode contemplated suicide. Had he been standing on London Bridge, he would certainly have jumped off it, howling the name of Applegarth with defiance before hitting the cold water and drowning with alacrity.

While he was at the very nadir of his career, Fate stepped in to save him. It came in the shape of Rose Marwood, the landlord's daughter, a vivacious young woman with long dark hair and a readiness to please. How two parents as physically repellent as Alexander and Sybil Marwood could prduce such an attractive creature between them he did not know, but it often exercised his mind. It was rather as if two gargoyles had copulated in order to produce a statute of a Madonna.

Hoode had once conceived a foolish passion for her that led only to humiliation, and so he tended to keep clear of the landlord's daughter. Rose's shining face was now an embarrassment to him.

'I have a message for you, Master Hoode,' she said.

'For me?'

'Put it into his hands, I was told.'

'By whom?'

'The lady who gave it to me.'

'Lady? What lady?'

'She would not tell me her name, sir.'

Rose handed over the missive and gave a little curtsey.

'Can you describe this lady to me?' he said.

'I saw her for only a moment, sir. She said that I was to give the letter to you in person. It is a gift.'

'Gift?'

'From her mistress.'

Rose giggled, showed two exquisite dimples in her cheeks, and bounded off towards the taproom. Hoode was intrigued. He broke the seal on the letter and opened it to find a red rose pressed inside. Only three words had been written in an elegant hand, but they clutched at his very soul.

"To my love . . ."

Jonas Applegarth scratched his head as he quaffed his beer. The empty tankard was slammed back down on the table by way of a signal and it was soon filled by a serving-man.

'Who could wish to kill Cyril Fulbeck?' he wondered.

'That is what we must find out,' said Nicholas.

'I'd happily have hanged his partner, Raphael Parsons. If ever a man invited a noose, it is that rogue. But not that shuffling Master of the Chapel. He was a harmless fellow.'

'Everyone speaks well of him.'

'He was a dear man and a gifted teacher,' said James Ingram. 'Cyril Fulbeck was the epitome of goodness.'

'Then why ally himself to such a villain as Parsons?'

'I do not know.'

'Nor I,' added Nicholas, 'but the talk is that the two men did not agree. Geoffrey, the porter, often heard arguments between them.'

'There is your murderer, then,' decided Applegarth. 'Look no further than Raphael Parsons. He stands to gain most from Fulbeck's death.'

'He must be suspect, assuredly,' said Nicholas, 'but I would not accuse him without further evidence. Indeed, one clue suggests he may be innocent of the crime.'

'What is that, Nick?' asked Ingram.

'The key to the back door of Blackfriars Theatre.'

'But Master Parsons has such a key. He, and only he, had the means to gain entrance privily. Unless you believe that old Geoffrey was involved in some way. His key fits that same lock.'

'We may exclude him straight,' said Nicholas. 'You saw the

way he cried when he beheld the dead man. He was as shocked as we. The porter has no part in this.'

'You spoke of Parsons's innocence,' noted Applegarth.

'A suggestion of innocence,' corrected the book holder. 'If Raphael Parsons had a key that admitted him to the back door of the theatre, why did he steal Master Fulbeck's keys in order to get out again?'

'To prevent us from following him,' said Ingram.

'But we were unexpected visitors, and the keys had been stolen from the dead man's belt before we arrived.'

'I have it,' announced Applegarth. 'This Parsons is too devious and cowardly a man to do the deed himself. He hired a confederate, let him into the building and locked the door after him before quitting the scene. The killer stole the other keys to effect his escape.'

'This was no confederate,' affirmed Nicholas.

'How do you know?' said Ingram.

'You heard that man, James. He was no assassin, paid to kill a complete stranger. He *knew* Cyril Fulbeck and gloried in his death. The Laughing Hangman would never have delegated to another a task which gave him so much pleasure. He was connected in some way to the Master of the Chapel.'

'As his business partner,' asserted Applegarth.

'Master Parsons may be only one of many possibilities.'

'I'll help you to draw up a list,' offered Ingram.

'Thank you, James.'

It was early evening and they had moved to the taproom of the Queen's Head after the performance of *The History of King John.* The play had been a moderate success but seemed flat by comparison with *The Misfortunes of Marriage.* Jonas Applegarth had snored through the last two acts. Exhilarated at the thought that his own play would now be seen at The Rose, he was already working on refinements to the text. Considering himself now part of the troupe, he was ready to sit through their other work out of loyalty even if it bored him into slumber.

Nicholas emptied his tankard and rose from the table.

'I bid you farewell, my friends.'

'Hold,' said Applegarth, struggling to his feet. 'I'll walk part of the way with you. My house is close to Thames Street and there is something I would discuss as we walk.'

'Your company is most welcome.'

'What of Blackfriars?' said Ingram.

'We'll go again tomorrow, James. Meanwhile, gather what intelligence you can. You must have other old friends from the Chapel Children, choristers who stayed on when you left? Perhaps they can shed some light on this tragedy. I am certain that we look for someone who is, or once was, within Master Fulbeck's circle.'

'Leave it with me, Nick. I'll about it straight.'

They traded farewells, then Nicholas and Applegarth headed for the door, passing, as they did, Edmund Hoode. His feeling of betrayal had faded and a beatific smile now played around his lips. The rose from Rose Marwood had transformed him from a discarded playwright into a hopeful lover. Recognising the look on his friend's face, Nicholas glided past without comment and simply waved.

The book holder led Applegarth out into the fresh air.

'I have an idea for my play,' said the latter.

'It is already crammed full with ideas.'

'A scenic device. Something that we could lower from above with the winding-gear they have at The Rose.'

'They have it at Blackfriars, too,' observed Nicholas as he recalled the hanging man. 'What do you wish to lower onto the stage?'

The question remained unanswered because Jonas Applegarth stumbled over the uneven surface of Gracechurch Street and pitched forward. Clumsiness saved his life. Something whistled through the air with vicious speed and sank with a thud into the door of the house directly behind them.

The dagger missed Applegarth by a matter of inches.

# [ CHAPTER FIVE ]

The suddenness of the attack took them both by surprise. By the time that Nicholas Bracewell swung round, there was no sign of the assailant. Several other people were walking peacefully along Gracechurch Street, and he called out to those nearest, but none of them had seen anyone throw a dagger. Fear of danger made them scurry quickly away. Nicholas went swiftly up and down the street in search of the assassin, but to no avail. For the second time in twenty-four hours, he was chasing shadows.

He went back to help Jonas Applegarth up from the ground. The latter was more concerned about the state of his apparel than about the ambush.

'Mud on my new breeches!' he complained bitterly. 'And a tear in my sleeve.'

'Someone just tried to kill you, Jonas.'

'Look at the state of my shoes.'

'Does it not concern you?' asked Nicholas.

'Mightily. My wife will take me to task for it.'

'I speak of the attack.'

'A mild annoyance, no more,' said Applegarth, dusting

himself off. 'Why should I fear such a lame assassin? If he cannot hit a target as large as me, he must be blind. Besides, who says that *I* was his target? Perhaps the dagger was meant for you, Nick. Have you considered that?'

Nicholas had and dismissed the possibility. The weapon had been thrown directly at Applegarth and only the man's fall had helped him to evade it. Plucking the dagger from its resting place, Nicholas tried to work out from where it must have been thrown. A lane on the opposite side of the street turned out to be the vantage point. It would give the assailant good cover and an excellent view of anyone leaving the Queen's Head. He could have fled unseen while the dagger itself was still in flight.

After inspecting the weapon, Nicholas offered it to his companion. Applegarth showed scant interest.

'Do you recognise this?' said Nicholas.

'It is a dagger like any other.'

'Other daggers are not thrown at you, Jonas.'

'One or two have been in the past,' said the playwright with a grim chuckle. 'This one was as wayward as they were. No, Nick, I do not recognize it. A mean weapon, that is clear. Toss it away and forget all about it.'

'But it may lead us to your attacker.'

'Leave him to me.'

'You know who he is?'

'I have many enemies.'

'Match this dagger to one man and you have him.'

'Do not trouble yourself so. This is my battle.'

'And mine,' said Nicholas, slipping the dagger into his own belt. 'You are the property of Westfield's Men now. It is my duty to protect you as I would protect any other part of our property.'

Applegarth stiffened. 'I need no bodyguard.'

'You are in *danger,* Jonas.'

'I will live with that fear.'

They resumed their walk and the playwright returned to the subject of The Rose. His work would be seen by a larger and more perceptive audience at the Bankside theatre. He was anxious to improve the play in any way that he could. Applegarth was still explaining his ideas when they turned into Thames Street. The smell of the river invaded his nostrils and they could hear it lapping against the wharves down to their left.

Applegarth paused on the corner of the next street.

'Let me see it again, Nick,' he said.

'See what?'

'The dagger. Haply, I do recognise it.'

'Here,' said Nicholas, passing it to him. 'There are some marks upon the hilt that may be initials.'

'Ah yes. I see.'

After pretending to study the weapon, Jonas Applegarth turned round and pulled back his arm to propel the dagger with full force. It spun crazily through the air and landed with a loud splash in the river. Nicholas was bewildered by his friend's action, but the latter chortled happily.

'There. 'Tis all past now. Think no more about it.'

'But that dagger was to have been a murder weapon.'

'I have blocked it out of my mind.'

'You have thrown away the one clue that we had.'

'There will be other nights, other daggers.'

'Next time, you may not have such good fortune.'

'Next time,' said Applegarth, 'I will not be taken unawares. This was a useful warning, but there's an end to it. I'll not lose sleep over the matter.'

Nicholas was convinced that the playwright knew the name of his attacker, but it could not be prised out of him. Jonas Applegarth lapsed into a kind of jocular bravado that was proof against all questioning. Even though it took him out of his way, Nicholas insisted on walking back to his friend's house to make sure that he got home safely. The journey passed without further incident.

Applegarth beamed hospitably at his colleague.

'Will you step in to continue our debate?'

'Not tonight, Jonas.'

'But I have much more to say about my play.'

'We will find time tomorrow,' said Nicholas. 'Stay alert and keep your doors locked. Your attacker may return during the night.'

Applegarth shrugged. 'What attacker?'

Nicholas could not understand his apparent unconcern. An attempt had been made on the man's life, yet he was choosing to ignore it. The book holder foresaw further trouble ahead and his anxiety was for the company as well as for its newest recruit. Westfield's Men might yet live to regret their association with the brilliant talent of Jonas Applegarth.

'Are you sure that you will not stay, Nick?'

'Unhappily, I may not.'

'There is plentiful wine within.'

'Thank you. But I have another call to make.'

The study was on the first floor of the house in Thames Street. Around all four walls were oak shelves heavily laden with books, documents, maps and manuscripts. Two long tables occupied most of the space and they were covered with more books and rolls of parchment. Quill pens lay sharpened in a little wooden box. Ink stood ready in a large well. The whole room smelled of musty scholarship.

Caleb Hay sat beneath the sagging beams and pored over a medieval document with intense concentration. He used a magnifying glass to help him translate the minuscule Latin script. His eyes sparkled with fascination as he took a privileged walk through the past of his beloved London. So absorbed was he in his research that he did not hear the respectful tap on the door of his study. His wife had to bang more loudly before she caught his attention.

Bristling with annoyance, he glared at the door.

'What is it?' he snapped.

'Can you spare a minute, Caleb?' she asked tentatively.

'No!'

'He said that it was important.'

'I've told you a hundred times, Joan. My work must not be interrupted. For any reason.'

'But you have a visitor.'

'Send him on his way.'

'He is too persistent, husband.'

'I'll see nobody.'

'He claims to be a friend of yours.'

'Friends know better than to disturb my studies. They only come to my house by invitation, and that rarely. Persistent, you say? Who is this rogue?'

'Nicholas Bracewell.'

'Give him a dusty answer and bid him farewell,' Caleb said abruptly. 'No, tarry a while,' he added, as curiosity began to grapple with irritation. 'Nicholas Bracewell, is it? What does he want with me? Did he state his business?'

'No, Caleb.'

'But he told you that it was important?'

'Yes,' she confirmed. 'He is a most polite and courteous gentleman, but resolved on talking to you.'

Caleb Hay glanced down at his work. Pursing his lips, he shook his head in mild anger before finally relenting.

'Ask him to stay. I'll come down anon.'

'Thank you!'

Waiting in the parlour below, Nicholas Bracewell heard the relief in her voice. Joan Hay was a submissive wife, eager to avoid her husband's displeasure. The mild-mannered historian whom Nicholas knew was evidently a more despotic creature within his own home.

She came clattering down the stairs to rejoin the visitor. A short, slim, timorous woman in a plain dress, she gave him a nervous smile of apology and relayed the message before bowing out again. Nicholas listened to the sound of a heavy bolt being drawn back in the study. A key turned in a stout lock and the door creaked open. It was immediately closed and locked. Feet padded down the wooden steps.

Caleb Hay shuffled in with an irritated politeness.

'Well met, Master Bracewell!'

'I am sorry to break in upon your studies.'

'A matter of some significance must have brought you.'

'Yes,' said Nicholas. 'It concerns Blackfriars.'

'Go on, sir.'

'I need you to tell me something of its recent past.'

'This is hardly the moment for a lesson in history,' said his host with quiet outrage. 'Have you dragged me away from my desk to purvey a few anecdotes about a friary?'

'With good reason, Master Hay.'

'And what may that be?'

'It touches on a murder lately carried out there.'

'A murder?'

'The victim was Cyril Fulbeck.'

'Cyril Fulbeck?' echoed Hay incredulously. 'The Master of the Chapel has been *murdered?* How? When?'

'He was hanged on the stage of the Blackfriars Theatre but yesterday.'

'Dear God! Can this be true? Cyril Fulbeck was a true Christian. The soul of kindness. Who could have wrought such villainy upon him?' He grasped Nicholas by the arm. 'Have the rogues been caught? This heinous crime must be answered.'

'So it will be, Master Hay. With your help.'

'It is at your disposal, sir.'

His host waved Nicholas to a seat and sat beside him. Caleb Hay swung between agitation and sorrow. He pressed for more detail and Nicholas recounted the facts. The older man shook his head in disbelief.

'Cyril Fulbeck!' he sighed. 'I spoke with him not ten days ago. A gracious gentleman in every way.'

'You know him well, then?'

'Tolerably well. He gave me the kindest assistance in my work. The Master of the Chapel is a person of consequence. Through him, I gained access to many documents that would else have lain beyond my reach. He could not have been more helpful, nor I more grateful for that help.'

'How did you find him at that last meeting?'

'Not in the best of health, alas. Ailing badly.'

'I speak of his mood.'

'Sombre. Sombre and full of remorse. He seemed much oppressed by the cares of his office.'

'Did he confide the reasons?'

'No, no,' said Hay firmly. 'Nor did I seek them. It was not my place to meddle in his private affairs. I am a scholar and not a father-confessor.'

'What dealings did you have with Raphael Parsons?'

'None whatsoever—thank heaven!'

'Why do you say that?'

'Common report has him a most unprepossessing fellow. I wonder that Cyril Fulbeck allowed the man near him. I had no call to make the acquaintance of Master Parsons. If you seek intelligence about him, look elsewhere for it.'

'Tell me about Blackfriars,' said Nicholas.

Hay brightened. 'Ah! Now, there, I am on firm ground. I can teach you all that may be taught on that subject. A Dominican House was first founded in London in 1221 at a site in Chancery Lane. Some fifty years or more later, Robert Fitzwalter gave them Baynard's Castle and Montfichet Tower on the river, enabling them to build a much larger monastery. King Edward I, of blessed memory, offered his patronage, and the House became rich and influential as a result.'

'I am more interested in recent events there.'

'They can only be judged aright if set against the ancient traditions of Blackfriars,' insisted Hay with a pedagogic zeal. 'Parliament first met there in 1311. It was later used as a repository for records relating to matters of state. Later still—in the years

1343, 1370, 1376 and 1378, to be exact—it was the meeting place of the Court of Chancery. Parliaments and Privy Councils were often convened there. Visiting dignitaries from foreign lands stayed there as honoured guests. In our own century,' he said, sniffing noisily in disapproval, 'a court sat in Blackfriars to hear the divorce case against that worthy lady, Catherine of Aragon. In that same fateful year of 1529, Parliament met there to bring a Bill of Attainder against Cardinal Wolsey.'

'All this is fascinating,' said Nicholas patiently, 'but not entirely relevant to my inquiry.'

'But you need to understand the greatness of the House in order to appreciate how ruinously it has dwindled. Before the suppression of the Religious, it was a major presence in the city. But now . . .'

'Largely demolished.'

'And the Dominicans expelled.' He gave an involuntary shudder. 'To make way for members of your profession.'

'The playhouse was not built until some years later.'

'In 1576, to be precise. Consecrated ground, used as a scaffold for lewd performance. By children, no less! Sweet choristers, whose voices should have been uplifted in praise of their Maker.' He became sharply self-critical. 'But I go beyond the bounds of my purpose here. An antiquarian must report the progress of events without making undue comment upon them. What is done is done. Who cares one way or the other what Caleb Hay may think about the Children of the Chapel?'

'I do,' said Nicholas.

'You are too indulgent, my friend,' said the other with a smile. 'When I fulminate against plays and players, you take the blows on your back with Stoic resignation and never offer me a buffeting in return.'

'I admire plain speaking.'

'My guilt is unassuaged. You do not deserve to have my trenchant opinions thrust upon you. I console myself with the thought that a man of the theatre must hear harsher tongues than mine in the course of his working day.'

'That is certainly true,' said Nicholas, thinking of Lawrence Firethorn's blistering tirades. 'But you forget that I sailed around the globe with Sir Francis Drake. Modest language has no place aboard a ship. Men speak in the roundest of terms. Your gibes are holy scripture beside the profanities of seafarers. Rail against the theatre as much as you wish, Master Hay. Simply give me the instruction that I seek.'

'In what particular?'

'Describe the first Blackfriars Theatre.'

'A species of Hell!'

Nicholas laughed. 'I wish to know something of its appearance and dimensions. Did it have secret passages leading to it or an underground vault beneath it? What changes were made when it was refurbished? Describe, if you will, all possible ways into the building.'

'You have first to get into the precinct.'

'Of course.'

'Five acres of land is all that is left of the original monastic community. They form the liberty of Blackfriars. It preserves its ancient right of sanctuary. Do you know what other privilege is bestowed upon them?'

'Only too well,' said Nicholas enviously. 'They are within the city walls yet free from city jurisdiction. We have no such freedom. While we at the Queen's Head must perforce observe the Sabbath and forego performance, the Blackfriars Theatre is able to stage its plays on the Lord's Day with impunity. That is a most important liberty.'

'The theatre is only a small part of the whole. It shares the precinct with the fine houses of respectable families. The whole area is walled and its four gates are locked each night by the porter. Blackfriars is an address of note. You will know, I am sure, that many of its inhabitants fought hard to prevent a theatre from being re-opened on the site.'

'I believe that a petition was drawn up.'

'Drawn up and willingly signed. It kept the boards clear of actors for an interval. Then Cyril Fulbeck made his shameful arrangement with Raphael Parsons.'

'Is that how the Master of the Chapel described it?' said Nicholas. 'As a shameful arrangement?'

'I intrude my own prejudices once more,' said Hay with a note of apology. 'That is not good, not right, not scholarly. Henceforth, I'll keep to particulars. What is it you seek? Dimensions and alterations? You will not lack for detail here, Master Bracewell. I will tell you all.'

Caleb Hay fulfilled his boast. He took his guest on a guided tour of Blackfriars, measuring out each wall, noting each doorway, indicating everything of even moderate significance and generally painting such a vivid picture in words that Nicholas saw the remains of the monastery rising before his eyes. It was uncanny. The older man tried to speak with deliberate calm but a more passionate note crept in from time to time. Here was someone who cared so deeply for the glorious past of London that he still lived in it.

Nicholas absorbed the salient details and thanked him.

'I will speak further, if you wish,' offered his host.

'You have told me all I need to know, Master Hay.'

'Pray God that it may help you! If I thought that my knowledge of this flower of cities could somehow lead you to the devils who committed this unspeakable act, I would give you a different lecture on the history of Blackfriars every day of the week.'

'You have been most generous with your time.'

'Call on me again,' said Hay. 'I am desirous to know how well your enquiries go. Cyril Fulbeck was as decent a man as any in Christendom. Pursue his killers.'

'I will do so,' promised Nicholas, 'but I think that only one person is involved here. A perverse creature who takes delight in his villainy.'

He thought for a moment of the body swinging helplessly on

the stage at the Blackfriars Theatre. The Master of the Chapel had been given no chance to resist as the breath of life was squeezed out of him inch by inch. It was a brutal death and it sent a chilling message. Nicholas would not easily forget the pallid horror on the face of the victim. Nor could he erase from his mind the glee of the murderer. That was what appalled him the most. The sound filled his ears so completely and so painfully that he had to shake his head to escape the callous mockery of the Laughing Hangman.

Too much drink and too little conversation had left Edmund Hoode in a state of maudlin confusion. Seated alone in a corner of the taproom at the Queen's Head, he was oblivious to the raucous jollity all around him. He sipped, he meditated, he sank ever deeper into bewilderment. Hoode was not sure whether he should be devastated by the tidings from Lawrence Firethorn or inspired by the message from Rose Marwood, and so he shifted with speed between despair and hope until they blended in his mind. A look of inebriated perplexity settled on his moonlike face.

A friendly arm descended upon his shoulder.

'Come, Edmund,' said a lilting voice. 'Time to leave.'

'What's that?' he murmured.

'You need help to get home. Lean on me.'

'Why?'

'Because those legs of yours would not take you more than seven yards towards Silver Street.'

To prove his point, Owen Elias hoisted him up, then let go of him. Hoode swayed violently, steadied himself on edge of the table, then felt a surge of confidence. He took three bold strides across the floor before losing his balance and pitching forward. The Welshman caught him just in time.

'Let's do it *my* way,' he said jovially. 'Otherwise, you must crawl back to your lodging on all fours.'

'You are a true friend, Owen.'

'I know that you would do the same for me.'

'Indeed, indeed,' mumbled the other.

It was an unlikely eventuality. Hoode was frequently overcome by alcohol, grief or unrequited love, and sometimes by a lethal combination of all three. Elias, by contrast, could carouse endlessly without lapsing into anything more than merriment or music, rarely gave way to sorrow, and led a career of cheerful lechery among the womenfolk of London. Half-carrying the drooping poet, he came out into the night and headed slowly towards Cripplegate Ward.

'What is her name, Edmund?' he asked.

'Name?'

'Your heart is heavy, my friend. I can feel the full weight pressing down on me. It is an all too familiar burden. Who is she this time?'

'I do not know, Owen.'

'A lady without a name?'

'Without a name, a face or substance of any kind.'

'An invisible creature?'

'To all intents.'

'Explain.'

To provide anything as logical as an explanation placed an enormous strain on Hoode's shattered senses, but he did his best. As he ambled along, supported by his friend, he tried to piece together the events of a day which had both destroyed and resurrected him. No sooner had his new play been evicted than an anonymous tenant moved into his heart. He pulled out the flower which he had slipped under his doublet. Crushed and forlorn, it yet retained the fragrance of its message. Elias noted the irony of the situation.

'You have lost one Rose and gained another,' he observed. 'Two, if we count the landlord's comely daughter. Rose Marwood is a rose in full bloom. It is a source of great regret to me that even my skilful hands have not been able to pluck her from the stem. Her parents are entwined around the girl like prickly thorns. They have drawn blood from my lustful fingers on more than one occasion.'

'Leave we Rose Marwood to her own devices,' said Hoode. 'She was only the messenger here, and my concern is with the message itself. Or rather, with the lady who sent it.'

'Your inamorata.'

'If such she be, Owen.'

'No question of that. You hold the certain testimony of her love in your grasp.'

'I hold a rose, it is true,' said Hoode gloomily. 'But was it sent by a female hand?'

Elias guffawed. 'A male admirer! Have you awakened some dark passion in a love-struck youth? Do not tell Barnaby of this conquest or he will roast on a spit of envy.'

'You misunderstand.'

'Then speak more clearly.'

'I fear me that this is some trick.'

'On whose behalf?'

'Some fellow in the company who means to buy a laugh or two at my expense. Luck has never attended my loving, Owen. Cupid has used my heart for some cruel archery practice over the years. Why should fortune favour me now?'

'Because you deserve it, Edmund.'

'Fate has never used me according to my desserts before,' said Hoode. 'No, this is some jest. The love-token was sent to torment me. Someone in the company means to raise my hopes in order to dash them down upon the rocks of his derision.' He looked down at the rose. 'I would do well to cast it away and tread it under foot.'

'Stay!' said Elias, grabbing his wrist. 'Can you not see a rich prize when it stands before you? This is no jest, my friend. Westfield's Men love you too much to practise such villainy upon you. This message could not be more precise. You have made a conquest, Edmund. Take her.'

Hoode stopped in his tracks. 'Can this be true?'

'Incontestably.'

'I have at last won the heart of a lady?'

'Heart, mind and body.'

'Wonder of wonders,' Hoode said, sniffing the rose before concealing it in his doublet once more. 'I almost begin to believe it. It is such an unexpected bounty.'

'They are the choicest kind.'

'If this be love, indeed, it must be requited.'

'Enjoy her!'

'I will, Owen.'

'Go to your bed so that you may dream dreams of joy.'

'Press on.'

Still supported by the Welshman, Hoode lurched along the street with a new sense of purpose. Someone cared for him. He luxuriated in the thought for a whole glorious minute. A cold frost then attacked the petals of his happiness. The other Rose delivered a message of a different order.

'My occupation is gone,' he moaned.

'That is not so, Edmund.'

'I am pushed aside to make way for the ample girth of this Applegarth. There is not room enough in Westfield's Men for him and for me.'

'Indeed there is. Most companies lack one genius to fashion their plays. We have two. Our rivals are consumed with jealousy at our good fortune.'

'My talents have been eclipsed.'

'Never!'

'They have, Owen. *The Misfortunes of Marriage* is work of a higher order than I can produce. It ousts me from the Rose Theatre, and rightly so.'

'Your new piece will have its turn anon.'

'How will it fare in the shadow of Jonas's play? *The Faithful Shepherd* is a pigmy beside a giant. Why stage it and invite disgrace? I have suffered enough pain already.'

'You do yourself wrong,' said Elias earnestly. 'Jonas has one kind of talent, you have quite another. Both can dazzle an audience in equal measure. Jonas may invest more raw power in his verse, but you have a grace and subtlety that he can never match.'

'He is better.'

'Different, that is all.'

'Different in kind, superior in quality.'

'That is a matter of opinion.'

'It is Lawrence's view,' sighed Hoode, 'and his is the opinion that holds sway in Westfield's Men. He commissioned my new play for The Rose and could not have been more delighted with it. Until, that is, he espied this new star in the firmament. *The Faithful Shepherd* is then shunned like a leper and I become an outcast poet.'

'No more of this self-imposed melancholy!'

'I am finished, Owen. Dispatched into obscurity.'

'Enough!' howled the other, thrusting him against the wall of a house and holding him there with one hand. 'Jonas Applegarth will never displace Edmund Hoode. You have given us an endless stream of fine plays, he has provided us with one. You are part of the fabric of the company, he is merely a colourful patch which has been sewn on.'

'His play is the talk of London.'

'How long will that last?'

'Until he produces a new one to shame me even more.'

'No!' yelled Elias.

'He has robbed me of my future.'

'Look to the past instead.'

'Why?'

'Because there you will read the true story of Jonas Applegarth,' said the Welshman persuasively. 'A huge talent fills those huge breeches of his, it is true, but Westfield's Men are not the first to perceive this. Jonas has been taken up and thrown back by every other troupe in London. He was too choleric for their taste.'

'What are you telling me, Owen?'

'He will not stay with us for long. His blaze of glory will be no more than that. A mere blaze that lights up the heavens before fading away entire. We must profit from his brilliance while we may. Jonas will not survive.' Owen patted his friend of the cheek. 'You will, Edmund.'

Nicholas Bracewell was almost invariably the first member of the company to arrive at the Queen's Head at the start of the day. On the next morning, however, the thud of a hammer told him that one of his colleagues had risen even earlier than he. Nathan Curtis, the master carpenter, was repairing a table for use in the performance that afternoon. Busy at his trade, he did not see the book holder striding across the innyard towards him.

'Good-morrow, Nathan!' greeted Nicholas.

'Ah!' He looked up. 'Well met!'

'I wish that everyone was as diligent in their duties as you. You will have finished that table before some of our fellows have even dragged themselves out of bed.'

'There is much to do. When I have restored this, I must make some new scenic devices. And you spoke, I believe, about some properties that are in request.'

'One rock, one cage, one crozier's staff.'

'I'll need precise instructions.'

Nicholas passed them on at once and the carpenter nodded obediently. Curtis was a rough-looking man in working apparel, but his voice was soft and his manner almost diffident. His craftsmanship helped to put flesh on the bones of a play. Nicholas had another reason to be grateful of a moment alone with him. Curtis lived in Bankside. When the book holder lodged in Anne Hendrik's house, he and the carpenter were neighbours. The latter might well know one of the other denizens of the area.

'Are you acquainted with an Ambrose Robinson, by any chance?'

'Robinson the Butcher?'

'The same.'

'I know him as well as I wish to, Nick.'

'You do not like the man, I think.'

'I do not trust him,' admitted the other. 'He sells good meat and is polite enough in his shop, but he hides his true feelings from you. I never know where I am with the fellow. His mouth may smile but his eyes are cold and watchful. My wife cannot abide him.'

'He is not an appealing man,' agreed Nicholas.

'How came you to meet him?'

'Through a mutual friend.'

'Ah, yes!' said Curtis. 'I should have linked their names.'

'Why do you say that?'

'We talk of Mistress Hendrik, do we not?'

'We do, Nathan.'

'Then *she* will have introduced him to you. The butcher is fast becoming a close companion of hers.'

Nicholas bridled slightly. 'Indeed?'

'My wife has often seen him visiting her house and both of us have taken note of them on Sundays.'

'Why so?'

'Because we worship at the same altar, Nick. It has been going on for a month or more now.'

'What has?'

'Mistress Hendrik and Ambrose Robinson. I was surprised at first, my wife even more so. We both have the highest respect for Mistress Hendrik. Her late husband was as decent a neighbour as we could choose. Not so this butcher. He is not worthy of her. But there is no gainsaying what we saw.'

'And what was that?'

'They come to church together.'

The information was deeply unsettling, and Nicholas took time to assimilate it. If Anne Hendrik was allowing Robinson to accompany her to her devotions, their relationship must be on a more serious footing than Nicholas realised. Before he could speak again, an ancient voice interrupted them. Thomas Skillen, the venerable stagekeeper, was talking to a stranger on the other side of the yard and pointing a bony finger at the book holder. The visitor thanked him and bore down on Nicholas, giving the latter only a second or two to appraise him.

He was a man of moderate height and square build, wearing a black doublet and hose which was offset by a lawn ruff and by the ostrich feather in his black soft-crowned hat. His black Spanish cape had a red lining. Neat, compact and dignified, he was in his late thirties. His voice was remarkably deep and had a slight Northern tang to it.

'May I have a word alone?' the visitor said, giving his request the force of a command. 'It is needful.'

'Let's stand aside.'

Nicholas moved him a few yards away so that Nathan Curtis could resume his work. The carpenter's hammer was deafening and the stink of fresh horse dung was pungent. Wrinkling his nose in disgust, the visitor waved a dismissive arm.

'I'll not stay here in the middle of the yard like some idle ostler complaining about the price of hay. I desire some private conference.'

Nicholas stood his ground. 'What is your business with me?'

'The deadliest kind.'

'Who are you, sir?'

'Raphael Parsons.'

Nicholas was at once surprised and curious. The name explained the histrionic air about the man. Parsons moved with grace and spoke in almost declamatory fashion. His black beard and moustache were well trimmed and there was a studied arrogance in his expression. He was accustomed to being obeyed.

'Come with me,' suggested Nicholas.

'This is indoor work.'

'We have a chamber at hand.'

The book holder led him to the room which was used as the wardrobe by Westfield's Men. Raphael Parsons ran an expert eye over the racks of costumes, feeling some of the material between his fingers and grunting his approval. Nicholas closed the door behind him.

'How did you know where to find me?' he asked.

'James Ingram advised me to call here.'

'You have spoken with James, then?'

'Briefly. Geoffrey, our porter, put me in touch with him. I wanted to see if your account confirms, in every particular, what Ingram alleges.'

'My account?'

'Of what you found at the Blackfriars Theatre. My dear friend and partner, Cyril Fulbeck, hanged by the neck.' Parsons relaxed slightly and even managed a thin smile. 'Besides,' he continued, 'I have long wanted an opportunity to meet Nicholas Bracewell. Your fame runs before you, sir.'

'Fame?'

'You have a reputation, sir.'

'I am merely a book holder, Master Parsons.'

'Your modesty is a credit to your character but it betrays your true worth. You talk to a man of the theatre. I know that a book holder must hold a whole company together and nobody does that better than you. I have sat in your galleries a dozen times and marvelled at your work.' His face hardened. 'Though it is perhaps as well that I was not at the Queen's Head when Applegarth's latest piece of vomit was spewed out on your stage.'

'*The Misfortunes of Marriage* is a fine play.'

'It swinged us soundly, I hear.'

'There was some gentle mockery of boy actors.'

'Jonas Applegarth could not be gentle if he tried,' said Parsons vehemently. 'He tore our work to shreds and questioned our right to exist. Boy actors were innocent lambs beneath his slashing knife. It was unforgivable. Applegarth will pay dearly for his attack.'

'In what way?'

'You will see, sir. You will see.'

'Do you make threats against our author?'

'Let him watch his back, that is all I say.'

'Take care,' warned Nicholas, looking him hard in the eye. 'Touch any member of this company and you will have to deal with me.'

'Proof positive!' said Parsons with a disarming smile. 'You are no mere book holder. You are the true guardian of Westfield's Men. Its very essence, some say.'

'I stand by my friends.'

'Why, so do I, sir. And that is why I came here this morning. Away with that mound of offal known as Jonas Applegarth! Let's talk of a sweeter gentleman, and one whose death cries out for retribution. Cyril Fulbeck.'

'Ask what you will, Master Parsons.'

'Describe the scene in your own terms. When you and James Ingram entered the theatre, what exactly did you see?'

'I will tell you. . . .'

Nicholas reconstructed the events with care, as much for his own benefit as for that of his visitor. He wanted to sift every detail in the hope that it might contain a clue that had so far eluded him. Raphael Parsons was a patient audience. When he had heard the full tale, he stroked his beard pensively. There was a long pause.

'Well?' said Nicholas.

'Your version accords with that given by Ingram.'

'And so it should.'

'There is a difference, however,' noted Parsons. 'Your account is longer and more accurate. You are the more reliable witness, but that was to be expected.'

'Why?'

'Because you never met Cyril Fulbeck until that grim moment. What you saw was an old man dangling from a rope. James Ingram, we must remember, was looking at someone he revered, and was thus too shocked to observe all the detail which you just listed.'

'That is understandable.'

'Also,' said Parsons drily, 'you are older and wiser than Ingram, and far more closely acquainted with the horrors that man can afflict on man. You have looked on violent death before.'

'All too often, alas.'

'It has sharpened your judgement.' Parsons stroked his beard as he ruminated afresh. When he spoke again, his tone was pleasant. 'You have answered my enquiries willingly and honestly. I am most grateful to you for that. Allow me to return the compliment. I am sure that you have questions you wish to put to me.'

Astonished by the offer, Nicholas was nevertheless quick to take advantage of it. His interrogation was direct.

'Where were you at the time of the murder?' he said.

'At the house of a friend in Ireland Yard.'

'Close by the theatre, then?'

'Within a stone's throw.'

'When did you last see your partner?'

'An hour or so before his death, it seems,' said Parsons with a sad shake of his head. 'Had I known that Cyril was in such danger, I would never have stirred from his side. I blame myself for leaving him so defenceless.' He bit his lip. 'And the manner of my departure only serves to increase my guilt.'

'Your departure?'

'We had an argument. Strong words were exchanged.'

'On what subject?'

'What else but the Blackfriars Theatre? Cyril admired the plays I put upon the stage but criticised the means by which they got there. He thought I was too strict with my young charges.'

'How did you reply?'

'Roundly, I fear.'

'Was he upset by the altercation?'

'I did not stay to ask. I marched out of the building.' He clicked his tongue in self-reproach. 'Can you see what a weight on my conscience it now is? We parted in anger before but we soon became friends again. Not this time. A length of rope strangled any hope of reconciliation between us. Cyril went to his death with our quarrel unresolved. That cuts me to the quick.'

Nicholas was impressed by the readiness of his answers and by his apparent candour. Parsons seemed genuinely hurt by the demise of his friend and business partner. Here was a new and more compassionate side to the man. Others had spoken of a bully and a disciplinarian, and Nicholas had seen the odd glint of belligerence, but he had also discerned a sensitive streak. When Raphael Parsons offered his hand, he shook it without reservation.

'I must take my leave,' said the visitor.

'Let me teach you another way out.'

Nicholas took him through a second door and down a long passageway so that his visitor could step out into Gracechurch Street without having to go back through the yard. The book holder stopped him in the open doorway.

'There is another matter I would like to raise.'

'Be brief. I, too, have a rehearsal to attend.'

'One of your actors is a boy called Philip Robinson.'

'A gifted child in every way.'

'He was impressed against his will into the Chapel.'

'Who told you so?'

'The boy's father. He petitions for his son's return.'

'Then he does so in vain.'

'Why?'

'Because Philip is happy with us,' said Parsons bluntly. 'Extremely happy. Farewell, sir.'

With a brusque nod, he swept out into the street.

# [ CHAPTER SIX ]

For the rest of the morning, Nicholas Bracewell was so bound up in his duties that he had no time to reflect upon the unexpected visit of Raphael Parsons or to indulge in any speculation about the true feelings of Philip Robinson towards the Children of the Chapel Royal. Preparation for the afternoon's performance was his abiding concern, and *The Maids of Honour* gave him much to prepare. His first task was to prevent the stage-keeper from assaulting his smallest and lowliest assistant.

'No, no, no, George! You are an idiot!'

'If you say so.'

'I *do* say so because I know so!' shouted the irate Thomas Skillen. 'You have set out the wrong scenery and the wrong properties for the wrong play.'

'Have I?' George Dart scratched his head in disbelief. 'I thought *The Maids of Honour* called for a bench, a tree, a rock, a tomb, a well and three buckets.'

'You are thinking of *The Two Maids of Milchester.*'

'Am I?' he said, blushing with embarrassment. 'Why, so I am! We need no bench and buckets here. Our play demands a wooden canopy, a large bed, a stool, Mercury's wings and a rainbow. Tell me I am right.'

'You are even more wrong,' hissed the other, taking a first wild swipe at him. 'Dolt! Dunce! Imbecile! Mercury's wings and the rainbow belong in *Made to Marry*. Have I taught you nothing?'

Four decades in the theatre had made Thomas Skillen an essentially practical man. Actors might covet a striking role and authors might thrill to the music of their own verse, but the stagekeeper summarised character and language in terms of a few key items.

'Table, throne and executioner's block.'

'Yes, yes,' gabbled Dart.

'We play *The Maids of Honour*.'

'Table, throne and executioner's block. I'll fetch them straight.' He scampered off but came to a sudden halt. His face was puckered with concentration. '*The Maids of Honour*? There is no executioner's block in the piece. Why do you send for it?'

'So that I may strike off your useless head!'

The old stagekeeper lunged at his hapless assistant, but Nicholas stepped good-humouredly between them. Dart cowered gratefully behind his sturdy frame.

'Let me at the rogue!' shouted Skillen.

'Leave him be,' soothed Nicholas. 'George confused his maids of honour with his maids of Milchester. A natural mistake for anyone to make. It is not a criminal offence.'

'It is to me!'

'Does it really merit execution?'

'Yes, Nick. Perfection is everything.'

'Then are we all due for the headsman's axe, Thomas, for each one of us falls short of perfection in some way. George is willing and well intentioned. Build on these virtues and educate him out of his vices.'

Skillen's anger abated and he chortled happily.

'I frighted him thoroughly. He will not misjudge *The Maids of Honour* again.' He gave a toothless grin. 'Will you, George?'

'Never. Table and throne. I'll find them presently.'

'No need,' said Nicholas, pointing to the makeshift stage. 'The table stands ready. Nathan Curtis was here at first light to repair it. And he is even now putting some blocks of wood beneath the throne to heighten its eminence.'

'What shall I do, then, Master Bracewell?'

'Fetch the rest of the properties.'

Skillen took his cue. 'Act One. First scene, table and four chairs. Second scene, a box-tree. Third scene, curtains and a truckle-bed within. Fourth scene, the aforesaid throne. Fifth scene . . .'

The rapid litany covered all seventeen scenes of the play and left Dart's head spinning. He raced off to gather what he could remember and to stay out of reach of the old man's temper. Nicholas looked fondly after him.

'You are too hard on the lad, Thomas.'

'Stern schoolmasters get the best results.'

'George has too much to learn in too short a time.'

'That is because of his stupidity and laziness.'

'No, it is not,' said Nicholas reasonably. 'We overload him, that is all. This season, Westfield's Men will stage all of thirty-six different plays, seventeen of them, like Jonas Applegarth's, entirely new. Asking George Dart to remember the plots and properties of thirty-six plays is to put an impossible strain on the lad.'

'*I* know what each play requires,' said Skillen proudly.

'You are a master of your craft, Thomas. He is not.'

The old man was mollified. He loved to feel that his age and experience were priceless assets to the company. After discussing the play at greater length with him, Nicholas went off to tackle the multifarious chores that awaited him before the rehearsal could begin. He could spare only a wave of greeting to each new member of the company who drifted into the yard.

Edmund Hoode came first, buoyed up by the thought that his admirer might send him another token of her love or perhaps even reveal her identity. Barnaby Gill shared his mood of elation, though for a more professional reason. *The Maids of Honour* was one of his favourite plays because it gave him an excellent role as a court jester, with no less than four songs and three comic jigs. Owen Elias and James Ingram arrived together, deep in animated conversation. Three of the boy apprentices came into the yard abreast, giggling at a coarse jest. The fourth, Richard Honeydew, strolled in with Peter Digby, the director of the musicians.

Lawrence Firethorn, predictably, timed his entrance for maximum effect, clattering into the yard on his horse when everyone else was assembled there and raising his hat in salutation. From the broad grin on his face, his colleagues rightly surmised that he had tasted connubial delight that morning with his wife, the passionate Margery, a fact which was corroborated by the sniggers of the apprentices, who lived under the same roof as the actor-manager and who had heard every sigh of ecstasy and every creak of the bed. Silent pleasure was a denial of nature in the Firethorn household.

'Nick, dear heart!' he said, dismounting beside the book holder. 'Is all ready here?'

'Now that you have come, it is.'

'Then let us waste no more of a wonderful day.'

He tossed the reins to a waiting ostler, then strode off towards the tiring-house. Nicholas called the rest of the company to order and had the stage set for the first scene.

*The Maids of Honour* was a staple part of their repertoire, played for its reliability rather than for any intrinsic merits. A sprightly comedy with a political thrust, it was set in the French Court at some unspecified period in the past. The King of France is deeply troubled by rumours of a planned assassination. The Queen dismisses his fears until an attempt is made on his life but thwarted by the brave intercession of the Prince of Navarre, a guest at the Court.

Convinced that someone inside the palace is helping his enemies, the King lets his suspicions fall on the three maids of honour who attend the Queen. She is outraged by the suggestion that her most cherished friends could plot the overthrow of her husband, but the King follows his own intuition. Disguising himself as an Italian nobleman, he tests each maid of honour in turn to see if she can be corrupted by the promise of money. Two of them welcome his advances, proving that they have neither honour nor maidenhead; but the third, Marie, the plain girl matched with two Court beauties, vehemently rejects his blandishments.

The King removes his disguise and returns to his Queen. Presenting his evidence, he expects her to accept his word, but she flies into a rage and accuses him of trying to seduce her maids of honour. She flounces out of the Court and locks herself in her chamber. The Court Jester, acting as a mocking chorus throughout, takes especial pleasure in the marital discord. In his despair, the King confides in the handsome Prince.

Two of the maids of honour conspire with the exiled Duke of Brabant to overthrow the King. A second assassination attempt is planned, but it is foiled by Marie, who raises the alarm. The King is only wounded and the conspirators are captured by the Prince of Navarre. A contrite Queen tends her husband's wounds and promises that she will never misjudge him so cruelly again. As a reward for her loyalty, Marie, blossoming in victory, becomes the bride of the Prince. The play ends on a note of celebration with honour satisfied in every way.

The rehearsal was halting but free from major mishap. A large audience filled the yard of the Queen's Head for the performance itself. Jonas Applegarth sat in the upper gallery, paying for one seat but taking up almost three. Hugh Naismith sat where he could keep his mortal enemy in view. Lord Westfield and his cronies emerged from a private room behind the lower gallery to occupy their customary station and to whet their appetites for the play with brittle badinage over cups of Canary wine. Alexander Marwood circled his yard like a carrion crow.

*Your pleasure and indulgence, dearest friends,*
*Is all we seek and to these worthy ends*
*We take you to the glittering court of France,*
*Where gorgeous costume, music, song and dance,*
*Affairs of state and matters of the heart,*
*Mirthful jests, a Barnabian art,*
*With pomp and ceremonial display*
*Enhance the scene for our most honourable play*
*About three Maids of Honour. . . .*

Dressed in a black cloak, Owen Elias delivered the Prologue before bowing to applause and stealing away as a fanfare signalled the entry of the French Court. Lawrence Firethorn and Richard Honeydew made a magnificent entrance as King and Queen, respectively, in full regalia, and took their places at the head of a table set for a banquet. The solemnity of the occasion was soon shattered by the appearance of the Court Jester, who came somersaulting onto the stage to snatch a bowl or fruit and set it on his head like a crown. The Barnabian art of Barnaby Gill was in full flow and the spectators were enthralled.

Firethorn led the company with characteristic brio. James Ingram was a dashing Prince of Navarre, Owen Elias a truly villainous Duke of Brabant, and Edmund Hoode, in a flame-coloured gown, was a resplendent Constable of France. What *The Maids of Honour* also did was to furnish the four apprentices with an opportunity to do more than simply decorate a scene in female attire. Richard Honeydew showed regal fury as the Queen while Martin Yeo and Stephen Judd were suitably devious and guileful as the two dishonourable maids.

But it was John Tallis who really came to the fore. The boy was a competent actor but his lantern jaw and unfortunate cast of feature ruled him out of romantic roles. The part of Marie was a signal exception. Overshadowed by the external beauty of the other maids, he evinced an inner radiance that finally shone through. Tactfully concealing his lantern jaw behind a fan, he knelt gratefully before his King as the latter joined his hand symbolically with that of the Prince of Aragon.

It was then that the crisis occurred. Until that point, John Tallis had given the performance of his young lifetime. Puberty then descended upon him with its full weight. When the King of France invited Marie to accept the hand of the Prince of Navarre in marriage, he tempted Providence with his choice of words:

*Sing out your sweetest answer, soft-voiced Maid,*
*And let your music captivate Navarre.*

John Tallis put all the sweetness that he could muster into his reply, but what emerged from his mouth was the croak of a giant frog. His voice had broken, and with it broke the spell which had so carefully been woven throughout the preceding two hours. A tender moment between lovers became a source of crude hilarity. The audience rocked with mirth. When John Tallis tried to retrieve the situation with a series of mellifluous rhyming couplets, they came out as gruff entreaties which only increased the general hysteria.

Lawrence Firethorn tried to limit the damage by cutting in with the final speech of the play, but he took Peter Digby and the consort completely by surprise. Instead of a dignified exit to music, the French Court shuffled off in grim silence, and it was only when the stage was virtually empty that the instruments spoke from above. Fresh peals of laughter rang out. Firethorn brought the cast on stage to enjoy the applause, but even his broad smile cracked when the entry of John Tallis was greeted with a loud cheer.

When he quit the stage, the actor-manager was seething.

'Where is that vile assassin!' he roared.

'Do not blame the boy,' advised Nicholas.

'Oh, I'll not *blame* him, Nick. I'll belabour him! I'll pull off those bulging balls of his and roast them like chestnuts in a fire!

He killed my performance! He stabbed the play in the back!'

'It was not John's fault. His voice broke.'

'Then I'll break his arms, his legs and his foul neck to keep it company! You only *heard* the disaster, Nick. I had visible warning of its dire approach.'

'Warning?'

'Manhood reared its unlovely visage,' said Firethorn with a vivid gesture. 'When the Prince of Navarre stole that first kiss from Marie, the maid of honour's skirt twitched as if it had a flagpole beneath it. Had John Tallis been wearing a codpiece, it would have burst asunder and displayed his wares to the whole world. I wonder that James Ingram kept his composure! What man wants to spend his wedding night in the arms of a frog maiden with a monstrous pizzle!' He glared around the tiring-house. 'Where is that freak of nature? I'll geld him!'

'Calm down,' said Nicholas. 'The play is done.'

'Done and done for!'

'It was well received by the audience.'

'Jeers of derision.'

'Even the best horse stumbles.'

'This one stumbled, fell and threw us all from the saddle.' He made an effort to bank down his fury. 'Nobody can accuse us of denying John Tallis his moment of triumph. Marie can steal every scene in which she appears. We did all we could to help the oaf. We covered his lantern jaw with a fan, we hid much of his ugliness under a wig, and we dressed him in such rich and jewelled apparel that it took the attention away from what remained of his charmless countenance. And how did he repay us?'

'John lost control of his voice, alas. It has been on the verge of breaking these past few months.'

'It was a humiliation!' recalled Firethorn with a shiver. 'He could not have ruined the play more thoroughly if he had sprouted a beard and grown hair all over his chest. God's buttocks!' he howled, as his anger burst out once more. 'He made Westfield's Men the laughing-stock of London. Instead of a demure maid of honour, we have a hoarse-voiced youth afflicted with standing of the yard. Bring the rogue to me! I'll murder him with my bare hands!'

Nicholas diverted him by flattering him about his performance. When Barnaby Gill came up to complain that Firethorn had deliberately ruined one of his jigs by standing between him and the audience, the book holder saw his chance to slip away. John Tallis sat in the corner of the tiring-house, still wearing the costume of a maid of honour but weeping the tears of a young man. Richard Honeydew tried to console his colleague but his piping voice only reminded Tallis of his fatal loss.

'My hour on the stage is over!' he wailed.

'Do not talk so,' said Nicholas, crouching beside him. 'As one door closes, another one opens for you.'

'Yes! The door out of Master Firethorn's house. He will kick me through it most certainly. This morning, I was one of the apprentices; this afternoon, I am doomed.'

'You came of age, John. It happens to us all.'

'Not in the middle of the Court of France!'

He sobbed even louder and it took Nicholas several minutes to comfort him. Tallis eventually stepped out of a dress he would never be able to wear again and put on his own attire. The lantern jaw sagged with despair.

'What will become of me?' he sighed.

'We'll find occupation for you somewhere,' Nicholas reassured him. 'In the meantime, keep out of Master Firethorn's way and do not—this I beg you, John—do not let him hear your voice.'

The boy produced the deepest and harshest croak yet.

'Why not?' he said.

Even Nicholas had to suppress a smile.

She was there. He sensed it. Without knowing who she was or where she might be sitting, Edmund Hoode was certain only of her presence. It set his blood racing. Throughout the performance, he scanned the galleries whenever he came on stage, searching for that special face, waiting for that telltale smile, hoping for that significant gesture. When she chose not to reveal herself, he felt even more excited. In preserving her mystery, she became infinitely more appealing. Simply to know that she existed was an inspiration in itself.

Alone of the cast, the Constable of France was unmoved by the sudden transformation of a maid of honour into a husky youth. With a rose pressed to his heart beneath his costume, he was proof against all interruption. If John Tallis had turned into a three-headed dog and danced a galliard, he would not have distracted Hoode. She was there. That was all that mattered.

'What means this haste, Edmund?'

'I have somewhere to go.'

'Deserting your fellows so soon?'

'They will not miss me.'

'You have some tryst, I venture.'

'Venture all you wish, Jonas. My lips are sealed.'

Jonas Applegarth chuckled aloud and slapped Hoode on the back. The latter was just leaving the tiring-house after shedding the apparel of the Constable of France. Inspired by the hope that his admirer might make fresh contact with him, he was not pleased to find the massive Applegarth blocking his way.

'You have talent as a player, Edmund.'

'Thank you.'

'That is the finest performance I have seen you give.'

'Much thought went into it, Jonas.'

'To good effect. I could not fault you.'

'Praise, indeed.'

'The role was base, the play even baser, but you rose above those shortcomings. It is your true profession.'

'I am a poet. Writing plays is a labour of love.'

'But they show too much of the labour and too little of the love, Edmund. Abandon the pen. It leads you astray. Let sharper minds and larger imaginations create new plays. Your destiny is merely to act in them.'

The amiable contempt of his remarks did not wound Hoode. He was armoured against the jibes of a rival, even one as forthright as the corpulent Applegarth. Excusing himself with a pleasant smile, Hoode pushed past the portly frame and hurried along the passageway. Where he was going he did not know, but hope kept him on the move.

Chance dictated his footsteps, guiding him through the taproom, down another passageway, up one staircase, down a second, deep into a cellar, until he finally emerged in the yard once again. It was almost deserted. Most of the spectators had now dispersed, save for a few stragglers. Hoode halted with disappointment. There was no sign of his pining lover, no hint even of a female presence in the yard or up in the galleries.

Rose Marwood then materialised out of thin air and came tripping across the yard towards him. He revived at once. Another rose? A different token of love? A longer missive? But all that she bore him was a shy smile. Wafting past him, she went back into the building and shut the door firmly behind her.

Hoode was abashed. Had his instincts betrayed him? Was his secret admirer absent from the afternoon's performance? Or had she taken a second and more critical look at her quondam beloved before deciding that he was unworthy of her affections? His quick brain conjured up a dozen reasons why she was not there, each one more disheartening than its predecessor.

He gave a hollow laugh at the depths of his own folly. While he walked the boards as the Constable of France, he was supremely aware of her attention. His vanity was breathtaking. Why should any woman swoon over *him*? Set against the imperious charm of Lawrence Firethorn, the sensual vitality of Owen Elias, or the striking good looks of James Ingram, his qualities were negligible. It was idiocy to pretend otherwise. The rose which had warmed his heart all afternoon was now a stake which pierced it. His hand clutched at his breast to hold in the searing pain.

And then she came. Not in person, that was too much to ask. An innyard in the wake of a performance was not the ideal place for the first meeting of lovers. It was too public, too mundane, too covered in the litter of the departed audience. What she sent was an emissary. He was a tall, well-favoured youth in the attire of a servant. Walking briskly across to Hoode, he gave him a polite bow and thrust a scroll into his hand before leaving at speed.

The fragrance of the letter invaded Hoode's senses and confirmed the identity of the sender. He broke the seal and unrolled the parchment to read her purpose. His heart was whole again and pounding with joy. The elegant hand had written only one word, but it gave him a positive surge of elation.

'Tomorrow . . .'

When did you speak with Raphael Parsons?'

'Yesterday evening.'

'You sought him out?'

'He came to me, Nick. The porter told him how he might track me down. He was waiting for me at my lodging when I returned from here.'

Nicholas Bracewell and James Ingram were sharing a drink and comparing opinions in the taproom. Both had been astounded by the unheralded arrival of Raphael Parsons, but each had learned much from his visit.

'I found him at odds with expectation,' said Ingram. 'My first encounter with him was too fleeting for me to form a proper opinion. This time, I conversed alone with him. He did not seem at all like the ogre I had been led to expect. A strong-willed man, yes, and with strong passions. But he was too polite and reasonable to be a vile tyrant.'

'Tyranny can work in many ways,' observed Nicholas. 'A reasonable despot can sometimes be more difficult to resist. Master Parsons was civil with me but I sensed a capacity to be otherwise. We saw but one side of him.'

'A caring man, deeply shaken by the murder of a friend.'

'That was how he wanted to present himself, James.'

'It was a form of disguise?'

'I am not sure, but Raphael Parsons knew best how to engage our help. He was eager yet not overbearing, persistent but undemanding. He even invited me to question *him*. That was most enlightening. At the same time . . .'

'You had doubts about him?'

'I did.'

'He put mine to flight, Nick.'

'And most of mine, I must confess. He was very adept. Perhaps it was his ease in stilling my doubts which kept one or two of them alive. There is craft here. Deep cunning.'

'You saw qualities in him that eluded me.'

'I may be wrong, James. I hope that I am.'

'He spoke so warmly of Cyril Fulbeck,' said Ingram, 'and I can forgive a man most things if he does that. For what it is worth, my judgement is in his favour. I do not believe that Raphael Parsons was involved in this crime.'

'I delay my verdict on that.'

'He shook with grief when he talked of the murder.'

'It is a grief that is not allowed to interfere with his business affairs,' remarked Nicholas coolly. 'He may mourn his partner but he has not suspended performances at the Blackfriars as a mark of respect. His company are due to perform again tomorrow, young actors who must themselves be consumed with their own grief and beset by terror. Master Parsons tempers his sorrow with an instinct for gain.'

'That *is* strange behaviour.'

'Strange and unfeeling. What was his profession before he became a theatre manager?'

'He was a lawyer.'

'That explains much.'

They finished their drinks, then Nicholas took his leave. He crossed to the table at which Owen Elias was sitting with other members of the company, trading impersonations of the luckless John Tallis. Nicholas waited for the laughter to subside. Crouching beside the Welshman, he plucked his sleeve and kept his voice low.

'Will you undertake a special task for me?'

'Willingly, Nick.'

'Go about it privily.'

'A secretive assignment? You arouse my curiosity at once. What is it?'

'The rumour is that Jonas fought a duel.'

'More than a rumour. I know it to be a fact.'

'Find out who his opponent was.'

'Why?'

'Jonas was attacked last night as we walked home,' said Nicholas quietly. 'The ambush may be linked in some way to the duel. We need to recognise the face of the enemy so that we may safeguard Jonas from him.'

'He made no mention to me of any ambush.'

'He denies it happened in the same way as he refuses to admit that he was involved in a duel. But I was there when a dagger was thrown at him. Jonas is one of us now. Though he may spurn it, he needs our help.'

'This is work I'll readily accept, Nick,' said Elias with concern. 'I am grateful you chose me for the task.'

'You can get closer to him than me.'

'That is because Jonas and I are birds of the same feather. Roisterers with red blood in our veins. Lovers of life and troubadours of the tavern. We were both born to carouse.' Elias grinned. 'I need him alive to buy his share of the ale. Besides, he's asked me to teach him some Welsh songs. I'll not let an assassin kill my fellow-chorister.'

'Then we must find the man before he strikes again.'

'I'll about it straight.' He looked around the taproom. 'Jonas was here even now. Where is the fellow?'

'Returned home.'

'When danger lurks in the streets? He is too careless. Each time he goes abroad, he is at risk. Jonas needs protection.'

'I arranged it,' Nicholas assured him. 'Have no fear. He had a companion on his journey. By now, he will be safely bestowed in his house.'

*The Maids of Honour* had amused Jonas Applegarth for a couple of hours that afternoon, but it also fed his arrogance. He regarded the play as vastly inferior to anything he had written and voiced that opinion loudly in the taproom of the Queen's Head. Watching one comedy prompted him to work on another. After only one tankard of ale, therefore, he left the inn to waddle back to his house.

When Nathan Curtis fell in beside him, it never occurred to Applegarth that the carpenter had been assigned to act as his bodyguard. He was happy enough to have jocular company on the walk back home, not pausing to wonder for a moment why a man who lived in Bankside was walking in the opposite direction. The sturdy presence of Curtis kept any potential attacker at bay. Once Curtis saw the playwright enter his house, he turned his steps back towards the river. The duty which Nicholas Bracewell had given him was discharged.

Jonas Applegarth clambered up the stairs to the little room at the front of the house. He sat down before a table set under the window and covered in sheets of parchment. After sharpening his pen, he dipped it into the inkwell and wrote with a swift hand. The surge of creativity kept him bent over the table for an hour. Evening shadows obliged him to light a candle and he used its flame to read what he had written. Pleased with his progress, he took up his pen once more.

Hugh Naismith watched it all from the cover of a fetid lane opposite the house. While the actor stood in a stinking quagmire, the playwright sat in comfort in his window as he created a new theatrical gem to set before the playgoers of London. Naismith spat with disgust. The difference in their stations rankled. He was cast into the wilderness by a man whose career was now flourishing. It was unjust.

The sight of Jonas Applegarth made his rage smoulder. As he breathed in the foul air, he contemplated the various ways in which he could kill his enemy, dwelling longest on those which inflicted the greatest pain and humiliation.

Nicholas Bracewell approached the house from the far end of the street so that he did not have to walk past the premises owned by Ambrose Robinson. It irked him that since Anne Hendrik stepped back into his life, he had not yet managed to have a proper conversation alone with her.

When the servant opened the door to him, Nicholas heard voices within and feared that the truculent neighbour was already there, but the visitor was in fact a good friend.

'It is wonderful to see you again, Master Bracewell!'

'Thank you, Preben.'

'We have missed you in Bankside.'

'I lodge north of the river now.'

'That is our loss.'

Preben van Loew was the senior hatmaker in the business which Anne Hendrik had inherited from her late husband and which she managed in the adjoining building. A spectral figure in a black skull-cap, the old Dutchman embraced Nicholas warmly before quitting the house. Anne herself waited until they were alone in the parlour before she gave him her welcome.

'This is a lovely surprise, Nick!'

'Do I call at an inconvenient hour?'

Her answer came in the form of a light kiss on the cheek. He wanted to enfold her in his arms, but she moved to a seat and gestured for him to sit opposite her. There was a long pause as they simply luxuriated in the pleasure of being together again. Nicholas let a tidal wave of fond memories wash over him. When it passed, he was left with a profound sense of loss and of waste. Why had he walked away from a house which had given him so much happiness?

'What did you play this afternoon?' she asked.

*'The Maids of Honour.'*

'I have seen the piece more than once.'

'Not quite as it was performed today,' he said wryly. 'John Tallis came to grief at a most unfortunate moment. His voice broke as he was about to marry the Prince of Navarre.'

'Poor boy!'

'He is a man now.'

Nicholas recounted the incident in full and the two of them were soon sharing a chuckle. It was just like old times when the book holder would repair to his lodging and divert her with tales from the innyard of the Queen's Head. Each day brought new adventures. A theatre company inhabited a world of extremes. Anne was a kind audience, interested and responsive, always rejoicing in the heady triumphs of Westfield's Men while sympathising with their numerous disasters. Her bright-eyed curiosity in his work was one of the things that he missed most.

'How goes it with you?' he asked softly.

'The business fares well.'

'Good.'

'We are to take on a new apprentice.'

'Preben will teach him his trade.'

'I have learnt much from him myself.'

Nicholas nodded. 'And the house?'

'What about it?'

'Do you have a lodger here?'

'That is my affair,' she said with a note of gentle reprimand. 'As it happens, there is nobody here at the moment, but that situation may change.' She looked at him with a cautious affection. 'Why did you come?'

'To see you.'

'For what purpose?'

'My own pleasure. Do I need a larger reason?'

'No,' she said. 'Not when that pleasure is mutual.'

She met his gaze and Nicholas thought of a dozen compliments he wished to pay. All of them had to be held back because there was now an obstacle between them. Until the intrusive figure of Ambrose Robinson were removed, he did not feel able to express his true feelings to her.

'A peculiar visitor called on me this morning,' he said.

'Who might that be?'

'Raphael Parsons.'

'Peculiar, indeed! Why did he come?'

'To ascertain the facts about the discovery of Cyril Fulbeck's corpse. Master Parsons had already questioned James Ingram on the matter. This morning, it was my turn.'

'Is he the beast that he is reputed to be?'

'Far from it, Anne.'

'Maligned by report, then?'

'Not entirely,' said Nicholas. 'He is a lawyer by training. He knows what to hide and what to show. Like most lawyers, he has the touch of an actor about him. I found him pleasant enough and remarkably candid. The Chapel Children no doubt see aspects of him that were concealed from me.'

'They loathe him.'

'So I am told.'

'You saw the letters written by Philip Robinson.'

'I did, Anne.'

'They speak of a cruel master, who makes them work hard and who beats them into submission if they try to disobey. Philip is more or less a prisoner there.'

'That is not what Master Parsons says.'

'Oh?'

'He claims that the boy is very happy at Blackfriars.'

*'Happy?* It is one long ordeal for Philip!'

'So his father alleges.'

'You read the boy's own testimony.'

'Yes,' agreed Nicholas. 'That is why I found Master Parsons's denial surprising. Why does it contradict the lad's version of events so completely?'

'The man must be lying.'

'That was not my impression.'

'What other explanation can there be?'

Nicholas let her question hang in the air for a moment.

'How well do you know Philip?' he said at length.

'Reasonably well. He lived but a step away from here.'

'Did you see much of him?'

'No,' she said. 'He was a quiet boy. Always polite but rather diffident. And very lonely after his mother's sad death. Philip was almost invisible. Until Sundays, that is.'

'Sundays?'

'When he sang in the choir. He came alive then. I have never seen a child take such a delight in singing the praises of God. His little face would light up with joy.'

'Does he not have that same joy in the Chapel Royal?'

'I fear not.'

'What chorister would not relish the opportunity of singing before Her Majesty?'

'His pleasure is marred by the misery he endures at the Blackfriars Theatre, where he is forced to be an actor.'

'By Raphael Parsons.'

'Even so. Philip's father has told you all.'

'Has he?'

She grew defensive. 'Of course. Do you doubt Ambrose?'

'Not if you can vouch for him.'

'I can, Nick.'

'I see.' He felt a flicker of jealousy. 'You and he seem well acquainted.'

'He is a neighbour and a friend.'

'Does he have no closer hold on you?'

'What do you mean?'

'Nathan Curtis has observed you in church together.'

'So that is it!' she said, stiffening. 'You have set your carpenter to spy on us.'

'Not at all, Anne. He vouchsafed the information.'

'In answer to your prompting.'

'I simply wondered if he knew Ambrose Robinson.'

'This is unworthy of you, Nick.'

'If I am engaged to help the man, I am entitled to know as much about him as I can. Nathan's opinion of your friend was helpful. It confirms my own impression.'

'You do not like Ambrose, I know that.'

'My concern is that you *do,* Anne. Sufficient to walk to church with him on a Sunday and to kneel beside him.'

'That is my choice.'

'Is it?'

'Yes!' she said, rising angrily from her seat. 'If you have come to turn me against Ambrose, you have come in vain. I live my own life, Nick, and you are no longer part of it. I am grateful to you for the help you have offered, but it does not give you the right to meddle in my private affairs.'

'I do it out of affection.'

'Then express that affection in a more seemly way.'

'Anne . . .'

He got up and reached out for her, but she moved away. There was an awkward pause. Before he could frame an apology into words, there was a loud knock on the door. The servant answered it and Ambrose Robinson came blundering in. His face was puce with indignation.

'Fresh tidings from Blackfriars? Why was I not called?'

'I came to speak with Anne,' explained Nicholas.

'Philip is my son. I have prior claim on any news.'

'How did you know that I was here?'

'I met with Preben van Loew in the street,' said the butcher. 'He told me that you were here. What has happened? I demand to know.'

'Can you not first offer my guest a polite greeting?' chided

Anne. 'You burst in here with improper haste, Ambrose. Remember where you are.'

'I do, I do,' he whined, instantly repentant. 'Forgive my unmannerly behaviour, Anne. My anxiety over Philip robs me of my wits yet again.' He took a deep breath and turned back to Nicholas. 'Please allay my concern. What has happened?'

'I spoke with Raphael Parsons.'

'Did you insist on the release of my son?'

'I raised the topic with him.'

'What was his answer? How did that snake reply?'

'He told me that your son was content to perform on the stage at the Blackfriars Theatre. The boy has talent as an actor. He is keen to develop it.'

'Lies! Deception! Trickery!'

'That is all Master Parsons would say on the subject.'

'Falsehood!'

'Lower your voice!' urged Anne.

'Why did you not take hold of the rogue and beat the truth out of him?'

'He came to discuss the murder of Cyril Fulbeck,' said Nicholas firmly. 'It weighs heavily upon him. Set against the death of the Master of the Chapel, the fate of one chorister was an irrelevance.'

'It is not an irrelevance to me, sir!'

'I will try to pursue the matter with him.'

'Parsons is an arrant knave,' said Robinson. 'I should have done what a father's love told me to do at the very start. Attend a performance at Blackfriars and snatch Philip off the stage.'

'That would be madness,' argued Anne.

'I want my son back home with me.'

'Then achieve that end by peaceful means. Take him away by force and the law will descend on you with such severity that you'd lose both Philip and your own freedom.'

'Anne counsels well,' added Nicholas. 'What use are you to the boy if you're fretting away in prison? I'll speak with Master

Parsons again and use what persuasion I may. In the meantime, you must learn patience.'

Robinson's fury seemed to drain away. Face ashen and shoulders dropping, he stood there in silent bewilderment. He looked so wounded and defenceless that Anne lay a hand on his arm, like a mother comforting a hurt child. The gesture annoyed Nicholas but it had a different effect on the butcher.

It only served to ignite the spirit of vengeance until it glinted in his eyes. Taking her by the hand, Robinson led Anne gently out of the room and closed the door behind her so that he could speak to Nicholas alone. There was no ranting this time, no bluster and arm-waving, only a quiet and quite eerie intensity.

'Very well,' he said. 'Try once more, Nick. Work within the law. Use reason and supplication to restore my son to me.' His jaw tightened. 'But if you fail, if they keep Philip locked up, if they continue to spread malicious lies about him wanting to stay there, I'll seek Raphael Parsons out and play a part for him myself.'

'A part?'

'The Laughing Hangman.'

'Keep well away from Blackfriars.'

'That is what Anne advises,' he said, 'and for her sake, I have stayed my hand. But not for much longer. Unless Philip comes home to me soon, I'll hang Raphael Parsons by the neck from the tallest building in London and I'll laugh until my sides burst.'

The threat was a serious one.

# [ CHAPTER SEVEN ]

The Elephant was a large, low, sprawling inn, famed for its strong ale and unflagging hospitality. It stood near near The Curtain, one of the two theatres in Shoreditch which brought the citizens of London streaming out through Bishopsgate in search of entertainment. Banbury's Men, the resident company at The Curtain, used the inn as a place to celebrate their frequent successes or to drown their sorrows in the wake of occasional abysmal failures. When Owen Elias arrived at the Elephant that evening, the boisterous atmosphere told him that celebration was in order. Banbury's Men were basking in the triumph of their new play, *The Fatal Dowry*, performed that afternoon to general acclaim.

Elias ducked below a beam and surveyed the taproom through a fug of tobacco smoke. Westfield's Men were deadly rivals of the company at The Curtain and relations between them went well beyond bitterness. The Welshman would not normally have sought out the other troupe, especially as he had once belonged to it for a brief and acrimonious period. Necessity compelled him to come, and he looked for the swiftest way to discharge his business and leave the enemy lair.

Selecting his man with care, he closed in on him.

'Why, how now, Ned!'

'Is that you, Owen?'

'As large and lovely as life itself.'

'What brings you to the Elephant?'

'Two strong legs and a devil of a thirst. Will you drink some ale with me, Ned?'

'I'll drink with any man who pays the bill, even if he belong to that hellish crew known as Westfield's Men.' He turned to his friends on the adjoining table. 'See here, lads. Look what the tide has washed up. Owen Elias!'

Jeers of disapproval went up and Owen had to endure some stinging insults before he could settle down beside his former colleague. Ale was brought and he drank deep. Ned Meares was a hired man, one of the many actors who scraped a precarious living at their trade and who made the most of their intermittent stretches of employment while they lasted. A stout man in his thirties, Meares was an able actor with a wide range. In the time since he had last seen the man, Elias noted, regular consumption of ale had filled out his paunch and deepened the florid complexion.

'A sharer now, I hear,' said Meares enviously.

'I have been lucky, Ned.'

'Spare a thought for we who toil on as hired men.'

'I do. I struggled along that same road myself.'

'It will never end for me, alas.' He nudged the visitor. 'Come, Owen, you crafty Welshman. Do not pretend that you are here to renew old acquaintance. Westfield's Men lurk in the Queen's Head. You have no place at the Elephant. What do you want?'

'To talk about a playwright you will know.'

'What is his name?' asked Meares, quaffing his ale.

'Jonas Applegarth.'

Elias had to move sharply to avoid the drink which was spat out again by his companion. Meares coughed and spluttered until his eyes watered. A few hearty slaps on the back were needed to help him recover.

Elias grinned. 'I see that you remember Jonas.'

'Remember him! Could I ever forget that monster? Jonas Applegarth was like a visitation of the plague.'

'Why?'

'Because he infected the whole company.'

'He wrote only one play for Banbury's Men.'

'One play too many!' groaned Meares. *'Friar Francis.* The name of that dread piece is scrawled on my soul for ever.' He sipped his ale before continuing. 'Most authors sell us a play, advise us how best to stage it, then stand aside while we do our work. Not Jonas. He was author, actor and book holder rolled into one. He stood over us from start to finish. We were no more than galley-slaves, lashed to the oars while he whipped us unmercifully with his tongue and urged us to row harder.'

'He does have a warm turn of phrase,' conceded Elias.

'Threats and curses were all his conversation.'

'Did the company not resist?'

'Every inch of the way, Owen. Banbury's Men were to have played *Friar Francis* but that raging bull tried to turn us into Applegarth's Men. It could not be borne.'

Meares needed another fortifying drink of his ale before he could recount full details of the fierce battle against the arrogance of the author. Feigning sympathy, Elias took great satisfaction from the chaos which had been caused in the rival company while making a mental note to take precautions to stop the obstreperous playwright from wreaking the same havoc among Westfield's Men. Recrimination left Ned Meares shaking like an aspen. The visitor had to buy him another tankard of ale to restore his shattered nerves.

'Did anyone hate Jonas enough to kill him?'

'Yes,' said Meares. 'All of us!'

'Was there a special enemy of his in the company?'

'A dozen at least, Owen.'

'Who had most cause to loathe him?'

'Most cause?' The actor rubbed a hand ruminatively through his beard. 'Most cause? That would have to be Hugh Naismith.'

Nicholas Bracewell slept fitfully that night, dreaming of happier days at the Bankside home of Anne Hendrik and waking at intervals to scold himself for the way he had upset her during his visit. Both were strong-willed individuals and this had led to many arguments in the past, but they had usually been resolved in the most joyful and effective way in Anne's bed. That avenue of reconciliation had now been closed off to him, and he feared that as long as Ambrose Robinson stayed in her life, she would remain beyond his reach.

Jealousy of the butcher was not the only reason why he wanted to put the man to flight. Robinson had a temper which flared up all too easily and threatened to spill over into violence. Nicholas was worried that Anne might one day unwittingly become the victim of that choleric disposition. What mystified him was that she seemed to enjoy's the man's friendship, enough to attend church in his company and to fret about his enforced estrangement from his son.

The plight of Philip Robinson had drawn the two of them together and placed Nicholas in a quandary. If he helped to secure the boy's release from the Chapel Children, would he be pushing Anne even closer to the Robinson family, and was it not in his interests to keep father and son apart? His sense of duty prevented his taking the latter course. Having promised assistance, he could not now go back on his word.

His mind was still in turmoil and his feelings still in a state of ambivalence as he left his lodging in Thames Street. The morning cacophony enveloped him and he did not hear the soft footsteps which came scurrying up behind him.

'Stay, sir!' said a voice. 'I would speak with you.'

Caleb Hay had to pluck at his sleeve to get Nicholas's attention. The book holder turned and exchanged greetings with him. Boyish enthusiasm lit up the older man's features.

'I hoped that I would catch you,' he said.

'Why?'

'Because I have something for you. Step this way, sir. Let us rid ourselves of this tumult.'

'I may not tarry long, Master Hay.'

'This will take but a few minutes and I think that you will consider them well spent.'

He led Nicholas back down the busy street to his house. Once they were inside, the noise subsided to a gentle hubbub. Joan Hay was sitting in the parlour with her embroidery as they entered. A glance from her husband made her jump to her feet and give the visitor a hesitant smile before moving off into the kitchen.

Caleb Hay went to a box on the table. Taking a large iron ring from his belt, he selected one of the keys and opened the box. Nicholas was first handed a sheet of parchment. His interest quickened as he studied the sketch of the Blackfriars Theatre.

'Forgive my crude handiwork,' said Hay. 'As you see, I am no artist, but it may give you some idea of the shape and size of the building. It is yours to scrutinise at will.'

'Thank you. This will be a great help.'

'Every exit is clearly marked.'

The sketch was simple but drawn roughly to scale. It enabled Nicholas to see exactly where he had been when he heard the Laughing Hangman and why it had taken him so long to reach the door at the rear of the building. Names of the adjacent streets had been added in a neat hand.

Caleb Hay produced a second item from the box.

'I can take more pride in this,' he said with a mild chuckle. 'You asked about the petition that was drawn up to prevent a theatre being re-opened in Blackfriars. This is not the document itself but an exact copy. It must remain in my keeping but you are welcome to over-glance it, if you wish.'

'Please,' said Nicholas, taking the document from him. 'I am most grateful to you. Anything which pertains to Blackfriars is of interest to me.'

He read the petition with attention to its detail:

> *To the right honorable the Lords and others of her Majesties most honorable Privy Counsell—Humbly shewing and beseeching your honors, the inhabitants of the precinct of Blackfryers, London, that whereas one Burbage hath lately bought certaine roomes in the said precinct neere adjoyning unto the houses of the right honorable, the Lord Chamberlaine and the Lord of Hunsdon, which roomes the said Burbage is now altering and meaneth very shortly to convert and turne the same into a comon playhouse, which will grow to be a very great annoyance and trouble. . . .*

The complaints against public theatre were all too familiar to Nicholas. They were voiced every week by members of the City authorities and by outraged Puritans, who sought to curb the activities of Westfield's Men. The Blackfriars petition was signed by thirty-one prominent residents of the precinct, starting with Lord Hunsdon, who, ironically, was the patron of his own troupe—Lord Chamberlain's Men—but who drew the line at having a playhouse on his doorstep. Nicholas ran his eye down the other names, which included the dowager Lady Russell and a respected printer, Richard Field.

'Is it not strongly and carefully worded?' said Hay.

'Indeed, it is.'

'It represents my own view on the theatre. I was mightily relieved when the petition was accepted by the Privy Council.'

'With such names to sustain it, the plea could hardly be denied,' said Nicholas. 'But it was only a temporary measure. A public playhouse may have been kept out of Blackfriars, but a private theatre was re-opened.'

'Alack the day!'

'The audiences who flock there will disagree.'

'No doubt,' said Hay, taking the document back and locking

it in the box. 'This petition belongs to history.'

Nicholas moved to the door. 'You have been most kind. This drawing of Blackfriars will make a difficult task much easier.'

'Catch him! Catch this vile murderer.'

'I will bend all my efforts to do so.'

'Keep the name of Raphael Parsons firmly in mind.'

'You have evidence against him, Master Hay?'

'Nothing that would support his arrest,' confessed the other. 'But I have a feeling in my old bones that he is involved in this crime in some way. He is a man without scruple or remorse. Keep watch on him. From what I hear about this Master Parsons, he would be a ready hangman.'

Raphael Parsons endured the rehearsal for as long as he could but the lackluster performance and the recurring errors were too much for him to bear.

'Stop!' he ordered. 'I'll stand no more of this ordeal! It is a disgrace to our reputation!'

The young actors on the stage at the Blackfriars Theatre came to an abrupt halt in the middle of the second act. Even a play as well tried as *Mariana's Revels* seemed to be beyond their scope. Their diction was muted, their gesture without conviction and their movement sluggish. A drama which required a lightness of touch was accorded a leaden treatment. Parsons was livid.

'This is shameful!' he snarled. 'I would not dare to put such a miserable account of the play before a crew of drunken sailors, let alone in front of a paying audience. Where is your art, sirs? Where is your self-respect? Where is your pride in our work? We laboured hard to make the Children of the Chapel Royal a company of distinction. Will you betray all that we have struggled to create?'

The cast stood there with heads bowed while the manager harangued them. Some shook with trepidation, others shed tears, all were plunged into the deepest melancholy. Parsons came striding down the hall to bang on the edge of the stage with his fist.

'Why are you *doing* this to me!' he demanded.

The youngest member of the company was its spokesman.

'We are grieving, sir,' said Philip Robinson meekly.

'That performance was enough to make anyone grieve!'

'Master Fulbeck is ever in our minds.'

Nods of agreement came from several of the cast and more eyes moistened. Philip Robinson's own face was glistening with tears. Short, slim and pale, he wore the costume of Mariana as if it were a set of chains. Features which had a feminine prettiness when animated were now dull and plain. His body sagged. His voice was a pathetic bleat.

'We are too full of sadness, sir,' he said.

The manager's first impulse was to supplant the sadness with naked fear. It would not be the first time that he had instilled terror into his company in order to raise the level of their performance. Instinct held him back. These were unique circumstances, calling for a different approach. Instead of excoriating his juvenile players, therefore, he opted for a show of compassion.

Clambering upon the stage, he beckoned them closer.

'We all mourn him,' he said softly. 'And rightly so. The cruel manner of his death makes it an intolerable loss. Master Fulbeck was the only true begetter of this theatre. Though the Chapel Royal was his first love, he came to take an equal delight in your work here at Blackfriars. Hold to that thought. We do not play *Mariana's Revels* for our own benefit or even for the entertainment of our spectators. We stage it in remembrance of Cyril Fulbeck, late Master of the Chapel. Will you honour his name with a jaded performance?'

'No, Master Parsons,' said Philip boldly.

'Shall we close the theatre and turn people away? Is that what he would have wanted? Or shall we continue the noble work which he first started here? Cyril Fulbeck died in and for this theatre. The place to celebrate his memory is here on this very stage with a play which he held dear.'

'Yes!' called a voice at the back.

'We must play on!' added another.

'Under your instruction,' said Philip Robinson.

'So it will be,' decided Parsons, watching their spirits revive. 'But let us do it with no show of sadness or despair. *Mariana's Revels* is a joyful play. Speak its lines with passion. Dance its measures with vigour. Sing its songs with elation. Tell us why, Philip.'

'They were written by Master Fulbeck himself.'

'Even so. Most of them fall to Mariana to sing. Give them full voice, my boy. Treat them like hymns of praise!'

'Yes, sir!'

The rehearsal started again with a new gusto. For all his youth and inexperience, Philip Robinson led the Chapel Children like a boy on a mission, taking his first solo and offering it up to Heaven in the certainty that it would be heard and applauded by the man who had composed it for him.

Marriage to an actor as brilliant and virile as Lawrence Firethorn brought many pains but they were swamped beneath the compensating pleasures. Foremost among these for his redoubtable wife, Margery, was the never-ending delight of watching him ply his trade, strutting the stage with an imperious authority and carving an unforgettable performance in the minds of the onlookers. His talent and his sheer vitality were bound to make countless female hearts flutter and Firethorn revelled in the adulation. When Margery visited the Queen's Head, she could not only share in the magic of his art, she could also keep his eye from roving and his eager body from straying outside the legitimate confines of the marital couch.

*Vincentio's Revenge* was a darker play in the repertoire of Westfield's Men, but one that gave its actor-manager a superb role as the eponymous hero. It never failed to wring her emotions and move Margery to tears. Since it was being played again that afternoon, she abandoned her household duties, dressed herself in her finery and made her way to Gracechurch Street with an almost girlish excitement. Good weather and high hopes brought a large audience converging on the Queen's Head. Pleased to see the throng, Margery was even more thrilled to identify two of its members.

'Anne!' she cried. 'This is blessed encounter.'

'You come to watch *Vincentio's Revenge*?'

'Watch it, wonder at it and wallow in it.'

'May we then sit together?' suggested Anne Hendrik.

'Indeed we may, though I must warn you that I will use all the womanly wiles at my command to steal that handsome gallant away from your side.'

Preben van Loew blushed deeply and made a gesture of self-deprecation. Margery's blunt speech and habit of teasing always unnerved him. When the three of them paid their entrance fee to the lower gallery, the old Dutchman made sure that Anne sat between him and the over-exuberant Margery. It allowed the two women to converse freely.

'I have not seen you this long while,' said Margery.

'My visits to the Queen's Head are less frequent.'

'You are bored with Westfield's Men?'

'Far from it,' said Anne. 'It is work that keeps me away and not boredom. I love the theatre as much as ever.'

'Does Nicholas know that you are here?'

'No, he does not.'

'Then it were a kindness to tell him. It would lift his spirits to know that you were in the audience.'

'I am not so sure.'

'He dotes on you, woman,' said Margery with a nudge. 'Are you blind? Are you insensible? If a man as fine and upright as Nick Bracewell loved me, I would never leave his side for a second. He *misses* you, Anne.'

'I miss him,' she said involuntarily.

'Then why keep him ignorant of your presence?'

'It is needful.'

'For whom? You or him?'

'I simply came to watch a play, Margery.'

'Then why not visit The Rose, which is closer to your home and far more commodious? Why not go to Shoreditch to choose between The Curtain and The Theatre? Deceive yourself, but do not try to deceive me. You came here for a purpose.'

'To see *Vincentio's Revenge,'* insisted Anne.

'I will not press the matter.'

'What happened between Nick and myself is . . . all past.'

'Not in his mind. Still less in his heart.'

Anne grew pensive. Margery's companionship gave her joy and discomfort in equal measure. Anne's feelings were so confused that she was not quite sure why she had decided to find the time to attend the play, and to release Preben van Loew from his work in order to chaperone her. She had responded to an urge which had yet to identify itself properly.

'Forgive me,' said Margery, squeezing her wrist in apology. 'My fondness for Nick makes me speak out of turn. You and he need no Cupid. I'll hold my peace.'

'A friend's advice is always welcome.'

'You know what mine would be. I say no more.'

Anne nodded soulfully and a surge of regret ran through her. It soon passed. *Vincentio's Revenge* began and the forthright woman beside her turned into a sobbing spectator. Anne herself was caught up in the emotion of the piece and whisked along for two harrowing but glorious hours by its poetry and its poignancy. It was only when the performance was over that she realised why she had come to it.

Having piloted another play safely into port, Nicholas Bracewell supervised the unloading of the cargo and the crew. It was not until the last of the properties and the costumes had been safely locked away that he was able to spare the time to listen to Owen Elias's report of his findings. The two of them were alone in the tiring-house.

'His name is Hugh Naismith.'

'Can you be certain, Owen?'

'As certain as it is possible to be. The fellow was a regular member of Banbury's Men, a promising actor, secure in the company's estimation and likely to rise to the rank of sharer.'

'What happened?' asked Nicholas.

'*Friar Francis*. By one Jonas Applegarth.'

'I remember seeing the playbills for it.'

'Hugh Naismith did not like the piece. *Friar Francis* was a most un-Christian play, by all account, as full of fury as *The Misfortunes of Marriage*, and with an even sharper bite. This foolish actor dared to rail against it in the hearing of the author and the two of them had to be held apart for they squawked at each other like fighting cocks.'

'Was this Naismith his opponent in the duel?'

'Ned Meares confirms it,' said Elias. 'The varlet was so badly injured that his arm was put in a sling for weeks. Banbury's Men expelled him straight. The fight with Jonas has cost Naismith both his pride and his occupation.'

'Two strong reasons for him to seek revenge.'

'One arm was in a sling but he still might throw a dagger with the other. It *must* be him, Nick.'

'Where does he dwell?'

'In Shoreditch. I called at his lodging.'

'You met him?'

'He was not there. Out stalking his prey, no doubt. That thought made me straight repair to Jonas's house, where I found our fat friend, sitting at his desk in the window of his chamber, writing away as if he did not have a care in the world.'

'You and he arrived here together, I saw.'

'Yes, Nick,' said Elias. 'I felt compelled to go back to his house again this morning. An assassin may strike on the journey to the

Queen's Head just as well as on the walk back home. Four eyes offer better protection than two.'

'How did Jonas seem?'

'As loud and irreverent as ever.'

'Did you mention Hugh Naismith to him?'

'He affected not to know the man and would not discuss his time with Banbury's Men except to say that it was a species of torment.'

'For him or for them?' asked Nicholas with a wry smile.

'Both.'

The book holder checked that everything had been cleared out of the tiring-house before taking his friend through into the taproom. It was throbbing with noise. Players and playgoers alike were ready for drink and debate after the stirring performance of *Vincentio's Revenge.*

Jonas Applegarth was holding forth in the middle of the room, addressing his remarks to all who would listen. His lack of tact and restraint made the newcomers gasp.

'It is a miserable, meandering, worm-eaten play,' he argued.

'*Vincentio's Revenge* is a sterling piece,' countered James Ingram. 'You saw how the audience loved it.'

'Ignorant fools! What do they know of drama? If you put ten bare arses on the stage and farted at them for two hours, they would applaud you just as wildly. *The Maids of Honour* was base enough, but today's offering was putrid.'

'That is unkind! Unjust!'

'And untrue!' added Barnaby Gill, entering the fray. '*Vincentio's Revenge* has been a loyal servant to the company. It fires my imagination each time we play it and raises the pitch of my performance.'

'Then is it time for you to retire,' said Applegarth with scorn. 'You were a walking abomination up on that stage. I have seen sheep with more talent and less confusion. Show some benevolence to mankind, Barnaby, and quit the theatre for good.'

'I was sublime!' howled Gill.

'Scurvy!'

'Unparallelled.'

'In absurdity!'

'Barnaby was at his best,' defended Ingram stoutly.

'Then I would hate to see his worst,' retorted Applegarth, 'for it would beggar belief. Why wave his hands so, and pull his face thus?' His grotesque mime turned Gill purple with rage. 'It was a barbarous performance, almost as bad as that of Vincentio himself.'

Lawrence Firetorn came sailing into the taproom.

'What's that you say, sir?' he growled.

'The play was ill-chosen.'

'Not as ill-chosen as your words, Jonas,' warned the other. 'Have a care, sir. We like *Vincentio's Revenge.'*

'Can any sane man admire such a botch of nature?'

'Yes!' challenged Firethorn. 'He stands before you.'

'Then I will list my complaints against the piece in order,' said Applegarth, quite unabashed. 'Firstly . . .'

'Save your strictures for another time,' insisted Nicholas, diving in quickly to take the heat out of the argument. 'Master Firethorn is entertaining his wife and does not wish to be led astray by idle comment that smells too strongly of ale. Our play found favour this afternoon and there's an end to it.'

With the aid of Owen Elias, he shepherded Applegarth to a table in the corner and sat him down on a bench. Barnaby Gill was still pulsating with anger and James Ingram with disgust, but the quarrel was effectively over. Lawrence Firethorn mastered his fury. Reminded that Margery was still waiting for him in the adjoining chamber, he ordered wine and withdrew to the urgent solace of her embrace. An uneasy peace descended on the taproom.

Jonas Applegarth was still in a bellicose mood.

'I am entitled to my opinion,' he asserted.

'Not when it offends your fellows so,' said Nicholas.

'Can they not cope with honesty?'

'Honesty, yes, but this was random cruelty.'

'I will not praise where praise is not due, Nick.'

'Then hold your tongue,' counselled Elias, 'or you'll lose every friend you have made in Westfield's Men. Insult Master Firethorn again and your career with us is ended.'

'This play was lame stuff.'

'Why, then, did you force yourself to watch it?' said Nicholas. 'If *Vincentio's Revenge* is not to your taste, avoid it. That way, you will not have to suffer its shortcomings and your fellows will not have to bear your gibes. How can you expect actors to give of their best in *your* play when you mock their performances in every other piece?'

'Stop biting the hand that feeds you,' said Elias. 'You have spat out enough fingers already. Respect our work and we might grow to respect yours.'

'My art demands reverence!' said Applegarth, slapping the table with a peremptory hand. '*The Misfortunes of Marriage* is an absolute masterpiece.'

'Only when it is played,' reminded Nicholas.

'Why, so it will be. At The Rose next week.'

'Not if you talk it off the stage.'

'Westfield's Men are contracted to perform it.'

'We were contracted to perform *The Faithful Shepherd* by Edmund Hoode until you came along. If one play can be ousted thus easily from The Rose, so can another.' Nicholas did not mince his words. 'And if Westfield's Men do not perform your work, it will remain as no more than words on a page. I gave you fair warning at the start, Jonas. You will be out of the company and we will cheer your departure.'

Applegarth was momentarily checked. 'But you saw my play, Nick. It blazed across the stage like a meteor. Owen will vouch for its quality. He tasted its true worth from the inside. Would any company be so prodigal as to cast aside a work of art?'

'Our doubts are not about *The Misfortunes of Marriage,*' said Nicholas. 'It is a rare phenomenon. We all agree on that. But the playwright obstructs our view of the play. In plain terms, you are making us regret the misfortunes of marriage between Westfield's Men and Jonas Applegarth. Divorce grows daily nearer.'

'Then let it come!' shouted the other.

'Listen to Nick,' said Elias. 'You need us.'

'Not if I must be bound and gagged. Fie on thee!'

'Sleep on what I have said,' suggested Nicholas. 'We would be friends. Why rush to make us mortal enemies?'

'God's blood!' exclaimed Applegarth. 'I'll not stand it!'

He rose to his feet and swayed over them. The smell of strong ale was on his breath. Applegarth had been drinking heavily before, during and after the performance. It made him even more pugnacious and fearless of consequence.

'A turd in your teeth!' he bawled. 'Oust me? I spurn you all like the knaves you are! There is a world elsewhere!'

Kicking the bench aside, he lurched towards the door. Owen Elias was outraged by his behaviour but his affection for the playwright won through.

'Wild words spoken in haste,' he said.

'That tongue of his will talk him out of employment.'

'I'll after him and see the rogue safe home.'

'Counsel moderation, Owen.'

'What I counsel is a bucket of cold water over his foolish head before I deign to speak to him. If Jonas will not see sense, he loses my esteem. I'll not sew another patch on the torn sleeve of our fellowship.'

As soon as the Welshman left, Nicholas was joined by James Ingram, still in a state of agitation.

'Applegarth is a menace to us all, Nick!'

'But chiefly to himself.'

'Do not ask me to show him sympathy.'

'Jonas has supped too much ale.'

'Sober, he is merely obnoxious; drunk, he is beyond excuse. He poured contempt on the whole company.'

'I heard him, James.'

'He is one big barrel of arrogance.'

'His time with us may be very short indeed.'

'It will be,' said Ingram with feeling. 'If he takes the cudgel to us, we will fight back. I tell you, Nick, I'd willingly strike the first blow.'

Nicholas was surprised. James Ingram was not given to fits of anger. With the exception of Edmund Hoode, he was the most mild-mannered person in the company. Yet he was now curling his lip in a sneer of animosity. It was several minutes before Nicholas could calm him down. When he finally did so, he slipped his hand inside his buff jerkin to take out the sketch which Caleb Hay had drawn for him.

'I have something to show you, James.'

'What is it?'

'Blackfriars. Given to me by a friend.'

Ingram examined the sketch with great interest and traced the outline of the theatre with his finger. There was a hint of nostalgia in his voice.

'It is very accurate.'

'The artist is a keen historian of the city.'

'Then here, in this small drawing, is history writ large. Castle and tower are turned into a monastery. Monastery becomes a theatre. And this very week, theatre becomes a place of execution. Master Fulbeck's death is one more violent change in Blackfriars. God rest his soul!'

'Amen.'

'When will you go back there, Nick?'

'This evening.'

'Take me with you.'

'Gladly.'

'I am ready,' said Ingram, handing the sketch back to him. 'Why do we tarry here?'

'Because I have to pay my respects first.'

'To whom?'

Nicholas glanced towards a door on the far side of the room

and Ingram gave a smile of understanding. The book holder needed to exchange a greeting with Margery Firethorn.

'I'll be with you anon,' said Nicholas.

He crossed to the door and tapped lightly on it.

'Enter!' boomed the actor.

Husband and wife were seated at a table when he went in. Both rose to their feet instantly, Margery coming across to embrace the visitor and Firethorn seeing an opportunity to elude her matrimonial vigilance for a few minutes.

'Is that insolent braggart still here, Nick?'

'Jonas Applegarth has gone back home.'

'He is like to stay there if he rail against me. I was Vincentio to the life this afternoon. Was I not, my dove?'

'Beyond compare,' cooed Margery.

'Yet that wrangling malcontent denied my genius. I'll fetch him such a box on the ears, he'll not wake until Doomsday! Let me see that he has quit the premises or I'll not rest.'

Firethorn slipped out of the room and closed the door behind him. Margery was clearly delighted to be left alone with Nicholas. Taking him by the hand, she led him across to a small bench and they sat down together. She spoke in a conspiratorial whisper.

'Thank heaven that you came to me, Nick.'

'Why?'

'You'd else have missed the glad tidings.'

'Tidings?'

'She was here.'

'Who?'

'Who else, man?'

'Anne? Here at the performance?'

'Sitting as close to me as you are now. She loved the play as much as I did and wept almost as many tears. Anne sent a private message to you.'

'Did she?'

'I am to give you her warmest regards,' said Margery. 'What

she really meant me to convey was her undying love but she could not put that into words.'

Nicholas was pleased that Anne had made contact through an intermediary, though disappointed that she had not delivered her message in person.

'Did Anne come to the Queen's Head alone?' he said.

'No,' replied Margery with a teasing grin. 'She was on the arm of the most striking young man I have seen for a long time. Were I not a contented wife, I would have fought her tooth and nail for the privilege of being escorted by so dashing a partner. An exquisite fellow.'

'What was his name?'

'Preben van Loew.'

Nicholas laughed with relief. There was no point in trying to hide his love for Anne Hendrik from her. Margery had seen them together in earlier days and never ceased to tax him over their parting. Unwilling and unable to talk about Anne with anyone else, he was now with the one person who had some insight into the relationship.

'Go to her, Nick,' she advised.

'It is not the answer, I fear.'

'She wastes away without you.'

'That is not my impression.'

'I can tell when a woman is grieving.'

'It is not for me,' he said with a sigh. 'When I called on her yesterday, I only managed to upset her. We have lost the way of speaking to each other.'

'Use deeds instead of words. Embrace her with love.'

He shook his head. 'My suit is unwelcome.'

'Press it with more diligence.'

'I am too late. There is another man in her life.'

'Ambrose Robinson.'

He blinked in astonishment. 'She spoke of him?'

'Not a word.'

'Then how did you learn of his existence?'

'From her handsome escort.'

'Preben van Loew?'

'Yes,' she said airily. 'Anne would not talk of her personal affairs and so I bided my time until I could speak with the Dutchman alone. For some reason, the poor fellow is afraid of me. I cannot think why. I am Mildness itself. Is any woman in London less frightening than me?'

'I think not,' said Nicholas tactfully.

'As we were leaving the gallery, Anne met a neighbour and exchanged a few words with her. I seized my opportunity. Preben was most forthcoming.'

'What did he say?'

'He does not like this Ambrose Robinson, I know that.'

'No more do I.'

'Anne does, it seems. And with some reason.'

'What might it be?'

'Money,' she said. 'The Dutchman was too loyal to betray the full details, but he gave me hints and nudges enough for me to piece together the story. Earlier in the year, her business was in grave difficulty.'

'Anne told me that it was faring well.'

'Only because of the butcher. Thieves broke into the shop three times. Hats were destroyed, patterns stolen. They were unable to meet their orders and lost business. To make matters worse, the shop was damaged by fire and much of their material went up in smoke.'

'Why did not Anne turn to me?' Nick asked anxiously.

'Because you had drifted out of her life. What she needed was money to rebuild and restock her premises. That is when Ambrose Robinson came on the scene.'

'Now I understand her sense of obligation.'

'Understand something else, Nick. She came to see *you*.'

'But I was hidden from sight.'

'You were here, that was enough. Anne wanted to be close.'

'Is that what she told you?'

'She did not need to.'

Nicholas was touched. Margery had been active on his behalf, and for all her outspokenness, he knew that she could be discreet. What she had found out explained much that had been puzzling him. Though she did not feel able to speak with him directly, Anne Hendrik had taken a definite step towards him. It was something on which to build.

Edmund Hoode waited for well over an hour before disillusion set in. Standing alone in the empty innyard, he began to feel decidedly conspicuous. He had been like a mettlesome horse at first, prancing on his toes and quivering with pent-up energy. His high expectation slowly trickled away and he was now as forlorn and motionless as a parish pump in a rainstorm.

Her message had been explicit. *Tomorrow.* Surely that was a firm promise? He was at the same spot, in the same yard at more or less the same time. Why did she not send word? A sleepless night in a fever of hope had been followed by a morning rehearsal. Knowing that she would be watching, he dedicated his performance in *Vincentio's Revenge* to her and invested it with every ounce of skill and commitment.

After changing out of his costume in the tiring-house and waiting for the yard to clear of spectators, he began his vigil with a light heart. It was now a huge boulder which weighed him down and which threatened to burst out of the inadequate lodging of his chest. Could any woman be capable of such wanton cruelty? A rose. A promise. Betrayal. Hoode was devastated.

There was no hint of Rose Marwood this time, no sign of a well-groomed servant with a secret missive. All he could see were a couple of ostlers, sniggering at him from the shadow of the stables and wondering why a man in his best doublet and hose should be standing in the middle of a filthy innyard. Hoode gave up. With weary footsteps, he trudged towards the archway which led to Gracechurch Street.

When the horse and rider trotted into the yard, he stood swiftly to one side to let them pass, never suspecting that they had come in search of him. The young man in the saddle brought his mount in a tight circle and its flank brushed Hoode as it went past. About to protest, the playwright suddenly realised that he was holding something in his hand. Another missive had been delivered.

Spirits soaring once more, he tore the seal off and unrolled the sheet. Hoping for a letter, he was at first dumbfounded to find no words at all on the page. In their place was what appeared to be the head of a horse with a spike protruding from between its eyes. Was it a message or a piece of mockery? It was only when his brain cleared that he was able to read its import.

'The Unicorn!'

A rose. A promise. A tryst. Love was, after all, moving in ascending steps. She was waiting for him at the Unicorn. It was an inn no more than a hundred yards away. His first impulse was to run there as fast as his trembling legs could carry him, but a more sensible course of action recommended itself. Since she had kept him on tenterhooks, he would make her wait as well. It would only serve to heighten the pleasure of their encounter.

Adjusting his attire and straightening his hat, he left the Queen's Head and strolled along Gracechurch Street with dignity. He was no love-lorn rustic, rushing to answer the call of a capricious mistress. He was a conqueror about to enjoy the spoils of war. That illusion carried him all the way to the Unicorn and in through its main door. It was shattered the moment he was confronted by a smiling young woman with a fawnlike grace and beauty. His jaw dropped.

She gave him a curtsey, then indicated the stairs.

'My mistress awaits you, sir. Follow me.'

With uncertain steps, Edmund Hoode climbed towards Elysium.

# [ CHAPTER EIGHT ]

When he reached the landing, he made an effort to compose his features and to straighten his back. It was as a man of the theatre that his admirer had first seen Edmund Hoode. She would lose all respect for him if he were to slink apologetically into her company and behave like a callow youth in a fumbling courtship. A dramatic entrance was called for and he did his best to supply it.

The maidservant tapped on a door, opened it in answer to a summons from within and then stepped back to admit the visitor. Pretending that he was about to face an audience in the innyard, Hoode went into the chamber with a confident stride and doffed his hat to bow low. The door closed soundlessly behind him. When he raised his eyes to take a first long look at the mysterious lady in his life, he was quite bedazzled.

She was beautiful. Fair-skinned and neat-boned, she had an alabaster neck which supported an oval face of quiet loveliness. She wore a dark blue velvet dress but no jewellery of any kind. Well-groomed blond hair was brushed back under a blue cap. Gloved hands were folded in her lap as she sat on a chair, framed by the window.

Hoode was struck by her poise and elegance. Her voice was low and accompanied by a sweet smile of welcome.

'It is a pleasure to see you, Master Hoode,' she said.

'Thank you,' he replied politely, 'but I fear that you have the advantage over me.'

'My name is Cecily Gilbourne.'

A second bow. 'At your service, Mistress Gilbourne.'

'Pray take a seat, sir.'

She motioned him to a chair opposite her and he lowered himself gingerly onto it, his gaze never leaving her. Cecily Gilbourne was a trifle older than he had expected—in her late twenties, perhaps even thirty—but her maturity was to him a form of supreme ripeness. He would not have changed her age by a year or her appearance by the tiniest emendation. It was reassuring to learn that she was no impressionable child, no giggling girl, no shallow creature infatuated with the theatre, but a woman of experience with an intelligence that positively shone out of her.

*'The Merchant of Calais,'* she announced.

'A workmanlike piece,' he said modestly.

'I thought it brilliant. It was the first of your plays that I saw and it made me yearn to meet the author.'

'Indeed?'

'Such an understanding of the true price of love.'

'Your praise overwhelms me.'

'Not as much as your work overwhelms *me,'* she said with a sigh of admiration. 'You are a true poet of the soul. *The Corrupt Bargain.'*

'Another apple plucked from the orchard of my brain.'

'Delicious in the mouth. *Love's Sacrifice.* We have all made that in our time, alas. Your play on that theme was so profound.'

'Drawn from life.'

'That is what I guessed. Only those who have suffered the pangs of a broken heart can understand the nature of that suffering. *Love's Sacrifice* gave me untold pleasure and helped me to keep sorrow at bay during a most troubling time in my life. Your plays, Master Hoode—may I call you Edmund?'

'Please, please!' he encouraged.

'Your plays, Edmund, are a source of joy to me.'

'For that compliment alone, they were worth writing.'

*'Double Deceit.'*

'Juvenilia. When I was young and green.'

'Its humour bubbled like a mountain stream.'

*'Pompey the Great.* That is Edmund Hoode at his finest.'

'I regret that I have never seen it played.'

'You must, you must, Mistress Gilbourne.'

'Call me Cecily . . . if we are to be friends.'

'Thank you, Cecily,' he gushed. 'And we will.'

'Be friends?'

'I earnestly hope so.'

'No more than that?'

She gave him an enigmatic smile. Hoode was not sure if she was enticing him or merely appraising him. It did not matter. He was ready to surrender unconditionally to her will. A rose. A promise. A tryst. Cecily Gilbourne was a kindred spirit, a true romantic, someone removed from the sordid lusts of the world, a woman of perception who loved the way that he wrote about love.

'Well?' she said. 'Do I surprise you?'

'Surprise me and delight me, Cecily.'

'Am I as you imagined I might be?'

'Oh, no.'

'You are disappointed?'

'Overjoyed. The reality far exceeds my imaginings.'

She laughed softly. 'I knew that I had chosen well.'

'Did you?'

'Yes, Edmund. Your plays let me look into your heart.'

'What did you find there?'

The enigmatic smile played around her lips again.

'I found you.'

The words caressed his ears and he almost swooned. He could

not believe that it was happening to him. Years of rejection by the fairer sex had sapped his self-esteem. Romantic disaster was his natural habitat. Women like Cecily Gilbourne did not exist in his life except as phantoms. There had been no chase, no agonising period of courtship, no sequence of sonnets to express his desire in honeyed phrases. She had come to him. It was the most natural and painless relationship he had ever enjoyed with a beautiful woman, intensified as it was by an element of mystery, and given a deeper resonance by the fact that she adored his work as much as his person.

'Will you come to me again, Edmund?' she whispered.

'Whenever you call.'

'It will be very soon.'

'I will be waiting.'

'Thank you.'

She offered her hand and he placed the lightest of kisses upon it, his lips burning with pleasure as they touched her glove.

'Farewell, my prince,' she said.

Cecily turned to stare out of the window, allowing him to see her in profile and to admire the marmoreal perfection of her neck and chin. Caught in the light, her skin was so white and silky that Hoode had to resist the urge to reach out and stroke it with the tips of his fingers. Instead, he gave her the lowest bow yet, mumbled his farewell and backed towards the door with his mouth still agape.

Their first meeting was over. He was ensnared.

When they reached the precinct of Blackfriars, they explored the surrounding streets and the church before going into the theatre itself. Geoffrey, the old porter, gave them a subdued welcome and told them that Raphael Parsons was still in the building. Nicholas Bracewell went briskly up the staircase with James Ingram at his side.

What met them in the theatre itself was a far less gruesome

sight than the one which had greeted them on their earlier visit. Raphael Parsons was talking to a group of young actors, who were sitting on the edge of the stage in costume. Behind them was the setting for the final scene of *Mariana's Revels.* His voice was loud but unthreatening. None of the Chapel Children evinced any fear of the man.

Hearing their approach, Parsons swung round to face them.

'You trespass on private property,' he said crisply.

'The theatre is open to the public,' reminded Nicholas. 'You performed here this very afternoon, it seems. *Mariana's Revels.* Not that we come as spectators, Master Parsons. We would speak with you.'

'The time is not convenient.'

'Then we will wait.'

Nicholas and his companion folded their arms and stood there patiently. They would not easily be dismissed. The manager clicked his tongue in exasperation before snapping his fingers to dismiss the actors. They scampered off into the tiring-house. Nicholas looked after them.

'Was Philip Robinson in your cast?' he asked.

'He was,' said Parsons. 'He played Mariana herself.'

'The boy can carry a leading role?'

'Exceeding well. His plaintive songs moved all who heard him sing. But you did not come here to discuss the talents of my actors. I see that by your faces.'

'We are here on Master Fulbeck's behalf,' said Ingram.

'There is something you did not tell me?'

'It is the other way around,' explained Nicholas. 'We have questions to put to you.'

'To what end?'

'The arrest and conviction of a killer. A Laughing Hangman, who turned your stage into a gallows. You and I and James here, each working on his own, would never track him down. But if we pool our knowledge, if we share opinion and conjecture, we may perchance succeed.'

'I do not need your help,' said Parsons sharply.

'You know the murderer, then?'

'Not yet, Master Bracewell.'

'Then how do you propose to root him out?'

'By cunning, sir. Alone and unaided.'

'We came by Ireland Yard,' said Ingram, pointedly.

'So?'

'That was where you claimed to be when Master Fulbeck was dangling from a noose in here.'

'You doubt my word?'

'Not in the slightest.'

'We would simply like to know which house you visited,' said Nicholas reasonably. 'Your host would confirm the time of your arrival and departure.'

'Damn your impudence, sir!'

'What number in Ireland Yard?'

'I'll not be harried like this,' warned Parsons. 'Where I went that day was and will remain my business. I am not under scrutiny here. Do you dare to suggest that *I* was implicated in the crime in some way? Cyril Fulbeck was my partner. I worshipped the man.'

'Yet argued with him constantly.'

'That was in the nature of things.'

'Why did you open the theatre today?' said Ingram.

'Because a play had been advertised.'

'The murder of Master Fulbeck notwithstanding?'

'He would have sanctioned the performance.'

'I beg leave to question that.'

Parsons was blunt. 'Our beloved Master of the Chapel may have died but life goes on.'

'With no decent interval for mourning?'

'This theatre itself is his memorial.'

'And your source of income,' observed Nicholas.

'That, too.'

'Therein lies the true reason for performance.'

'I run this theatre the way that I choose!'

'No,' corrected Nicholas. 'The way that you *have* to run it, Master Parsons. By cramming in every performance that you possibly can and by working your actors like oxen in the field. That is why you staged *Mariana's Revels* today. Not by way of a memorial to Cyril Fulbeck. You wanted the money.'

'The theatre has expenses.'

'Is that why you wrangled with your partner?'

'Leave off this, sir!'

'Did you argue over profit?'

'I'll not account to you or anyone else for what I do within these four walls!' yelled Parsons, waving his arms. 'Blackfriars is my theatre. I live for this place.'

'Master Fulbeck died for it.'

Anger building, Parsons looked from one to the other. 'Envy drives you both on,' he sneered. 'I see that now. Blackfriars is without peer. We offer our patrons a real playhouse, not an innyard smelling of dung and stale beer. Here they sit in comfort to watch the best plays in London, protected from the rain and wind, marvelling at our skill and our invention. Westfield's Men are vagabonds beside my Chapel Boys.'

'We pay our actors,' said Nicholas. 'Do you pay yours?'

'I'll hear no more of this!'

'Answer me but one thing.'

'Away with you both or I'll summon a constable!'

'Master Fulbeck's keys.'

'What of them?'

'Have they ever been found?'

Raphael Parsons made them wait for a reply, his eyes flicking around the theatre before finally settling on Nicholas with a defiant glare.

'They have not been found.'

'So they are still in the possession of the murderer?'

'We may presume as much.'

'Beware, Master Parsons,' said Nicholas. 'He can gain access to this theatre again by means of those keys.'

The manager was unperturbed. He walked to the door and

opened it for them to leave. The visitors exchanged a nod. To remain any longer would be a waste of time. Nicholas felt that they had learned far more from the manner of his answers than from anything that Raphael Parsons had said. When he questioned the two friends earlier, the theatre manager had been calm and plausible. Cornered by surprise on his own territory, he was resentful and unco-operative.

As they walked to the door, Parsons stopped them.

'Come tomorrow and pay to gain entrance,' he suggested.

'Why?' said Nicholas.

'Because you will not only see a fine play finely acted on a stage fit to bear it. You will witness our revenge.'

'Against whom?'

'Master Foulmouth himself. Jonas Applegarth.'

'What do you play tomorrow?'

'*Alexander the Great.* An old play on an old theme but with a Prologue newly minted to cut the monstrous Applegarth down to human size. Westfield's Men are soundly whipped as well. They who attack Blackfriars will suffer reprisals.' He wagged an admonitory finger. 'Deliver that message to your lewd playwright. We'll destroy his reputation entire. We'll hang him from the roof-beam with a rope of rhyming couplets and strangle the life out of his disgusting carcass!'

Easing them through the door, he closed it firmly behind them. They heard a key turning in the lock. As they descended the stairs, Ingram glanced over his shoulder.

'Master Parsons has grown testy,' he said.

'We came unannounced into his domain and caught him on the raw. He has a malignant streak, no question of that. I would not care to be one of his young actors.'

'Nor I, Nick. It was never thus in my day.'

'You were trained as well as any of our apprentices.'

'And shown great kindness. Times have changed.'

The porter was waiting at the foot of the staircase to detain Ingram in conversation. Nicholas drifted out of the building and retraced the steps he had taken when in pursuit of the murderer on the earlier visit. Pausing at the rear of the theatre, he looked at the various avenues of escape which the man could have taken. If he had run fast, he might have been clear of the precinct before Nicholas reached the spot where he was now standing. Or he might have gone to ground in any one of the nearby streets and alleyways.

By way of experiment, Nicholas broke into a trot and dodged around a few corners. When he came to a halt, he saw that he was standing in Ireland Yard. He studied the houses with interest before he walked back towards the theatre. As he strolled past it, the rear door was unlocked and a dozen or more figures emerged. Wearing white surplices over black cassocks, they lined up in pairs and march away in step, the choirboys at the front and the vicars choral behind them.

'Philip!' called Nicholas.

One of the boys turned in surprise to look at him. The resemblance to Ambrose Robinson was clear. His bright young face was puzzled by the salutation. The boy was pushed gently from behind by another chorister and the procession wended on its way. Nicholas was impressed by the sense of order and assurance about them. Philip Robinson was an integral part of the whole. He did not look like an unwilling prisoner. Nicholas watched him until the column vanished out of sight.

The journey took an eternity. Owen Elias was soon regretting his offer to safeguard the drunken Jonas Applegarth. The playwright kept stopping in the street to accuse innocent bystanders of unspeakable crimes, to hurl verbal thunderbolts at every church they passed, to kick at the stray dogs which yapped at his heels and to relieve himself unceremoniously against any available wall. When Elias tried to remonstrate with him, Applegarth either turned his vituperation on the Welshman or embraced him tearfully while vowing undying friendship.

Celtic patience finally snapped. Applegarth reviled him once too often and Elias expressed his displeasure in the most direct way. Grabbing the bigger man by the scruff of the neck, he dragged him towards a horse-trough and threw him in head-first. Applegarth hit the water with a fearsome splash. His face was submerged for a full minute as he emitted a hideous gurgling sound. Then he managed to haul himself out of the trough and fell to the ground.

He lay there twitching violently like a giant cod on the deck of a fishing vessel. His clothes were sodden, his hair and beard dripping and his hat floating in a puddle beside him. After expelling a pint of water from his mouth, he let out a bellow of anger and tried to get up. Elias put a foot in the middle of his chest to hold him down. Applegarth replied with an even louder bellow but it soon gave way to rumbling laughter. Instead of lambasting his colleague, he turned his derision upon himself.

'Look at me!' he said, wobbling with mirth. 'The most brilliant playwright in London, flat on his back in the mire! The greatest ale-drinker in England, spewing out rank water. The fattest belly in Christendom, staring up at the sky! Is this not a pretty sight, Owen?'

'You deserved it.'

'Indeed, I did.'

'You went well beyond the bounds of fellowship.'

'I am the first to acknowledge it.'

'The horse-trough was the best place for you.'

'No, my friend,' said Applegarth, as remorse wiped the grin from his wet face. 'It is too elevated a station for me. A swamp would be a fitter home. A ditch. A dunghill. Find me a hole big enough and I'll crawl into it with the other vermin. Why do I *do* it, Owen?'

'I'll tell you in the morning when you're sober.'

Reaching down, he took the other in a firm grip and heaved backwards. Jonas Applegarth swung slowly upright. He looked down at the state of his apparel with revulsion.

'My wife will assault me!' he moaned.

'There may be others keen to do that office for her.'

'My doublet is stained, my breeches torn, my stockings past repair. I am an insult to her tailoring.' He felt his head in a panic. 'Where's my hat? Where's my hat?'

'Here,' said Elias, retrieving it from the puddle.

'I dare not go home like this.'

'You will and you must, Jonas.'

'What will my wife say?'

'That is her privilege. But I marvel that you rail against religion so when you must be married to a saint. Who else would put up with you?'

'True, true, Owen,' agreed the other. 'She *is* a saint.'

'A martyr to her husband.'

Applegarth remained solemn and silent all the way home. He was a sorry sight as he was admitted to the house by a servant. Elias waited long enough to hear the first shriek of complaint from the resident saint before turning away. Movement in the shadows then alerted him. He was reminded why he had accompanied Applegarth in the first place.

Pulling out his dagger, he ran diagonally across the street to the lane on the opposite side but he was too slow. All he caught was the merest glimpse of a man, darting down the lane before disappearing into the rabbit warren of streets beyond it. Elias stabbed the air in his anger.

They had been followed.

Anne Hendrik counted out the coins and handed them over.

'There, Ambrose,' she said with relief. ' 'Tis done!'

'Thank you.'

'My debt is cleared at last.'

'There was no hurry to repay me,' he said, putting the coins into his purse. 'And I am far more in your debt than you in mine. No amount of money can ever discharge that obligation.'

'I have done nothing.'

'Is saving a man's life nothing? Is giving him fresh hope nothing? You did all that for me and more.'

'I think not.'

'Every penny I have is yours for the asking.'

'We can pay our own way again now.'

'You *must* know how much you mean to me, Anne.'

She turned away and resumed her seat in order to avoid what she sensed might be an embarrassing declaration. They were in the parlour of her house in Bankside. The butcher stood awkwardly in the middle of the room, peeved that the settlement of her debt had deprived him of an excuse to call on a regular basis and searching for a means to secure a more permanent mooring in her affections.

'I acted out of simple friendship,' she said.

'Is that all that it will remain?'

'For the moment, Ambrose.'

'And in time?'

'Who knows what the future will hold?'

'Who indeed?' he agreed, shaking his head ruefully. 'A year ago, I was the most contented of men. I had a happy marriage, a son I adored and a business that was thriving. What else could anyone ask? Then, suddenly . . .' He clapped his hands together. 'I lost it all. My dear wife died, my son was taken from me by deed of impressment, and I had no pleasure from my occupation. What was the point in struggling on?'

'There is always a point, Ambrose.'

'You taught me that.'

'I, too, lost my dearest partner.'

'But not your child as well.'

'No,' she conceded sadly. 'Not my child. The joys of motherhood were denied me and that is a grievous loss in itself.' She brightened. 'Besides, your son has not left you for ever. Philip is still alive and like to return to you before too long. Nick will see to that.'

'Will he?'

'Put your trust in him.'

'It is growing difficult to do so.'

'Ambrose!' she scolded.

'You saw the way he rounded on me. He is supposed to be helping Philip, not accusing the boy's father with such severity. I am sorry, Anne, but I begin to have serious doubts about Nick Bracewell.'

'Then you do not know him as well as I.'

'That is another cause of my discomfort.'

He moved away to hide the surly expression on his face. When he turned back to her, it was with a slow smile and a surge of ungainly affection.

'I have written to Philip again today,' he said.

'Your letters will be a comfort to him.'

'He is old enough to be told now. To understand.'

'Understand?'

'What an angel of mercy you have been. Without you to rescue me, I would have given in. Philip knows that. He always liked you, Anne. He always talked kindly of you. It will make such a difference to him. Philip was much closer to his mother than to me but that is only natural. It will make such a difference.'

'I do not follow.'

'A child needs a proper home, Anne.'

'He has one.'

'He has a house but something is missing from it.'

Anne realised what he was trying to say to her and steeled herself. In paying off her debt she had hoped to lighten the weight of his friendship, but she had merely given him the cue to translate it into a deeper relationship.

'I know that I have little enough to offer,' he began, planting himself before her. 'Jacob Hendrik was a decent, God-fearing, conscientious man and I could never be the husband to you that he was. But I swear to you—'

'That is enough,' she interrupted. 'I would prefer it if you said no more on that subject.'

Robinson was hurt. 'Have I offended you?'

'No, Ambrose.'

'Do you find me so revolting, then?'

'You are a good man with many qualities.'

'But not good enough for you?'

'That was not my meaning.'

'Then why do you spurn me?'

'I do not,' she said, standing and crossing to the window. 'I am just not ready to consider . . . what you wish to propose, that is all.'

'Not ready now?' he said, brightening. 'But one day . . .'

'I make no promises.'

'One day . . .'

'My life is happy enough as it is.'

'A husband and a son will make it even happier.'

'No,' she said, turning to face him. 'We are friends. I like to think that we are close friends. You helped me when others would not and I will always be grateful to you for that. It made me want to help you to bring Philip home.'

Robinson stared at her. A resentful note intruded.

'It is him, is it not?'

'Who?'

'Your precious Nick Bracewell. He is the canker here.'

'What do you mean?'

'It has all changed,' he said bitterly. 'Until he came back into your world, you had time for me and interest in my affairs. We talked together, supped together, even walked to church together on a Sunday. All golden times for me. Then this friend, this Nick Bracewell, appears again and my chances go begging.'

'That is not true.'

'He changed everything.'

'No, Ambrose.'

'But for him, you would have been mine. I know it.'

'Nick changed *nothing*!'

The force of her rejection was like a slap in the face. His body tensed and his eyes blazed but he made no comment. Swinging on his heel, he went out of the house and slammed the door behind him.

Lawrence Firethorn was just about to climb into bed when he heard the thunderous knocking on his front door. Margery was already lying among the pillows in her nightgown with a smile of lustful anticipation on her face. *Vincentio's Revenge* had sent them early to their bedchamber and they knew that nobody in the house would dare to interrupt them.

When more knocking came, Firethorn stamped a bare foot on the floor to signal to the servant below.

'Whoever that is, send them on their way!' he yelled.

'Ignore them, Lawrence,' purred his wife.

'When you lie before me like that, my sweet, I would ignore the Last Judgement. Was ever a man so blessed in his wife? Was ever lover so well matched with lover?' He moved in to bestow a first tender kiss on her lips. 'Was ever an actor given such a fine role as this that I play now?'

He embraced her with fiery passion and buried his head between her generous breasts. Digging her fingers into his hair, she pulled him close and urged him on with cries of delight, groaning with even more pleasure when his hands slipped under her nightgown to explore her warm thighs. The bed soon began to creak rhythmically but a louder noise rose above it. Somebody was actually pounding on their door.

Ecstasy froze on the instant. Firethorn could not believe it. At a time when he and his wife most wanted to be alone, they were being rudely disturbed. It was unforgivable. Leaping from the bed half-naked, he stalked across the room, determined to castigate the servant in the roundest of terms before hurling her out into the street. When he snatched open the door, he fully expected the girl to be cowering in terror. Instead, he was met by the improbable sight of Edmund Hoode, hands on hips, standing there with his legs set firmly apart.

'I have come to speak with you, Lawrence,' he asserted.

'*Now?* Must it be now? Must it be here?' Firethorn stepped outside the bedchamber and pulled the door shut after him. 'Do you know what you have just interrupted?'

'I care not.'

'Margery is waiting for me within.'

'I will not keep you from your sleep much longer.'

'Sleep was the least of our concerns!'

'I had to see you.'

'Well, see me, you do. So turn tail and leave my house before I speed you on your way!' His eyes glowed in the half-dark. 'Come not between the dragon and his mate!'

'Who is it?' called Margery from within.

'Edmund!'

'At this hour?'

'Begone, sir!' snarled Firethorn. 'You hold up destiny.'

'That is why I am here,' said Hoode calmly. 'To discuss my own destiny. When I sensed danger in the person of a rival, my impulse was to shrink away and yield up my place. Not any more, Lawrence. I intend to fulfil my destiny. I am here to fight for my place in Westfield's Men.'

Firethorn exploded. 'If you tarry any longer, you will be fighting for your life! God's tits, man! The most wonderful woman in the world is waiting for me in that bed.'

'Not for ever,' cautioned Margery. 'I grow weary.'

'Come back tomorrow, Edmund!'

Firethorn tried to push him away, but Hoode held his ground with a determination that was unprecedented in so reserved a man. Five minutes alone with Cicely Gilbourne had transformed him. He was loved. His plays were admired. His life had purpose after all. What thrilled him most was her appreciation of his work. It was this which had restored his confidence in himself and made him reflect on the shabby treatment he had been accorded by Westfield's Men. With fire in his belly, he walked all the way to Shoreditch to beard Firethorn in his own den. Margery's presence was a minor disadvantage.

'Will *you* box his ear or will I?' she shouted.

'I will, my pretty one,' cooed Firethorn before glowering at the intruder. 'Leave now while your legs still carry you or I'll not be answerable for my actions!'

'If I leave now, Lawrence, I leave for good!'

'That will content us.'

'Who will pen your plays then, I wonder?'

'Still there?' wailed Margery. 'Throttle the idiot!'

'I talk of my place,' continued Hoode, unruffled. 'I talk of my destiny. Westfield's Men are contracted to perform *The Faithful Shepherd* at The Rose yet I am thrust aside to make way for Jonas Applegarth.'

Firethorn gasped. 'You have invaded my bedchamber in order to talk about a paltry *play*?'

'That paltry play means much to me. Thus it stands. Perform it at The Rose and I remain in the company. Supplant me with another playwright and I will henceforth offer my talent to Banbury's Men. Do you understand, Lawrence?'

The other was so stunned that all he could offer was a meek nod. Hoode's fearless manner and dire threat robbed him of the organs of speech. Panting on the bed, Margery Firethorn was more concerned with other organs.

'Lawrence!' she bawled. 'Get in here *now*! Your kettle is no longer boiling, sir. It needs more heat to make it sing. Light my fire again. Where are you, man?'

Hoode tapped politely on the door and inched it open.

'We are done now, Margery,' he said. 'I'll send him in.'

Unable to sleep for more than a few hours, Nicholas Bracewell rose before dawn and strolled down to the edge of the Thames.

The river lapped noisily at the wharf and vessels bobbed in the gloom as they lay at anchor. Born and brought up in a seaport, Nicholas felt at home beside the dark water as it curled between its banks with lazy power. When the first specks of light began to dapple the river, he inhaled the keen air and was at peace with himself. Gulls cried, a winch squealed into life, the plash of oars could be heard in the distance.

His eye then travelled across to Bankside and the demons returned to plague his mind. The Thames did not just snake through London on its way to the sea. Its broad back kept Anne Hendrik and him far apart. They would need more than a bridge to join themselves together again.

Nicholas was still brooding by the quayside when the river was teeming with boats and flanked by scores of people about their daily work. Kneeling down low, he cupped his hands to scoop up some water and let it run over his face. As he began the noisy walk to the Queen's Head, he felt refreshed and ready to begin his own day.

Blackfriars displaced Anne Hendrik from his thoughts. The second visit to the theatre had yielded much. Aided by Caleb Hay's sketch, he had been able to take his bearings with more accuracy and James Ingram had pointed out aspects of the precinct which had gone unremarked before. A most fashionable quarter of London had baulked at the notion of a public playhouse in their midst, yet the most successful private theatre in England stood in its place. He wondered how many of the residents who had signed the earlier petition were keen spectators at Blackfriars.

Raphael Parsons now came into the reckoning as a murder suspect. Their first meeting, Nicholas believed, had been deliberately engineered to throw suspicion off the victim's business partner. Pretending to investigate the crime on his own account, Parsons sought to put himself beyond any investigation. No stage management had been possible before their second encounter. He was taken unawares. His truculent manner, his wild threats and his refusal to account for his precise whereabouts at the time of the murder combined to make him a potential killer.

Nicholas was convinced that the man's vicious rows with his partner were as much over money as over the treatment of the young actors. Long service with Westfield's Men had given the book holder an insight into the perilous finances of a theatre company. Blackfriars might not be at the mercy of the elements in the same way as the Queen's Head, but there was still rent to pay, costumes to buy, scenery and properties to provide, expensive stage equipment to be installed, and the theatre itself to be cleaned and maintained.

When Nicholas added the fees for commissioning new plays with unceasing regularity, he could see how high the running costs must be. The Blackfriars audience might pay higher prices to view the entertainment, but it was much smaller in size than the public playhouses and the gatherers would take less at a performance even than at the Queen's Head. Raphael Parsons had to drive his actors hard to make a profit. He would not thank the soft-hearted Cyril Fulbeck for standing in his way.

Consideration of the theatre manager inevitably brought him around to the case of Philip Robinson and that let Anne Hendrik back into his mind. He brooded afresh on her until a voice hailed him. Nicholas looked up to see Nathan Curtis emerging from the crowd to join him as he turned into Gracechurch Street.

'Early again, Nathan. You put the rest to shame.'

'There are two benches to repair, a coffin to strengthen and a wooden leg to make.'

'A carpenter is always in request.'

'Until you go on tour. My trade falls asleep then.'

'Theatre is a cruel master.'

They were still chatting as they turned in through the archway of the Queen's Head and made for the rooms which they rented as storage areas. Costumes, properties and scenic devices were expensive items, kept under lock and key at all times.

Nicholas was alarmed, therefore, when he tried the first door and found it already unlocked.

'Someone is here before us?' said Curtis.

'Not from the company. Only I have the key.'

'Who, then, can it be?'

Nicholas drew a cautionary dagger before opening the door. With Curtis behind him, he stepped into the room used as their wardrobe. Nothing seemed to be missing, but he was certain that someone had been in there. A creaking sound took his attention to the room beyond. It was the place where they stored their properties and scenery, and where the carpenter stowed his tools overnight. Nicholas crept over to the door and lifted the latch gently. The door was unlocked but it would only open a matter of inches before it met an obstruction.

Putting his shoulder to the timber, he applied more pressure and there was a scraping noise as a heavy object was pushed across the floorboards. The creaking sound continued throughout and the two of them froze in their tracks when they saw what was causing it.

Jonas Applegarth was hanging from the central beam by a thick rope. As he swayed to and fro, the stout timber creaked under his weight. His face was bloated, his eyes staring, his body twisted into an unnatural shape. His shoes were dangling only inches above the floor, but that short distance was enough to separate him from life. A man of enormous vitality and power had been reduced to an inert hulk.

The object which had impeded them was an open coffin jammed against the door. Reeling from the shock, Curtis bent over his handiwork and spewed uncontrollably into it. Nicholas recovered more quickly. He saw that the rope went over the beam and was tied off on a wooden cleat fixed to the wall. After unwinding it carefully, he took the full strain and lowered Applegarth's body to the ground with as much consideration as he could.

Nathan Curtis turned to help him but their examination of

the body was cut short by another noise. It was a weird and maniacal cackle, which seemed to come from an adjoining room and which rose in volume and intensity until it filled the whole place. The carpenter was terrified by the sound but Nicholas had heard it once before. The Laughing Hangman had returned.

Diving to the other door in the room, Nicholas tried to open it but found it locked. He fumbled for his key and inserted into quickly into the lock. The adjoining chamber was the company's tiring-house. By the time that Nicholas burst into it, the laughter had stopped and the place was empty. He went through the door that led to the yard but could see no sign of a fleeing figure. Guests were departing, ostlers were going about their business, a servant wielded a broom. When he dashed back into the tiring-house, he tried a third door in the chamber. It opened on to the passageway that led all the way down to the taproom.

Nicholas raced along it, searching each room and alcove that he passed. When he reached the taproom, the door opened before him and he came face to face with Alexander Marwood.

'What's amiss?' demanded the landlord.

'Did anyone come through this door a moment ago?'

'I saw nobody.'

'Are you certain, sir?'

'My eyesight is sound.'

'Where, then, did he go?'

Nicholas went back along the passageway to see if he had missed anything. Scenting trouble, the landlord trotted at his heels with face aghast and hands clutching the air.

'What new calamity has befallen me?' he wailed.

'Send for the law, Master Marwood.'

'Thieves have got in? Property has been stolen?'

'It is a more serious crime than that.'

'Fire has been started on my premises?'

'Summon the constables.'

'Dear God!' howled Marwood, fearing that the worst had

finally happened. 'My daughter, Rose, has been ravished by one of your goatish actors!'

Nicholas took him by the shoulders to calm him.

'Be still, sir,' he soothed. 'No theft, no arson and no assault upon your daughter. A greater affliction has struck us. There has been murder at the Queen's Head.'

'Murder!'

The word sent the landlord into a fresh paroxysm of apprehension. His body shuddered, his hands slapped his balding head and three nervous twitches united together to turn his eyebrows into a pair of mating caterpillars. Nicholas propelled him back towards the taproom.

'Fetch assistance!' he ordered. 'Raise the alarm!'

Marwood scuttled off like a chicken pursued by an axe.

'Murder! What, ho! Help!'

Abandoning the search, Nicholas made his way swiftly back to the room where Applegarth lay. It was important to look for clues and to guard the body from the invasion of ghoulish interest which the landlord's cries were bound to excite. Other members of the company would soon be arriving. They had to be shielded from the horror of viewing the corpse. Death would deprive them of the day's audience. There could be no performance that afternoon.

When Nicholas entered the room, the body lay in the exact position where he had left it. Nathan Curtis was still there but he had been joined by someone else. Nicholas was jolted. While the carpenter gazed down reverentially at Jonas Applegarth, his companion stared at the murder victim with a smile of quiet satisfaction.

James Ingram turned away to look across at Nicholas.

'Do not ask me to mourn him,' he said. 'I will not.'

# [ CHAPTER NINE ]

Lawrence Firethorn was still bemused as his horse trotted in through the looming bulk of Bishopsgate that morning. A promised night of passion with an uninhibited lover had turned into an unseemly squabble with a disappointed wife. Thanks to the intercession of Edmund Hoode, the actor-manager spent the hours of darkness in a cold and cheerless bed. And yet he was not really angry with the playwright. Irritation was the most he could muster. Where he should have been thirsting for the man's blood, he was instead stupefied by his boldness.

Hoode entered the lion's den to deliver his ultimatum. He had to be admired for that. Even in the face of extreme conjugal frustration, he did not flinch. Firethorn could usually stifle him at will and his wife could vanquish Hoode with a glance, yet their combined powers had no impact on him this time. He had lain between them like a naked sword and kept two urgent bodies agonisingly chaste.

Who had changed a taciturn playwright into a brave knight? What had made him enter the lists so purposefully on behalf of his work? Why had he chosen to interrupt lawful copulation in a Shoreditch bedchamber at that particular moment? Only one explanation sufficed.

'A pox on his pizzle!' groaned Firethorn. 'He's in love.'

It posed a real problem for Westfield's Men. They could no longer take their resident playwright for granted. Hoode was forcing them to choose between his proven reliability and Jonas Applegarth's potential wizardry. What should they stage at The Rose—*The Faithful Shepherd* or *The Misfortunes of Marriage*? Hoode's romantic comedy would be an undoubted success, but it was Applegarth's trenchant satire which would reverberate throughout London.

Firethorn was in despair. To lose Hoode would cause him deep personal pain; to sacrifice Applegarth would be an act of professional folly. He was still weighing the two men in the balance as his horse picked its way through the crowd and turned into the yard of the Queen's Head.

Chaos awaited him. Bodies dashed hither and thither in wild confusion. Alexander Marwood charged around in ever-decreasing circles, bewailing his lot to those who would listen and upbraiding those who would not. Thomas Skillen was shaking his head in disbelief, George Dart was pacing up and down in cold fear, and the four apprentices were weeping openly. Edmund Hoode sat on a barrel in a complete daze. Owen Elias strutted frenziedly around the edge of the yard with a sword in his hand.

Firethorn saw a large coffin being unloaded from a cart by two men. He kicked his horse to take him across to Hoode.

'Edmund!' he said. 'What means this commotion?'

'Jonas Applegarth has been murdered!'

'Here at the Queen's Head?'

'Hanged by the neck.'

The news hit Firethorn like a body blow. He quivered in the saddle. The implications would be horrendous and far-reaching. One problem had been solved: Hoode would now stay with the company which Applegarth had deserted for ever. But a hundred other problems had just been created. On top of a night of enforced celibacy, it was too much to endure.

Nicholas Bracewell worked as quickly as he could in the limited time at his disposal. To prevent any unnecessary intrusion, he stationed James Ingram and Nathan Curtis, respectively, outside each of the two doors. Ingram's reaction to the murder had been almost callous, but Nicholas could not spare a moment to reflect upon such an unexpected response from such a caring man. Jonas Applegarth pushed all else from the book holder's mind. Before examining the dead body, he first removed the rope and noted how carefully the noose had been tied. The playwright had not been dispatched from the world with the aid of a crude knot. The Laughing Hangman knew his craft.

Inspecting the body, Nicholas was surprised to find no sign of blood. Applegarth would not have gone willingly to the makeshift gallows. His killer would have had to disable him first or he would have fought and yelled. Nicholas eventually located the large swelling on the back of the victim's head. He had been knocked unconscious from behind. A sturdy mallet lay on the floor. The carpenter had unwittingly provided the weapon just as Westfield's Men had unwittingly provided the rope. The scene of the execution had been chosen with care.

When he turned the body on its side, Nicholas was puzzled by the sight of sawdust sticking to the doublet and breeches. Curtis was a tidy carpenter. Though he used the room as his workshop, he always swept the floor clean. Nicholas went over to the roughhewn table in the corner. Pinches of sawdust still lay in the grooves and knot-holes of the carpenter's workbench. How had it found its way onto the victim's attire?

Bending over the prostrate Applegarth once more, he searched the man's pockets but found only one item that might be a clue. The brief note scribbled on a piece of paper went into Nicholas's own pocket. Mute and unprotesting, Applegarth lay on his back with his eyes searching the ceiling. In his brief stay with Westfield's Men, he had made a forceful impact and he would be missed. Nicholas offered up a silent prayer for him, then reached down with delicate fingers to close his eyelids.

The sound of raised voices outside the door told him that he did not have much time left. He used it to search for parallels between this murder and that of Cyril Fulbeck. The similarities were too obvious to ignore. Both were rendered unconscious before the noose was fitted. Both were hanged by a man who celebrated his crime with mocking laughter. Both died in buildings from which the killer could make an easy escape. Nicholas was musing on the other common factors when there was a banging on the door.

Constables had arrived and the official investigation began. Nicholas and Curtis gave statements, the scene of the crime was thoroughly searched and the body was scrutinised. Unable to get it into their coffin, the two men had to perch it on top and cover it with a black cloth. More tears were shed in the yard as the corpse of Jonas Applegarth was carried solemnly out to the cart and driven away to the morgue. Westfield's Men were bereaved.

When Nicholas finally emerged, Lawrence Firethorn was standing outside the door. He took the book holder by the arm and led him aside for a hissed interrogation.

'Do you know what this will do to the company?'

'My thoughts are with his poor wife.'

'Mine, too,' said Firethorn defensively. 'Mine, too. The woman will be destroyed. But we suffer an act of destruction as well. Today's performance has been hanged by the neck and Marwood is in such a state of superstitious panic that he is talking of renouncing our contract. What are we to *do,* Nick?'

'Try to keep calm.'

'When one of our number has been murdered?'

'Reassure the rest of the company,' advised Nicholas. 'They need kindness and support at a time like this. I'll speak with the landlord and smooth his ruffled feathers.'

'Who did this, Nick?'

'I do not know.'

'And why did he have to do it *here*?'

'That question is easier to answer.'

'Why not stab Jonas in some dark alleyway?'

'Because the killer wanted to inflict the most damage on Westfield's Men. You see the disarray it has caused.'

'It was like Bedlam out in that yard,' said Firethorn. 'Marwood was prancing around like some lunatic at full moon. Why could not the hangman put *his* scrawny neck into a noose? If our landlord were swinging from the rafters, we'd have something to celebrate.' He pulled Nicholas close. 'Tell me what happened from the moment you arrived here.'

Nicholas was succinct. Firethorn frowned.

'What was Jonas doing here so early?' he wondered.

'Answering your summons.'

'My what?'

'You were the only person who could get him to the Queen's Head at the crack of dawn. The murderer knew that and set his trap accordingly.'

'Trap?'

'Here is the bait,' said Nicholas.

He handed over the letter which he had found in pocket of the dead man. His companion read the scribbled words.

> *If you would remain with Westfield's Men, meet me at the Queen's Head at dawn. . . . Lawrence Firethorn.*

'I never sent this!' protested the actor-manager.

'Jonas believed that you did.'

'This is not my summons.'

'I know,' said Nicholas. 'It is a death warrant.'

* * *

Anne Hendrik was at once saddened and relieved by her exchange with Ambrose Robinson on the previous evening. She was sorry to wound the feelings of someone who was already suffering a degree of emotional pain. A powerful man in a brutal profession, he was nevertheless remarkably sensitive and she had been touched that he felt able to reveal this side of his character to her. At the same time, however, she did not want her friendship to be misinterpreted. His unwelcome proposal had forced her to be more open with him about her own affections, and that brought a measure of relief. She may have hurt him but at least he would not pester her again.

'What time is he coming?'

'At noon, Preben.'

'Do you wish me to be there?'

'I shall insist,' she said, pleasantly. 'I would never dream of taking on a new apprentice without your full approval.'

'Where does the boy's family come from?'

'Amsterdam.'

'That is recommendation enough.'

Preben van Loew was, as usual, first to arrive at work. Anne came in from her adjacent house to discuss plans for the day. She took a full and active part in the running of the business. The old Dutchman and his colleagues might make the hats, but it was Anne who often designed them and she was solely responsible for gathering all the orders and for ensuring delivery. When demand was especially pressing, she had even been known to take up needle and thread herself.

By the time her other employees drifted in, the discussion with Preben van Loew had ended. Her first task was to buy some new material for the shop. She went back into her house and put on her own hat before she was ready to leave. A dull thud at her front door made her turn. A figure flitted past her window but far too quickly to be identified. She was mystified.

Anne crossed to the door and opened it tentatively. There was nobody there. Something then brushed against her dress. It was a large bunch of flowers in a wicker basket. She picked it up to inhale their fragrance. The scent was quite enchanting. Anne was moved by the unexpected present and she wondered who could have bestowed it on her.

The sender soon declared himself. Stepping around the corner of the street, Ambrose Robinson waved cheerily to her. His expression was apologetic and the flowers were clearly meant as some kind of peace offering. Accepting them as such, Anne replied with a grateful flick of her hand and a token smile. He grinned broadly before ducking out of sight again. She put the basket of flowers on a table without pausing to consider for a moment the real significance of the gift that she was taking into her house.

That was nobly done, Nick. No man could have handled it better.'

'I wanted to be the one to break the sad tidings.'

'Thank heaven that you were!'

'Your presence was a help, Owen.'

'I said almost nothing.'

'You were there. That was enough. Mistress Applegarth drew strength from your sympathy.'

'It was your compassion which sustained her. You delivered the roughest news in the most gentle way. She will ever be grateful to you for that.'

Owen Elias and Nicholas Bracewell had just left the home of Jonas Applegarth. It had fallen to the book holder to inform her that she was now a widow, and he had done so by suppressing all the gruesome details of her husband's death. Neighbours had been brought in to sit with the woman until other members of the family could arrive to share the burden of the tragedy.

'She is a brave woman,' observed Owen. 'She bore up well

throughout that ordeal. It was almost as if she were expecting something like this to happen.'

'I think she was. Jonas seemed to court destruction.'

'Yes, Nick. The wonder is not that he is dead but that he lived for so long.'

Nicholas looked back at the house with deep sadness. 'Jonas Applegarth was a playwright of distinction—we have not seen a finer at the Queen's Head—but his talent was marred by a perversity in his nature. His work won him friends, yet he thrived on making enemies.'

'One, in particular!'

'I fear so.'

'Let's after him straight,' urged Elias. 'Now that we have done our duty by his widow, we must seek revenge. We know who the murderer was.'

'Do we?'

'Hugh Naismith. Late of Banbury's Men.'

'I think not.'

'He has been stalking Jonas for days. You were there when Naismith hurled a dagger at him. And I dare swear that he followed us here last night.'

'That does not make him our man, Owen.'

'Why not?'

'Because he would not go to all the trouble of setting up a gallows at the Queen's Head when he could dispatch his victim more easily with sword or dagger. You forget something.'

'What is that?'

'Naismith was injured in his duel with Jonas. How could a man with his arm in a sling haul up so heavy a load over a beam? It is not possible.'

'It is if he had a confederate.'

'I heard one Laughing Hangman, Owen, not two.'

'Naismith had cause and means to kill Jonas.'

'Granted,' said Nicholas. 'But what cause and means did he have to murder Cyril Fulbeck at the Blackfriars Theatre?'

'The cause is plain enough, Nick.'

'Is it?'

'Fulbeck put those Chapel Children back on the stage to take the bread out of the mouths of honest actors. I am one with Hugh Naismith there. I'd happily wring the necks of those infant players myself and the man who put them there.'

'You are wrong, Owen.'

'It *has* to be Naismith.'

'Never!'

'Your reason?'

'He was too obvious an enemy,' argued Nicholas. 'Jonas would be on his guard as soon as he saw the man. Naismith might have forged a letter to lure him to the Queen's Head, but how did he entice him into our storeroom? The person who killed him was a man he did not fear. Remember the Master of the Chapel.'

'Cyril Fulbeck?'

'He also let someone get close enough to strike. A stranger would never have gained entry to Blackfriars.'

'Then Naismith was not a stranger to him.'

'He has no part in this, Owen.'

'But he does,' insisted the Welshman. 'You saw a dagger aimed at Jonas's back. Did that come out of thin air?'

'No, it was thrown by an enemy. But not by our hangman.'

'There are *two* villains here?'

'Most certainly,' said Nicholas, thinking it through. 'One of them haunts the shadows and strikes from behind. The other is a more calculating killer. Why was Master Fulbeck hanged on his own stage? Why did Jonas have to be enticed to the Queen's Head? There is method here, Owen. And it is way beyond anything that Hugh Naismith could devise.'

Elias nodded reluctantly. 'You begin to persuade me. Haply, he is not our man.' His ire stirred again. 'But that does not rule him out as the street assassin. Naismith trailed Jonas and hurled that dagger at him.'

'That may yet be true.'

'It is, Nick. Let's track him down and beat a confession out of him. Attempted murder must not go unpunished.'

'Nor shall it. But you must pursue Naismith alone.'

'And you?'

'I must to the Coroner to sign a sworn statement of how the body of Jonas Applegarth came to be discovered. Nathan Curtis waits for me there. Then I'll to the playhouse.'

'The Curtain? The Theatre? The Rose?'

'Blackfriars,' said Nicholas. 'That is where this riddle first started and where it will finally be solved.'

As the finger of guilt pointed at him once more, Edmund Hoode shut his eyes against its silent accusation. He only half-heard the argument that was raging nearby. Barnaby Gill and Lawrence Firethorn were sitting with him in the taproom of the Queen's Head. Inflamed with drink, they locked horns.

'Why was the performance canceled?' demanded Gill.

'Out of respect for the dead,' said Firethorn.

'I was not consulted.'

'The decision was taken for us, Barnaby. Even you must see that. We could not stage a play in the yard while Jonas Applegarth was dangling from a beam in the storeroom.'

'He was cut down and carted away hours ago.'

'His memory remains.'

'I believe that you did this out of spite, Lawrence.'

'Spite?'

'Yes!' screamed Gill, working himself up into a full tantrum. '*Cupid's Folly* should have been played today. A piece tailored to my genius. Audiences clamour for it time and again. You tore it off the stage to spite me.'

'That is madness!'

'You know how I rule the roost in *Cupid's Folly*. They adore me. They love to see my performance as Rigormortis.'

'Why, so do I!' said Firethorn with sarcasm. 'I would give anything to look upon your *rigor mortis.'*

'Spite!'

'Go rot!'

'The play was cancelled out of spite.'

'Is that why Jonas Applegarth got himself hanged? In order to spite you? "Pray, good sir, put that noose around my neck so that I may aggravate Barnaby Gill." Think of someone else for a change, man. Sigh for the loss of a friend. That is what Edmund does.' He nudged the playwright hard. 'Do you not?'

Hoode opened his eyes. 'What's that you say?'

'You are in mourning for Jonas, are you not?'

'Yes, Lawrence. I mourn and I repent. As God is my witness, I must speak honestly. I writhe with guilt.'

'Why?'

'Because I wished the poor fellow dead.'

'So did I and so did every man,' said Gill. 'Why deny it? We hated him. Jonas Applegarth was an earthquake in our midst. See how we shake at his passing.'

'I would rather remember how the audience shook at his play,' said Firethorn proudly. 'They trembled with amazement at the sorcery of his imagination and shook with laughter at the sharpness of his wit. What use is theatre if it be not a two-hour earthquake? Why do the spectators come if not to feel the ground move beneath their feet?'

'Lawrence is right,' admitted Hoode. 'Jonas Applegarth had the power to move mountains.'

'Yes,' snapped Gill. 'He did that every time he opened his bowels. His buttocks were mountains indeed.'

'Do not speak ill of the dead!' chided Firethorn.

'It is unjust,' said Hoode. 'In a moment of envy, I may have wished for his death, but I regret his passing now. He brought much to Westfield's Men. Mark it well. A great value has gone out of our lives.'

'He had whispers of genius,' said Gill grudgingly. 'I give him that. But he might have chosen another day to die. *Cupid's Folly* is an appalling loss. I have seventeen magical moments in the play and he has robbed me of every one of them!' He rose to his feet. ' "Cruel death hath stolen my Rigormortis from me." '

Quoting his lines from the play, he flounced off. Hoode poured them both more wine from the jug. Alexander Marwood came buzzing around them with his woes.

'What am I to do? Where am I to go?'

'As far out of my sight as you can,' said Firethorn.

'Murder was committed on my premises. Guests have fled. Spectators have stayed away. My serving-men and ostlers are too frightened to do their offices. My wife is distraught. My daughter had taken to her bed. I am dead, sirs.'

'We'll sing lustily at your funeral.'

'I blame you, Master Firethorn.'

'For what?'

'Bringing that heathen among us,' said the landlord. 'His play all but caused an affray in my yard. Jonas Applegarth dared to mock God and the Almighty has given His reply. You should not have let that heathen befoul my yard with his irreverence!'

'Let him rest in peace,' said Hoode. 'He is gone.'

'And taken my livelihood with it!'

Marwood's twitch suddenly broke out around his mouth and both lips trembled so dramatically that they looked like a pair of fluttering wings. His words were distorted into grunts and whines. It rescued them from further persecution and the landlord stole away, holding his mouth in both hands lest it take flight.

'Which is worse?' asked Firethorn. 'Marwood with his twitch or Barnaby with his *rigor mortis*?' He lifted his cup of wine. 'Let's drink to Jonas!'

'I'll say Amen to that!' added Hoode.

'We have lost a playwright but his play lives on. *The Misfortunes of Marriage* must be staged again in tribute.'

'But not at The Rose next week.'

'Are we to have that argument all over again?'

'No, Lawrence,' said Hoode, becoming more assertive. 'The matter is settled. My new play will grace The Rose, as you promised. Choose another time for the tribute to Jonas Applegarth. I'll not forfeit my right.'

There was a glint in his eye which forbade any further debate. Hoode was reaffirming his position in the company. Firethorn gave a nod of agreement, then leaned in close.

'What is her name, Edmund?'

'Whose name?'

'This fairy princess who has waved a wand over you.'

'I know of no fairies or wands.'

'Come, sir. You talk to a master of the sport. I am a denizen of dark bedchambers. I know how a woman can make your blood race. Love has put this vigour into you. Some enchantress has stroked your manhood upright at last.' He slipped an arm around Hoode. 'Who is she?'

'An invention of your mind.'

'Am I never to meet this goddess?'

'What goddess?'

'Share her wonder with me.'

'How can I?' said Hoode, coolly. 'She does not exist.'

'*Someone* has put this new spirit into you.'

But Edmund Hoode would not be drawn. Cecily Gilbourne was a secret he would share with no-one. She had enlarged his mind and captured his soul. With her in his life, he felt, he could achieve anything. He recalled the one omission in her catalogue of his work.

'When do we play *Pompey* again?' he asked.

'It has fallen out of our repertoire.'

'Insert it back in, Lawrence.'

'Why?'

'Because I tell you. I, too, can make the earth quake on occasion, nowhere more so than in my tale of Pompey. See him put upon the stage once more. Those who remember him will welcome him back and he is sure to win fresh hearts.'

He thought of Cecily Gilbourne and smiled serenely.

Blackfriars Theatre brought a steady flow of spectators into the precinct. The reputation of the Chapel Children grew with each performance and the murder of their Master seemed to encourage interest rather than to deter it. Some came out of love for Cyril Fulbeck and others out of morbid curiosity, but the result was that the whole precinct was soon swarming with playgoers. Where the Dominican Order once held sway, Alexander the Great would now march in triumph.

Nicholas Bracewell arrived well before the performance was due to begin and loitered in the Great Yard to study the composition of the milling crowd. The audience differed markedly from that normally seen at the Queen's Head. Westfield's Men played to patrons drawn from every rank of society. Aristocrats, artisans and apprentices would share the same space as lawyers, landowners and local politicians. Merchants and mathematicians sat in the balcony while punks and pickpockets mingled with the standees in the pit.

Blackfriars had a more exclusive clientele. It was less a heterogeneous mix than a parade of sumptuary legislation. The laws designed to regulate the dress of men and women were strictly applied. Flashes of gold, silver and purple told Nicholas how many members of the hereditary peerage were present. Velvet denoted a large number of gentlemen and their ladies. Satin, damask, taffeta and grosgain spoke of the eldest sons of knights and all above that rank, or of an income of at least one hundred pounds per annum. And so it went on.

Since costume was such an important element of theatre and accuracy of detail vital, Nicholas had a close acquaintance with the regulations, and he took wry amusement from the fact that gifts of old clothing to actors were one of the few permitted exceptions to the rules. A deeper irony often impressed itself upon him. Actors who struggled to make ten pounds a year would appear on stage in apparel worth far more than that. Popes and princes at the Queen's Head were hired men who rubbed shoulders with poverty when they left it.

A face came out of the crowd to startle him. Nicholas had not expected to see James Ingram there. He was about to hail his colleague when he recalled the latter's strange behavior beside the corpse of Jonas Applegarth. It had seemed so mean-spirited. What, in any case, was Ingram doing at the Queen's Head so early? Was his sudden appearance in the storeroom coincidental? Nicholas stepped back out of sight as the actor went past, wondering if past loyalty had brought him to Blackfriars or if a more sinister motive was at work. Ingram would repay watching.

Waiting until the majority of the spectators had taken their places, he paid sixpence for a seat at the rear. Ingram was three rows in front of him but on a diagonal which allowed Nicholas a clear view of his profile. He did not dwell on it for long. His attention was captured by the splendour of the private playhouse. Shutters had been closed to block out the afternoon sun but the stage was ablaze with light. Candles burned in branched candelabra, many of them hanging and operated by pulleys. The auditorium itself was illumined by numerous small flames as well but full radiance was concentrated on the stage.

Musicians kept the audience entertained while they awaited the performance and Nicholas once again noted a stark contrast. Peter Digby and his consort inhabited a narrow balcony above the stage at the Queen's Head, a cramped and windswept arena in which to practice their art. Their music had to complete with the jostling hubbub of the innyard, the strident yells of vendors selling refreshment and the relentless uproar of the adjacent Gracechurch Street.

Blackfriars was more benevolent to its musicians. Seated in complete comfort, they were given an attentive audience in a building that was designed to catch and amplify the beauty of their work. No raucous yells disturbed the concert, no violent quarrels broke out between onlookers. Music was able to create the perfect mood for the presentation of *Alexander the Great.*

Additional light flooded the acting area as fresh candelabra were brought in and set in position. All eyes were trained on the stage without distraction. Martial music played and the Prologue entered to a burst of applause. The attack began after only half a dozen lines:

*Monstrous body with the Head of a Queen,*
*A maggot-filled apple, so sour and so green,*
*A running sewer of repulsive jest*
*Besmearing grass in the field to the west.*

Nicholas was stung by the jibe at Westfield's Men, but it was the sustained assault on the character and work of Jonas Applegarth which really offended him. Tasteless enough while the playwright was alive, it was disgusting when aimed at a victim of murder. Nicholas told himself that those who laughed at the vicious abuse were unaware of the fate of the man at whom it was aimed, but that did not ease his mind.

His acerbic mockery of child actors had set Applegarth up for a counter-blast. Nicholas accepted that. But while his had been a general satire on despised rivals, the playwright was now suffering a vindictive onslaught of the most personal kind. Every aspect of his appearance, his plays, his opinions and his alleged atheism was held up to ridicule. Nicholas could almost see the man, dangling from a rope in the middle of the stage while he was pelted with rotting fruit and sharp stones.

Alexander the Great stormed onto the stage with his entourage and the tale of heroism began. Military prowess and stirring poetry wiped out the Prologue for everyone else, but it wriggled like a tiny worm in Nicholas's brain. The play itself was a skilful drama, yet it lacked any of the sheer power which had made the work of Jonas Applegarth so compelling and controversial.

Ideal for Blackfriars, the piece would not have survived on the stage at the Queen's Head. Its language was too high-flown, its action too stylised and its moral judgements too oblique. Much of its political commentary would have been incomprehensible to the standees and there was none of the earthy humour with which even the most serious plays in the repertoire of Westfield's Men was liberally salted. The greatness of Alexander did not extend to a sense of humour.

At the same time, it was an instructive experience. As a member of one theatre troupe, Nicholas rarely had the opportunity to view the work of the others. Adult companies were scathing in their dismissal of juvenile actors, but he now saw how unfair that attitude was. The Chapel Children deserved to be taken seriously. They were worthy rivals to Westfield's Men and had one supreme advantage over them. While a typical season at the Queen's Head would last at most for five months, the Blackfriars company could perform for twelve. In the interests of commercial gain, and regardless of the pressure on his actors, Raphael Parsons would keep the theatre open for the whole year.

*Alexander the Great* showed the strengths and exposed the weaknesses of the Chapel Children. They spoke the verse well, they sang superbly and they moved with the grace of dancers. What they lacked was physical presence and this was a failing in a play about recurring warfare. Battles were described in soaring language by children who did not look strong enough to carry spears, let alone to wear full armour. Older members of the company bore the principal roles with honour but there were occasional sniggers as the mighty Alexander entered with an army of boy soldiers.

Two things impressed Nicholas above all else. The first was the clear evidence of the manager's rich abilities. Whatever the defects of his character, Raphael Parsons had a flair for theatrical presentation. His cast was well drilled, his use of scenic devices was masterly and he brought off some stunning dramatic effects. Control of light was a feature of the performance.

Candles were whisked on in profusion to create the sun-baked deserts of Persia, then removed in a flash to leave Alexander's tent in virtual darkness for a dream sequence. As the play moved faultlessly on, one book holder admired the work of his counterpart behind the scenes.

The other striking feature was the performance given by Philip Robinson. Dressed as a Greek goddess, he wafted in and out of the action with ethereal charm. Three songs were allotted to him, each sung in the most sweet and affecting voice. Enjoyment shone out of the boy. Nicholas wondered if this Greek goddess really did wish to return to family life with a heavy-handed butcher in Bankside.

The final scene was the best. Having used all the stage equipment with consummate skill, Parsons saved the most arresting moment until the end. As life slowly ebbed away from the dying Alexander, a silver cloud descended from above with the goddess reclining in front of it. High above the stage, Philip Robinson declaimed a valedictory tribute to the great commander. Light slowly faded on his epic career.

While the audience was profoundly moved, Nicholas was shocked. The winch used to lower Philip Robinson was the one which had hauled Cyril Fulbeck up to his death.

An ovation greeted the cast as they came out to take their bows and several spectators rose to their feet in salute. When they began to file out of the theatre, nothing but praise was heard on every side. Nicholas waited until he reached the Great Yard before he accosted James Ingram.

'Nick!' Ingram said. 'I did not look to find you here.'

'It was a temptation too big to resist.'

'They acquitted themselves well, I feel, though they would fare better with a better play. Boys make wonderful goddesses but sorry soldiers.'

'Why did you come?' asked Nicholas.

'Out of interest.'

'Interest or envy?'

'Both, Nick.'

'There is certainly much to interest.'

'But even more to envy. Just think what we could do with that winding-gear at the Queen's Head. And that scenery! Jonas was so wrong in his attack on the children's companies. So wrong and so vilely unfair.'

'What did you think of the reply?'

'In the Prologue?'

'Was not that vilely unfair?'

'No,' said Ingram evenly. 'Jonas deserved it.'

Before Nicholas could discuss it further, the actor wheeled away and was soon lost in the crowd. It was abrupt behavior for a man who was unfailingly polite as a rule. The book holder was not left alone for long.

'I see that we have a spy in our midst.'

'Merely another spectator.'

'Our spectators do not come to sneer.'

'Nor more did I. There was much to admire.'

'I cannot say the same of Westfield's Men.'

Raphael Parsons was circling the Great Yard to garner praise and eavesdrop on opinion. He gazed around with a proprietary air and spoke to Nicholas over his shoulder.

'I wonder that you could spare the time, sir.'

'You advised me to come.'

'Not with any expectation of a response,' said Parsons. 'Should you not have been at the Queen's Head this afternoon to prop up that rabble of actors?'

'I should have been there, it is true.'

'Then why did you choose Blackfriars instead? And why did you not bring Jonas Applegarth with you so that we could throw his insults back in his teeth?'

'Jonas, I fear, is dead.'

Parsons turned to him in surprise. It quickly shaded into a pleasure that was fringed with disappointment.

'Then the rogue has escaped me, has he?'

'Not by design,' said Nicholas. 'Jonas was murdered at the Queen's Head early this morning. Hanged from a beam.'

'Hanged? Was there a rope strong enough?'

'A rope strong enough and a killer determined enough. We have seen his handiwork here at Blackfriars.'

Parsons blinked. 'You believe it to be the same man?'

'I am convinced of it.'

'Then he is enemy and friend in one.'

'How so?'

'I hate him for what he did to Cyril Fulbeck but I love him for the way he dealt with Jonas Applegarth.'

'You dealt cruelly enough with him yourself.'

'He invited it.'

'The dead invite respect.'

'True,' said Parsons. 'But when I commissioned that Prologue to *Alexander the Great,* I thought he would be alive to hear of it. How was I to know that he would be dead?'

'And if you *had* known?'

'What do you mean?'

'If you had been made aware of his death,' said Nicholas, 'would you have removed that offensive attack in your Prologue?'

Parsons grinned. 'By no means. I'd have called for a few more couplets to celebrate the happy event.'

Nicholas struggled to control a powerful urge to strike him. The manager stood his ground, almost inciting some form of violence so that he could bring an action for assault against the book holder. A former lawyer would assuredly win any legal battle and penalise him severely. Nicholas held back. Delight danced in the other man's eyes. He was taking such pleasure in the death of Jonas Applegarth that Nicholas began to wonder if he might not have been directly involved in it. The egregious manager certainly hated the playwright enough to kill him. Had the surprise he expressed at the news been real or feigned?

Still grinning broadly, Parsons moved away to collect more

congratulations from members of the audience. There was a blend of arrogance and obsequiousness about him which was unpleasant to watch. He was alternately boasting and bowing with mock humility. When a generous compliment was paid to him by a lady, Parsons let out a high laugh of gratitude. It made Nicholas prick up his ears. He had an uncomfortable feeling that he might have heard that sound before.

Speculation was not enough. It was time to support it with evidence, and he was in the correct place to begin the search. The audience was fast dispersing and Ireland Yard was all but empty when he reached it. Starting at the first house on the left, he knocked hard and waited for the servant to open the door.

'Is Master Parsons at home?' he asked politely.

'There is no Master Parsons here, sir.'

'Does Raphael Parsons not live at this address?'

'I have never heard the name.'

It was a painstaking process, but Nicholas stuck to his task until he had been to every house. Several of the residents did not even know him. Of those who did, a number were resentful of the fact that he ran a theatre in the precinct and thus disturbed their peace. Nicholas found no close friends of Raphael Parsons. Where, then, had the man been at the time when Cyril Fulbeck was killed?

He was deep in meditation when a figure came around the corner towards him. He threw the woman a half-glance and let her go past before he realised that he knew her.

'Mistress Hay!' he called.

'Oh,' she said, turning around. 'Good-day, sir.'

He could see from her expression that she did not recognise him, largely because she was too shy to look at his face properly. He walked over to her.

'I am Nicholas Bracewell,' he said. 'I called at your house to speak to your husband.'

She gave a nervous laugh. 'I remember now.'

'Have you been to the play at the theatre?'

'God forbid, sir!'

'Then what are you doing in Blackfriars?' he asked.

'Visiting old friends. I was born and brought up here.'

'In the precinct?'

'Around the corner,' she explained, pointing a hand. 'My father was a bookseller. That is how Caleb and I . . . how my dear husband and I first met. He came into the shop to buy books and prints.' A timid enthusiasm flickered. 'He is such a learned man. Nobody in London knows as much about the history of the city as my husband. I am married to a genius. How many women can say that, sir?'

'Very few, Mistress Hay. Your husband has been kind and helpful to me. I am grateful.'

Anxiety pinched her. 'I must return home now. He will be expecting me back. I must be there for him.'

'Your father was a bookseller, you say?'

'Yes, sir.'

'What name?'

'Mompesson. Andrew Mompesson. I must go.'

'Adieu!'

Nicholas waved her off and watched her shuffle along with her shoulders hunched and her head down. Joan Hay was a woman whose whole purpose in life was to obey her husband's bidding. A bookseller's daughter was an ideal helpmeet for him.

'Mompesson,' repeated Nicholas. 'Andrew Mompesson.'

He had a vague feeling that he knew the name.

Hugh Naismith used his free arm to lift the tankard and drain the last of his ale. It was good to be back in the Elephant again and to share in the banter with his old friends from Banbury's Men, even though he was no longer a member of the company. His wounded arm would heal in time and he would be fit for employment again. Meanwhile, he could cadge a few drinks from Ned Meares and his other fellows.

When he got to his feet, he swayed slightly and bade his farewells. Meares and the others sent him on his way with shouts and laughs. It was early evening when Naismith came reeling out of the inn, adjusting the sling around his neck. His lodging was only a few streets away but he did not get much closer to it.

As soon he passed the lane beside the Elephant, a strong hand reached out to grab him by his jerkin and swing him hard against a wall. All the breath was taken out of him and his wounded arm was jarred. The point of a dagger pricked his throat and made him jerk back his head in terror.

'Leave me alone!' he begged. 'I have no money!'

'That's not what I want,' growled a voice.

'Who are you?'

'A friend of Jonas Applegarth's.'

'That rogue!'

'Yes,' said Owen Elias. 'That rogue.'

He let the blade of his weapon caress the man's neck.

'Tell me why you tried to kill him.'

# [ CHAPTER TEN ]

An air of gloom hung over the Queen's Head like a pall. The murder of Jonas Applegarth changed a haven of conviviality into a murmuring tomb. There was desultory movement in the yard with few guests seeking a bed for the night once they heard about the crime on the premises. The atmosphere in the taproom was funereal. Westfield's Men sat over their ale with a sense of foreboding. Superstitious by nature, they were convinced that a curse had descended on their company and that a violent death presaged an even worse catastrophe.

Alexander Marwood was in his element. A man whose whole life was agitated by imaginary disasters now had a real one to make him truly despondent. Revelling in his misery, he circled his premises like a lost soul, chanting a monologue of black despair and pausing each time outside the storeroom where the horror had occurred to wonder if it should be exorcised, boarded up or torn down completely. Partnership with a theatre company had visited many tribulations upon his undeserving head but this, he felt, was easily the worst. The ghost of Jonas Applegarth would haunt him for ever.

When Nicholas returned from Blackfriars, the landlord was still perambulating the yard with enthusiastic grief. He swooped on the book holder at once, bony fingers sinking into his arm like the talons of a bird of prey.

'Why have you done this to me?' he groaned.

'It was not deliberate.'

'My trade blighted, my womenfolk prostrated, my happiness snatched away! Ruination, sir!'

'A cruel twist of Fate,' said Nicholas. 'Westfield's Men cannot be blamed. You must see that.'

'Who brought that heretic to the Queen's Head? Who staged his blasphemy in my yard? Who permitted him to fetch the wrath of the Lord down on my inn?'

'Jonas Applegarth was a brilliant playwright.'

'His brilliance has destroyed me!'

'It cost him his own life, certainly,' admitted Nicholas. 'Had he not written *The Misfortunes of Marriage,* he would still be with us. It was too powerful a piece for its own good. Someone was deeply offended by it.'

'Yes!' howled Marwood. 'God Almighty!'

'Jonas was killed by a human hand. I can vouch for that.'

Another torrent of self-pity gushed from the landlord but it washed harmlessly over the book holder. He was diverted by the sight of the woman who had just come hurrying in through the archway of the yard. Detaching himself from Marwood, he ran to greet Anne Hendrik. There was a spontaneous embrace. She hugged him with relief.

'I am so glad to see you safe, Nick!'

'What brought you here?'

'The grim tidings,' she explained. 'I met with Nathan Curtis as he was returning home to Bankside. He told me of the murder here this morning and I had to come. I feared for you.'

'But I am in no danger, Anne.'

'If you pursue a killer, you must be. He has two victims already. Do not become the third, I beg you. Nathan told me how determined you were to avenge this death. Why put yourself in such peril?'

Nicholas soothed her as best he could, then led her across to the tiring-house, unlocking it with his key to give them some privacy. As they stepped into the room, Nicholas felt a pang of remorse. Jonas Applegarth had been hanged in the adjoining chamber and his unquiet spirit hovered over the whole building.

'Nathan was still trembling at what he saw.'

'It was a grisly sight indeed. The mere thought of it has thrown the company into chaos. Jonas Applegarth was one of us.'

'Why was he murdered?'

'To silence his voice.'

'I do not understand.'

'He was a man of strong opinions, who used his art to express them and his wit to belabour his enemies. Jonas was killed for something that he wrote.'

'But what of Cyril Fulbeck?' she asked. 'Did you not tell Nathan that he was killed by the same fell hand? The Master of the Chapel was a gentle man with quiet opinions. He made no enemies. Why was his voice silenced?'

'I will find out in time,' he said confidently. 'But you are wrong about him. Meek as he was, Cyril Fulbeck did make enemies. You introduced me to one of them in this very inn.'

She gave a sigh. 'Ambrose Robinson.'

'He would cheerfully have practised his butchery on the Master of the Chapel.'

'That is not so.'

'Your friend has too much anger swilling inside him.'

'He has a temper but is learning to govern it.'

'The wonder is that he has not descended on Blackfriars in a fit of rage and seized his son by force. How have you prevented him from doing so?'

'I urged him to proceed by legal means. That is why I brought him to you, Nick. I hoped that you could help.'

'I have tried, Anne.'

'What have you found?'

Nicholas hesitated. Delighted to see her and touched by her concern for him, he was anxious not to provoke another quarrel. He took her hand and led her to a bench against the wall. They sat down together.

'We parted unhappily the last time we met,' he said.

'That was as much my fault as ours.'

'I was unmannerly with you, Anne.'

'You could never be that.'

'Too bold in my enquiries, then.'

'They carried the weight of accusation,' she explained. 'That was what distressed me. Your tone was possessive.'

'I can only beg forgiveness.'

'You harassed me, Nick. I am not bounden to you. In my own house, I am entitled to make my own decisions.'

'I accept that.'

'To choose my own friends without first seeking your approval. Is that so unreasonable a demand?'

'No, Anne,' he conceded. 'I am justly rebuked.'

'I deserve some censure myself for being so harsh.'

'The fault is mended.'

'You were only drawn into this business because of me. I should have borne that in mind. You did not choose this situation. I did, Nick, and I was wrong to foist another man's domestic problem on to you.'

'I embrace it willingly if it makes us friends again.'

She smiled and kissed him softly on the cheek.

'This you must know,' she said quietly, 'and then we may put it aside so that it does not come between us again. Ambrose Robinson is a kind and generous man. Thefts and damage to my property left me in difficulty. Many offered sympathy but he alone offered me the money I needed at that time. It saved me, Nick. It let me rebuild. I cannot forget that.'

'Nor should you.'

'It brought us close. When his son was taken into the Chapel Royal, he was distraught. I could not deny him my help. That brought us even closer. And yes, you were informed correctly, I *have* been to church with Ambrose—but only to pray beside him on my knees and not for any deeper reason.'

Nicholas took both comfort and regret from her words.

'Why did you not confide your troubles in me, Anne?'

'You were not there.'

'And he was.'

'Yes.'

He lowered his head in dismay. The thought that she had been in dire financial straits was upsetting, all the more so because he was unaware of her predicament. It was a disturbing reminder of how far apart they had drifted. If the butcher had come to her aid, the man deserved gratitude. Nicholas felt slightly ashamed. He squeezed her hand in apology.

'My debt has been fully repaid,' she continued. 'I owe Ambrose nothing now. What I do for him, I do out of simple friendship for I would see him reunited with his son.'

'That may prove difficult.'

'You have looked further into it?'

'The deed of impressment has the might of the law behind it. Philip Robinson belongs to the Chapel Royal.'

'Can he not be released by any means?'

'It seems not.'

'Have you spoken again to Raphael Parsons?'

'He is not the stumbling block,' said Nicholas. 'Nor was he responsible for having the boy impressed. That was Cyril Fulbeck's doing. He is now dead and the lad is answerable to the Assistant Master of the Chapel.'

'But Master Parsons is the real tyrant here.'

'Not so.'

'He is the one who makes Philip's life such an ordeal. He shouts at the boy, beats him and forces him to act upon the stage. He makes the whole company work from dawn till dusk without respite. It is cruel. Complain to him. Exert pressure there. Raphael Parsons is the problem.'

'One problem, perhaps. But there is a bigger one.'

'What is that?'

'Philip Robinson himself.'

'In what way?'

'He enjoys being one of the Chapel Children.'

'There is nothing he loathes more.'

'I have seen the boy, Anne,' Nick argued. 'I watched him play in *Alexander the Great* this afternoon. He was a delight to behold. He acted well and sang beautifully, all with true zest. I tell you this. I would make Philip Robinson an apprentice with Westfield's Men without a qualm. We will need a replacement for John Tallis now his voice has deepened into manhood. If he were not already ensconced at Blackfriars, the lad would be ideal.'

'I find this hard to believe. Philip *enjoys* it?'

'He has found his true profession.'

'Then why are his letters so full of misery? Why does he rail at Raphael Parsons so? Why does Philip beg his father to come and rescue him from his imprisonment?'

'He does none of these things, Anne.'

'He does. I read his tales of woe and so did you.'

'What we read were letters given to us by the father,' said Nicholas. 'We only have his word that they were written by his son. Ambrose Robinson has been a good neighbour to you and I respect him for that, but I beg leave to doubt his honesty. I believe that we have been misled.'

It was an unsatisfactory confessional box. The lane beside the Elephant in Shoreditch was too public for Owen Elias's liking. Revellers kept arriving at the inn or tumbling out of it. Grabbing his quarry by the neck, therefore, Elias marched him through a maze of back streets until they found a small house which had collapsed in upon itself. The Welshman kicked Hugh

Naismith into the ruins and made him sit on a pile of rubble.

'Peace at last!' said Elias. 'Now—talk!'

'I've done nothing to you,' bleated Naismith.

'You offend my sight. Apart from that, you have the stink of Banbury's Men about you and that's even more revolting. Tell me about Jonas Applegarth.'

A slow smile spread. 'He's dead. That's why I went to the Elephant. To drink to his departure.'

'Take care I do not drink to yours!' warned Elias, still brandishing his dagger. 'Jonas was a friend. Remember that if you wish to stay alive.'

'He was no friend of mine.'

'So I hear. You fought a duel. He bested you.'

'Only by chance.'

'He should have run you through like the dog you are.'

'He gave me this,' said Naismith, holding up the sling. 'Banbury's Men had no work for an actor with only one arm.'

'Is that why you sought to kill Jonas?'

'No!'

'Is that why you threw a dagger at his back?'

'I never did that!'

'Do not lie to me or I'll cut your mangy carcass to pieces and feed it to the crows. You stalked him, did you not?'

'That I do admit,' grunted Naismith.

'You followed him home last night and ran away when I saw you. Do you admit that as well?'

'Yes. It was me.'

'Hoping for a chance to throw another dagger.'

'No! That would have been too merciful a death. Jonas Applegarth deserved to be roasted slowly over a hot fire with an apple in his mouth like any other pig.'

'Enough!'

Elias slapped him hard across the face and the man keeled over onto the ground. The Welshman knelt beside him.

'Insult his memory again and you will join him.'

'Stay, sir!' pleased Naismith.

'Then tell me the truth.'

'I have done so. I despised Jonas Applegarth. I wanted him dead but lacked the opportunity to kill him.'

'You mean, you hurled a dagger and it missed.'

'How *could* I?'

Naismith help up his free hand. The bandage was now removed but the hand was still badly swollen and a livid gash ran from the wrist to the back of the forefinger.

'I can hardly lift a tankard,' he said bitterly. 'How could I hope to throw a dagger? It was not me!'

Elias saw the truth of his denial. Naismith was not their would-be assassin. He had been watching Applegarth in order to feed his hatred of the man, waiting until his wounds healed enough for him strike back at his enemy.

'Why did you fight the duel?' asked Elias.

'He challenged me.'

'Something you said?'

'And something I did not say,' explained Naismith. 'We played *Friar Francis* at The Curtain. It was a clever comedy but full of such sourness and savagery that it was not fit for the stage. I said as much and he took me to task. I hated the play. It bubbled like a witch's brew. He cursed the whole world in it. Then came the performance itself.'

'What happened?'

'We were all at odds with Applegarth by then. He made *Friar Francis* a descent into Hell for us. Everyone swore to hit back at him but I alone had the courage.'

'What did you do?'

'I changed his lines.'

'Jonas would not have liked that.'

'Why speak such slander against mankind when it stuck so in my throat? I wrote my own speeches instead. They had less wit but far more sweetness.'

'No wonder he wanted to cut your heart out!'

'Jonas Applegarth put words in my mouth I simply could not say. What else could I do?'

But Elias was not listening. Convinced that Naismith did not throw the dagger at his friend's back, he was already asking himself a question.

Who *did*?

Edmund Hoode ascended the staircase at the Unicorn with far more alacrity this time. Summoned that evening by another sketch of the fabled beast, he responded immediately. A day of mourning might yet be redeemed. Bereavement was dragging him down with his fellows. He had sighed enough for Jonas Applegarth. Sighs of a different order were now in prospect.

Only when he reached the landing did he stop to consider how little he really knew of Cecily Gilbourne. Was she married? A lady of her age and beauty was unlikely to have remained single. Was she widowed? Divorced even? And where did she live? In London or beyond? Alone or with her family? He winced slightly. Did she have *children?*

'My mistress is ready for you, sir.'

The maidservant was holding the door of the chamber open for him. All his doubts melted away. Cecily Gilbourne was sublime. Her age, her marital status, her place of abode and her familial situation were irrelevant. It mattered not if she had three husbands, four houses and five children. She was evidently a lady of wealth and social position. More to the point, she was a woman of keen discernment where drama was concerned. One feature set her above every other member of her sex. Cecily Gilbourne was his.

Hoode entered the room to take possession of his prize.

'You came!' she said with a measure of surprise.

'Nothing would have kept me away.'

'Not even the death of a friend? The performance at the Queen's Head was cancelled because of him. We were turned away. I feared that you would stay there to grieve for him.'

'I would rather celebrate with you.'

'That is what I hoped.'

There was nothing enigmatic about her smile now. It was frank and inviting. Cecily Gilbourne was dressed in a subtle shade of green which matched the colour of her eyes. Perched on a chair near the window, she wore no hat and no gloves. He noted that a single gold band encircled the third finger of her left hand. Seeing his interest, she glanced down at the ring with a wan smile.

'I was married at seventeen,' she explained sadly. 'My husband was a soldier and a statesman. He was killed in action at the Siege of Rouen. No children blessed our union. I have only this to keep his memory bright.'

'I see.'

'Have you been married, Edmund?'

'No. Not yet.'

'It is something which should happen when you are very young, as I was, or very old, as I will be before I consider a second marriage. A husband should provide either excitement for your youth or companionship for your dotage.'

'What may *I* provide for you, Cecily?'

'You give me all that I need.'

Another candid smile surfaced and she beckoned him over to sit close to her. Hoode was enraptured. The hideous murder at the Queen's Head that morning was not even a distant echo in his mind. The Laughing Hangman had been obliterated by the smiling inamorata.

'I spoke with Lawrence Firethorn,' he told her.

'About me?'

'Indirectly. I wanted to fill the one gap in your knowledge of me. You have not seen my *Pompey* and so I instructed him to put it back on the stage soon for your delectation. It is a work in which I take much pride. *Pompey the Great* has a true touch of greatness.'

'Then my delight is assured. And your new play?'

'*The Faithful Shepherd* will be seen at The Rose next week,' he said, beaming. 'I insisted that it was. With your permission, I will write a sonnet in praise of you, to be inserted cunningly in one of the longer speeches so that its true meaning may be disguised from the common herd.'

'Can this be done without corrupting your tale?'

'It will enhance it, Cecily. My play is partly set on the island of Sicily, allowing me to conjure endlessly with your magical name. I'll move the action from midsummer's night to St Cecilia's Day to give my fancy even more scope and pen you fourteen lines of the purest poetry ever heard on a stage. Will this content you?'

'Beyond measure.'

'Look for pretty conceits and clever rhymes.'

'I will savour the prettiness of the conceits but I do not look to find a rhyme that is half so clever as this before us.'

'What rhyme is that?'

'Why, Cecily and Edmund. Can two words fit more snugly together than that? Edmund and Cecily. They agree in every particular. Set them apart and neither can stand for much on its own. Put them together, seal them tight, lock them close in a loving embrace and they defy the laws of sound and language. Edmund and Cecily. Is that not the apotheosis of rhyme?'

'They blend together most perfectly into one.'

'Edmund!'

'Cecily!'

No more words were needed.

Nicholas Bracewell escorted her back over London Bridge and on to Bankside. It was pleasant to have Anne Hendrik on his arm again and it rekindled memories for both of them. The long walk was far too short for them to exchange all the information they would have wished, but he now had a much clearer idea of the life she had been living since their separation, and she, for her part, filled in many blank pages of his own recent history.

Anne invited him into her home for some refreshment before he journeyed back. Over a glass of wine, they let nostalgia brush seductively against them.

'Have you missed me?' she asked.

'Painfully.'

'How did you cope with that pain?'

'I worked, Anne. There is a dignity in that.'

'That was also my escape.'

'Westfield's Men have kept me busier than ever. I was able to lose myself in my work and keep my mind from straying too often to you and to this house.'

'Did you never think of straying here in person?'

'Daily.'

She laughed lightly, then her face clouded over.

'I worried deeply about you, Nick.'

'Why?'

'Westfield's Men thrust too much upon you. The burden would break a lesser man. Yet still they ask for more from their book holder. It is unfair.'

'I do not complain.'

'That is your failing. They will overload you and you will not raise your voice in protest. You always put the company first.'

'Westfield's Men are my family. Without them, I would be an orphan. That is why I always seek to advance them. And why I rush to defend them, as I do in this instance.'

'What instance?'

'The murder of Jonas Applegarth,' he said. 'It was no random killing. Only one man died, but the whole company will suffer as a result. That was the intention. Victim and place were selected with deep guile.' He made to leave. 'Our Laughing Hangman wants to strangle Westfield's Men as well.'

'Why?'

'He keeps his reason private.'

'Take care,' she said, moving close. 'For my sake.'

'I will.'

After a brief kiss, he forced himself to leave. The temptation to linger was almost overwhelming, but Nicholas resisted it. A year's absence could not be repaired in a single evening. Anne's feelings towards him had changed slightly and he could no longer trust his own promptings. They needed time to find more common ground.

Other commitments took priority over Anne Hendrik. Only when two murders had been solved and the fate of a chorister had been decided could he feel free to renew his friendship with her, properly and at leisure.

Instead of crossing the bridge, he walked down to the river to hail a boat. It felt good to be back on the water again and he let a hand trail over the stern like a rudder. His boatman rowed hard. Thames Street drifted slowly towards them. When he landed, Nicholas went straight to the house of a friend.

'I will not take much of your time.'

'Come in, come in, sir,' said Caleb Hay.

'I feel guilty at dragging you away from your history.'

'It will wait, Master Bracewell.'

'How many hours a day do you spend working on it?'

'Not enough, not enough.'

Caleb Hay looked weary. He rubbed his eyes to dispel some of the fatigue and conducted Nicholas into his parlour. His wife had answered the door, but he had come down from his study when he heard the name of the visitor. Joan Hay crept nervously away to leave the two men alone.

'Well, sir,' said Hay. 'How may I help this time?'

'In a number of ways. You were, I believe, a scrivener.'

'That is so.'

'How did you discover your aptitude for history?'

'In the course of my work. A scrivener spends much of his time copying documents of various kinds. I was fortunate enough to be commissioned to make fair copies of ancient records in the

Tower of London. It was an inspiration. From that moment on, I knew what my life's work would be.'

'Were you ever called upon to write letters?'

'Frequently.'

'Of what kind?'

'All kinds. Most of London is illiterate. If people need to send an important letter, they will often dictate it to a scrivener. We are like parish priests. We hear a man's most intimate thoughts.' He gave a chuckle. 'Letters of love were my special joy. You have no idea how many times I ravished beautiful women with my quill. I must have seduced a hundred or more on paper. I knew the tricks and the turn of phrase.'

'Could you always tell the hand of a scrivener?'

'Of course.'

'How?'

'By the neatness of his calligraphy,' he said. 'And by a dozen other smaller signs. Why do you ask?'

'I read some letters from a boy to his father on a matter of some consequence. I took them at face value and the father is eager for me to do so. But I now suspect that the lad did not write them at all.'

'Bring one to me and I'll tell you for sure.'

'If I can contrive it, I will.'

'How old is the boy?'

'Eleven.'

'Then we have a certain guide,' said Hay blithely. 'I've taught many lads of that age to hold a pen. I know what an eleven-year-old hand can do.' He cocked his head to one side to peer at Nicholas. 'But is this not a trivial affair for so serious as man as yourself? When my wife told me you were here, I thought you'd come for more advice to help you catch the man who murdered Cyril Fulbeck.'

'There is a connection.'

'I fail to see it.'

'The boy is a chorister in the Chapel Royal. Against the

express wishes of his father, he was taken there by deed of impressment at the behest of Master Fulbeck.'

'I begin to understand.'

'What distresses him most is that his son spends much of his time at Blackfriars as a child actor. The father is demanding his release, but to no avail.'

Hay's face darkened. 'Then we have one suspect before us. What father would not feel ready to commit a murder in such a case? Might not this same parent be the fellow who killed Cyril Fulbeck?'

'He might well be,' agreed Nicholas, 'but I think that it is unlikely. And I am certain that he is not guilty of the other hanging.'

'There has been a *second*?' gasped the old man.

'This morning. At the Queen's Head.'

'What poor wretch has died this time?'

'Jonas Applegarth.'

'Ah!' His tone became neutral. 'The playwright. I will not speak harshly of any man on his way to the grave. But I cannot pity him so readily as I do the Master of the Chapel. And this Applegarth was hanged, you say?'

'In the same manner. By the same hand.'

'But why? What is the link between them?'

'It is there somewhere.'

'One was a saint, the other a sinner.'

'Our hangman treated them with equal savagery.'

'The animal must be caught!'

Hay moved away and rested a hand against the wall while he stared into the empty fireplace. He was lost in contemplation for a few minutes. Nicholas waited. His host eventually looked over at him.

'I am sorry, I am sorry. My mind wandered.'

'It is gruesome news. Anyone would be jolted.'

'How else may I help you, sir?'

'Does your history of London touch on its inns?'

'In full detail,' said Hay, brightening. 'They are one of the splendours of the city and I give them their due.'

'Will the Queen's Head be mentioned?'

'It would be a crime to omit it. The history of that inn would fill a book on its own. Such a landmark in Gracechurch Street. Do you know when it was first built?'

'No,' said Nicholas, 'but I would love to hear.'

Caleb Hay launched himself into another impromptu lecture, taking his guest on a tour through almost two hundred years. His account faltered when he reached the point where Westfield's Men entered the action, and Nicholas cut him short.

'That was astonishing,' he complimented. 'I have worked at the Queen's Head for years but you have revealed aspects of it which I have never even noticed.'

'The scholar's eye.'

'You certainly have that. It showed in your sketch of Blackfriars. That has been a godsend to me.' Nicholas walked to the door and threw a casual remark over his shoulder. 'It is strange that you did not mention your personal interest in the precinct.'

'Personal interest?'

'Your wife grew up there, I believe.'

'Well, yes,' said Hay with a chuckle, 'that is true but hardly germane. Her father was a bookseller there, but he died years ago. How did you come by this intelligence?'

'From your wife herself. We met in Ireland Yard.'

'She was visiting old friends.'

'So she informed me.'

Caleb Hay opened the door to usher him out. He gave Nicholas an encouraging pat on his arm.

'Work hard to catch Cyril Fulbeck's killer.'

'He also murdered Jonas Applegarth.'

'You must sing the Requiem Mass for *him*. I will not. The Master of the Chapel is the loss I suffer. He was a dear friend. Do you know why?' He gave another chuckle. 'Here is something else that slipped my old mind. Cyril Fulbeck not only assisted my researches in Blackfriars. He rendered me a more important service than that.'

'Did he?'

'Yes,' said Hay, easing him out into the street. 'He once had me released from prison.'

Nicholas found the door closed politely in his face.

Anne Hendrik went through into the adjoining premises to check that all doors were securely locked. The shop was kept in meticulous condition because Preben van Loew believed that cleanliness was next to godliness and that an ordered workplace was a Christian virtue. He would certainly have closed the shutters and bolted the doors before leaving, but Anne still felt the need to see for herself. In the wake of the thefts from her property, she had become more conscious of the need to protect both house and shop.

When she went back through into her parlour, she saw that her servant had admitted a visitor. Ambrose Robinson was in his best apparel. His hands had been thoroughly scrubbed to rid of them of the smell of his trade. His expression was apologetic, his manner docile.

Anne was not pleased to see him but she suppressed her feelings behind a smile of welcome. She indicated the basket of flowers standing on a table.

'Thank you, Ambrose. A kind thought.'

'It was the least I could do.'

'Their fragrance fills the room.'

'And so does yours!' he said with heavy-handed gallantry. 'You are a flower among women.'

Anne shuddered inwardly. She hoped that she had heard the last of his clumsy compliments but he was back again with more. Robinson inclined his head penitentially.

'I have come from church,' he said.

'At this hour?'

'I went to pray for forgiveness. On my knees, I can think more clearly. I saw the error of my deeds. After the way I left this house, I have no right to be allowed back into it. You should bar the door against me.'

'Let us forget what happened,' she suggested.

'I cannot do that, Anne. My disgrace is too heavy to be shrugged off so easily. I sought forgiveness in church but I also appealed for guidance. My ignorance is profound. I blunder through life. I revile myself for the way that I hurt those I cherish most. When my intentions are good, why are my actions often so bad?'

He sounded quite sincere but she remained on her guard.

'You will find me a changed man,' he promised.

'In what way?'

'I will be a true friend and not an angry suitor. I offer you my humblest apologies, Anne. Please accept them.'

'I do.' There was a pause. 'With thanks.'

'And I will say the same to Nick Bracewell.'

'Why?'

'For mistrusting him. For abusing the man behind his back when I should be overcome with gratitude. What does Ambrose Robinson mean to him? Nothing! Why should he care about my dear son, Philip? No reason! Yet he has undertaken to help me with a free heart. That is kindness indeed.'

'Nick responded to my entreaty.'

'There is my chiefest source of shame,' he said, lifting his eyes to look at her. 'You, Anne. You took me to him. You engaged Nick Bracewell on my behalf. You did all this, then had to suffer my foul abuse of your friend.'

'It was uncalled for, Ambrose.'

'You are right to chide me.'

'I will not tolerate another outburst like that,' she warned him. 'Master your anger or my door *will* be barred to you. Wild accusation has no part in friendship.'

'I know, I know. My rudeness is only exceeded by my gross

stupidity. I love my son and would move Heaven and Earth to get him back. Yet what do I do? Carp and cavil. Malign the one man who may help me.'

'The one man?'

'Let us be frank,' he said with rancour. 'The law fails me. Were Philip the son of a gentleman, the case could go to court with some chance of success. Since he is only the child of a butcher, he is beyond salvation. That deed of impressment is a set of chains.' He took a step towards her. 'That is why we must work by other means. We must trust Nick Bracewell to insinuate himself into Blackfriars and use persuasion to set Philip free. Why did I dare to censure him? Nick is our only hope.'

Anne was in a quandary. She wanted Philip Robinson released from the Chapel Royal, partly because she believed that father and son should be together and partly because she felt that the boy's return would liberate her from the now irksome attentions of the butcher. A new factor had come into her calculations. Should she remain silent or should she confront Ambrose Robinson with it?

His earnest enquiry forced her to make a decision.

'Has there been further word from Nick?' he asked.

'I spoke with him at length.'

'And?'

'He visited Blackfriars this afternoon,' she said, 'and watched a play there. Philip was in the cast.'

'Dressed up as a woman, no doubt! Wearing a wig and daubing his face with powder! Strutting around the stage like a Bankside harlot for any man to ogle!' He scowled at her. 'I want my son to grow into a man. They do him wrong to force him into female attire. Philip detests it.'

'That was not Nick's impression.'

'He despises every moment of it.'

'Yet he gave a fine performance, it seems.'

'Under duress.'

'Of his own volition.'

'Never!'

'Nick loves the theatre. He spends every waking moment in the company of actors. When he admires a performance, he knows what lies behind it. I trust his judgement.' She inhaled deeply before confronting him. 'Your son enjoys working in the theatre. Nick says he has decided flair.'

'Blackfriars is a torture chamber for Philip.'

'That may not be so.'

'It *is* so. I know my son.'

'Nick has seen him on the stage—you have not.'

'The shame would be too much for me!'

'Philip was a most willing actor this afternoon.'

'Then why does he beg me to rescue him!' said Robinson with mounting rage. 'Why does he plead so in every letter that he sends me? You saw his pain, Anne, you saw his misery. Were those the letters of a boy who is *happy*?'

'No, Ambrose.'

'Then why did he write them? Let Nick answer that.'

'He has,' she said levelly. 'He does not believe that Philip sent those letters at all. They were written by someone else. Is that not so?'

Ambrose Robinson fell silent. He looked deeply hurt and betrayed. His fists bunched, his body tensed, and he began to breathe stertorously through his nose. Eyes narrowing, he glared at her with a mixture of animosity and wounded affection. Anne took a step backwards. She was suddenly afraid of him.

Nicholas Bracewell returned to the Queen's Head once more. As he turned into the yard, he heard the familiar voice of Owen Elias.

'So I told Barnaby that I'd translate *Cupid's Folly* into Welsh for him so that he could take it on a tour of the Principality and play to an audience of sheep!'

Appreciative guffaws came from the knot of actors around the speaker. When Nicholas came up, he saw with a shock that it was not Elias at all. James Ingram had been diverting his fellows with an impersonation of their Welsh colleague. It was the accuracy of his mimicry which had produced the laughter.

The mirth faded when they saw Nicholas. Actors who should have been mourning the death of Jonas Applegarth looked a little shamefaced at being caught at their most raucous. They slunk quietly away, leaving Ingram alone to talk with the book holder.

'You are a cunning mimic,' said Nicholas.

'Harmless fun, Nick. Nothing more.'

'Does Owen know that he has a twin brother?'

'He'd slaughter me if he did,' said Ingram. 'It was an affectionate portrait of him, but Owen would not thank the artist.' He became remorseful. 'But I am glad that we meet again. I was brusque and unmannerly at Blackfriars. You deserved better from me. I have no excuse.'

'Let it pass, James.'

'It will not happen again.'

'I am pleased to hear it,' said Nicholas. 'But you have still not told me what brought you to the Queen's Head so early this morning.'

'Eagerness. Nothing more.'

'It does not often get you here ahead of your fellows.'

'It did today.'

'Why did you come into the storeroom?'

'The door of the tiring-house was open. I wondered who was here. Nathan Curtis was in the storeroom with the body. I got there only seconds before you returned.'

Ingram spoke with his usual open-faced honesty and Nicholas had no reason to doubt him. The tension between the two of them had gone completely. The book holder was glad. Fond of the actor, he did not want a rift between them.

'Let's into the taproom,' he suggested.

'Not me, Nick,' said the other pleasantly. 'It is too full of reminiscence about Jonas Applegarth for me. You know my feelings there. I would be out of place.'

They exchanged farewells and Ingram left the innyard.

The atmosphere in the taproom had lightened considerably. Members of the company sat in a corner and traded maudlin memories of the dead man, but most of the customers were only there to drink and gamble. Laughter echoed around the room once more and the serving-men were kept busy. Alexander Marwood could never be expected to smile, but his despair was noticeably less fervent than before.

Nicholas joined the table at which Lawrence Firethorn and Owen Elias sat. Both had been drinking steadily. They called for an extra tankard and poured the newcomer some ale from their jug.

'Thank heaven you've come, Nick!' said Elias.

'Yes,' added Firethorn. 'We are in such a morass of self-pity that we need you to pull us out. Marwood still swears we have performed our last play in his yard.'

'He has done that often before,' said Nicholas, 'and we always return to confound his prediction. Tomorrow is Sunday and our stage would in any case stand empty. That will make our landlord think again. Two days without a penny taken in his yard! His purse will speak up for Westfield's Men.'

'I hope so,' said Firethorn. 'The last twenty-four hours have been a nightmare. One author turns my marital couch into a bed of nails, another gets himself hanged and my occupation rests on the whim of an imbecile landlord! I might as well become a holy anchorite and live on herbs. There's no future for me here.'

He drank deep. Elias saw the chance to impart his news.

'I found Naismith,' he said. 'The dog admitted that he had been shadowing Jonas through the streets.'

'Did he throw that dagger?' asked Nicholas.

'Unhappily, no. I'd have welcomed the excuse to carve him up and send him back to Banbury's Men in a meat-pie. Hugh

Naismith is too weak to throw anything, Nick. He is not our man.'

'Then we must look elsewhere.'

'What have you learned?'

'Much of interest but little that ties the name of the murderer to Jonas Applegarth.'

'Choose from any of a hundred names,' said Firethorn. 'Jonas spread his net widely. Enemies all over London.'

'That was not the case with Cyril Fulbeck,' reminded Nicholas. 'Few would pick a quarrel with him. That cuts our list right down. We look for a rare man, one with motive to kill both the Master of the Chapel *and* Jonas Applegarth.' A new thought made him sit up. 'Unless I am mistaken.'

'About what?' said Elias.

'The Laughing Hangman. Do I search for one murderer when there are really *two*?' He thought it through. 'Jonas was hanged in the same manner as Cyril Fulbeck, it is true. And I heard what I thought was the same laughter. But ears can play strange tricks sometimes. Sound can be distorted in chambers and passageways.'

'It *must* be the same man,' insisted Elias.

'Why?'

'Coincidence could not be that obliging.'

'We are not talking of coincidence, Owen, but of mimicry. Someone who saw the first man hanged could dispose of a second in the identical way. Someone who heard that peal of laughter at Blackfriars could bring the same mockery to the Queen's Head.'

'Why go to such elaborate lengths?' asked Firethorn.

'To evade suspicion,' said Nicholas. 'What better ruse than to use the method of one killer as your own and put the crime on his account?'

'Your reasoning breaks down,' decided Elias. 'Only someone who actually *saw* the first victim could know the necessary detail. Only a trained actor with a gift for mimicry could reproduce a laugh like that. Where on earth would you find such a man?'

Nicholas said nothing. He was preoccupied with the thought that he had just been talking with that very person in the inn-yard. Motive, means and opportunity. A perfect cloak for his crime. James Ingram had them all.

'I give up!' moaned Elias.

'Why?'

'The villains multiply before my eyes. First, I thought our killer and our dagger-thrower were one man. Then you separate them. Now you split the hangman into two as well to give us three in all. By tomorrow, it will have grown to four and so on until we are searching for a whole band of them!'

'I am lost,' admitted Firethorn. 'What is happening?'

'Confusion, Lawrence!'

'Do we have any idea at all who murdered Jonas?'

'Yes,' said Elias with irony. 'Nick pulls a new suspect out of the air every minute. Each one a possible killer. We'll get them all to sign a petition, then pick out the name that pleases us most and designate him as Laughing Hangman.'

'Mompesson!' muttered Nicholas.

'My God! He's added another suspect to the list.'

'Andrew Mompesson.'

Nicholas remembered where he had seen the name before.

# [ CHAPTER ELEVEN ]

The miracle had happened at last. After a lifetime's fruitless search, Edmund Hoode finally found his way into the Garden of Eden and discovered Paradise. Cecily Gilbourne was a most alluring Eve, soft and supple, at once virginal and seasoned in all the arts of love. She was a true symbol of womanhood. Hoode's ardour matched her eager demands, his desire soared with her passion. Hearts, minds and bodies met in faultless rhyme. Their destinies mingled.

It was several minutes before he regained his breath. He used the back of his arm to wipe the perspiration from his brow, then gazed up at the ceiling. The Garden of Eden, he now learned, was a bedchamber at the Unicorn. When he turned his head, he saw that his gorgeous and compliant Eve had freckles on her shoulder. She, too, was glistening with joy.

What thrilled him most was the ease with which it had all happened. A rose. A promise. A tryst. Consummation. There had been no intervening pauses and no sudden obstacles. No inconvenient appearances by returning husbands. Everything proceeded with a graceful inevitability. It was an experience he had always coveted but never come within sight of before. In Hoode's lexicon, romance was a synonym for anguish. Cecily Gilbourne offered him a far more satisfactory definition.

Her voice rose up softly from the pillow beside him.

'Edmund?'

'My love?'

'Are you still awake?'

'Yes, Cecily.'

'Are you still happy?'

'Delirious.'

'Are you still *mine*?'

'Completely.'

She pulled him gently on top of her and kissed him.

'Take me, Edmund.'

*'Again?'*

'Again.'

He kicked open the gate with his naked foot and went into the Garden of Eden, not, as before, with halting gait and wide-eyed wonder but with a proprietary swagger. Edmund Hoode had found his true spiritual home.

The silence seemed interminable. Anne Hendrik was petrified. She stood there unable to move, unable to call out for her servant and incapable of defending herself in any way. The menacing figure of Ambrose Robinson loomed over her. She felt like one of the dumb animals whom he routinely slaughtered.

Cold fury coursed through the butcher. The veins on his forehead stood out like whipcord as he fought to contain his violent instincts. When he took a step towards her, Anne was so convinced that he was about to strike her that she shut her eyes and braced herself against the blow. It never came. Instead, she heard a quiet snivelling noise. When she dared to lift her lids again, she saw that Robinson was now sitting on a chair with his head in his hands.

Her fear slowly shaded into cautious sympathy.

'What ails you?' she asked.

'All is lost,' he murmured between sobs of remorse.

'Lost?'

'My son, my dearest friend, my hopes of happiness. All gone for ever.' He looked up with a tearful face. 'It was my only chance, Anne. I did it out of love.'

'Love?'

'The loan, those letters . . .'

'You are not making much sense, Ambrose.'

'It was wrong of me,' he said, lurching to his feet. 'I should not have deceived you so. You deserved better of me. I will get out of your life for ever and leave you in peace.'

Wiping his tears away, he lumbered towards the door.

'Stay!' she said, curiosity roused. 'Do not run away with the truth untold. What *is* going on, Ambrose?'

He stopped to face her and gave a hopeless shrug.

'You were right, Anne.'

'Philip did not send those letters?'

'No,' he confessed, 'but they are exactly the letters that he *would* have sent, had he the time and opportunity to write. I know my own son. Philip is in torment at Blackfriars. Those letters only said what he feels.'

'Did you write them yourself?'

'With these clumsy hands?' he said, spreading his huge palms. 'They are more used to holding an axe than a pen. No, Anne. I only wrote those letters in my own mind. A scrivener put them on paper at my direction.'

She was baffled. *'Why?'*

'To reassure me. To tell myself that my son really did love me and want to come home to me. When I'd read those letters enough times, I truly began to believe that Philip had indeed sent them.' His chin sank to his chest again. 'And there was another reason, Anne.'

'I see it only too clearly.'

'It was a mistake.'

'You used those letters to ensnare *me*,' she said angrily. 'To work on my feelings and draw me closer. And through me, you brought Nick Bracewell in to help.'

'You spoke so highly of him. Of how resourceful he was and what a persuasive advocate he would be. That was why I was so keen and willing to meet Nick.'

'And to deceive *him* with those false letters!'

'They are not false. Philip might have written them.'

'But he did not, Ambrose. You beguiled us!'

'How else could I secure your help?'

'By being honest with me.'

'Honesty would have put you straight to flight.'

'Why so?'

'Because of the person I am,' he said, beating his chest with a fist. 'Look at me. A big, ugly, shambling butcher. What hope had I of winning you with honesty? When you thought I lent that money out of friendship, you took it gladly. Had I told you I gave it because I cared, because I loved, because I wanted you as mine, you would have spurned it.' A pleading note reappeared. 'What I did was dishonest but from honest motives. I worship my son and so I inveigled you and Nick Bracewell into working for his release. Because I dote on you—and this is my worst offence—I used Philip as a means to get close to you. To make you think and feel like a mother to him. I was trying to *court* you, Anne.'

'There was a worse offence yet,' she said vehemently.

'That is not so.'

'I see it now and shudder at what I see. You dangled your own son in front of me like a carrot in front of a donkey. That was disgusting enough. To mislead Philip as well was despicable.'

'I did not mislead him.'

'Yes you did,' she accused. 'We were not the only dupes. He had his share of false letters. You wrote to him to tell him that he would come back to a happy home with a second mother. You used *me* to tempt Philip back.'

'No!'

'It was the one thing that might bring him home.'

'You don't know Philip.'

'I know him well enough to understand why he likes it in the Chapel Royal. He has escaped from his father. No wonder he enjoys it so at the Blackfriars Theatre.'

'I want him *home*!' shouted Robinson.

Anne walked to the front door and opened it wide.

'Do not expect me to help you, sir,' she said crisply. 'There lies your way. Do not let me detain you. I'll be no man's false hope to wave in front of an unwitting child. Farewell, Ambrose. You are no longer welcome here!'

He glared at her for a moment, then skulked out.

Sunday morning turned London into a gigantic bell-foundry. The whole city clanged to and fro. Bells rang, tolled, chimed or sang out in melodious peals to fill every ear within miles with the clarion call of Christianity and to send the multifarious congregations hurrying in all directions to Matins in church or cathedral. Bells summoned the faithful and accused the less devout, striking chords in the hearts of the one and putting guilt in the minds of the others. Only the dead and deaf remained beyond the monstrous din of the Sabbath.

Nicholas Bracewell left his lodging in Thames Street on his way to his own devotions. Recognising a figure ahead of him, he lengthened his stride to catch her up.

'Good-morrow!'

'Oh!'

'May I walk with you?'

'I am late, sir. I must hurry.'

'May I not keep your haste company?'

Joan Hay was not pleased to see him and even less happy about the way he fell in beside her. Keeping her head down and her hands clutched tight in front of her, she bustled along the street. Nicholas guessed the reason for her behaviour.

'I think that I must beg your pardon,' he said.

'Why?'

'For putting you in bad favour with your husband. I should not have told him that we met in Blackfriars. I fear he may have upbraided you for talking to me as you did.'

'No, no,' she lied.

'Master Hay is a private man, I know that.'

'He is a genius, sir. I am married to a genius.'

'Why is he not with you this morning?'

'He has gone ahead. I rush to catch up with him.'

'Then I will ask one simple question before I let you get on your way.'

'Please do not, sir. I know nothing.'

'This is no secret I ask you to divulge. Your husband talked openly of it yesterday.'

'Then speak with him again.'

'I would rather hear it from you.'

When they reached a corner, he put a gentle hand on her shoulder to stop her. Joan Hay looked up into his face with frightened eyes. Timorous at the best of times, she was now in a mild panic.

'Master Hay told me that he was once in prison.'

'Only for one day,' she said defensively.

'There must have been some error, surely? Your husband is the most law-abiding man I have ever met.'

'He is, he is.'

'What possible charge could be brought against him?'

'I do not know.'

'You must have some idea.'

'It was a mistake. He was soon released.'

'Thanks to the help of the Master of the Chapel.'

'Yes, I believe that he was involved.'

'So why was your husband arrested?' pressed Nicholas.

'Truly, sir, I do not know.'

'He could not have been taken without a warrant. Did they come to the house? Was he seized there?'

Joan Hay glanced nervously around, fearful of being late for church and anxious to shake off her interrogator. She was patently unaware of the full details of her husband's temporary incarceration, but Nicholas still felt that he might winkle some clue out of her.

'Let me go, sir,' she said. 'I implore you.'

'When the officers came for your husband . . .'

'Discuss the matter with him.'

'Did they take anything away with them?'

'Some documents, that is all.'

'Documents?'

'Do not ask me what they were for I know not.'

Nicholas stepped aside so that she could continue on her way. He felt guilty at harassing an already harassed woman but the conversation had yielded something of great interest. It gave him much to ponder as he headed for his own church in the neighbouring parish.

The jangling harmonies of London finally brought Edmund Hoode out of his protracted sleep. Expecting to wake up in the Garden of Eden, entwined in the arms of his beloved, he was disconcerted to find himself alone in a dishevelled bed at the Unicorn with a draught blowing in through an open window. As his brain slowly cleared, the full force of the bells hit his ears and he put his hands over them to block out the sound.

There was no trace of Cecily Gilbourne, not even the faintest whiff of the delicate perfume which had so intoxicated him the previous night. Had she fled in disappointment? Was their love shipwrecked on its maiden voyage? Hoode closed his eyes and tried to remember what had actually happened. Paradise had been recreated on the first floor of a London inn. He had been offered an apple from the Tree of Knowledge and had eaten it voraciously. It had been inexpressibly delicious.

The problem was that Eve had given him another apple. Then a third, a fourth, a fifth and possibly more. Before he collapsed in sheer exhaustion, he recalled looking around a Garden of Eden that was littered with apple cores. Eve, meanwhile, was straining to pluck another down from a higher branch. Her pursuit of knowledge was insatiable.

When Hoode struggled to sit up, he realised just how insatiable Cecily Gilbourne had been. She had left him for dead. His muscles ached, his stomach churned and his body seemed to have no intention of obeying any of its owner's commands. After long hours of sleep, he was still fatigued. His mouth was parched and he longed for some water to slake his thirst.

With a supreme effort, he rolled off the bed and got his feet onto the floor. They showed little enthusiasm for the notion of supporting him and he had to clutch at a bench to stay upright. Blown by the wind and buffeted by the bells, he staggered across to the door, using a variety of props and crutches on his way. What kept him going was the thought that Cecily might be in the adjoining chamber, waiting for him to join her before breakfast was served. But the door was locked.

Hoode leant against it while he gathered his strength. A question began to pound away at the back of his skull. Why did he feel so unhappy? After such a night of madness, he should be overwhelmed with joy. Having tasted the sweet delights of Cecily Gilbourne, his mouth should be tingling with pleasure. Yet his palate was jaded. What had gone wrong?

His body rebelled and threatened to cast him to the floor. Legs buckled, arms went slack and his neck tried to disassociate itself from his head. The bed was his only salvation but it now seemed to be a hundred yards away. Marshalling his forces for one desperate lunge, he flung himself across the room, kicked over a stool, a table and a chamber-pot on the way, then landed on the bed with a thud, resolving never to move from it again.

He was still lying there, moaning softly and idly composing his own obituary, when he saw something out of the corner of his eye. It was a letter, protruding from beneath the pillow, clearly left by Cecily Gilbourne. His heart lifted. He was not, after all, an abandoned lover in a draughty bedchamber. She had penned her gratitude in glowing terms before stealing away and affirmed her love. That thought made him open the letter with fumbling enthusiasm, only to drop it instantly in alarm.

Cecily was a laconic correspondent. One word decorated the page and it struck an inexplicable terror into him:

*"Tonight."*

Royal command had delayed the funeral of Cyril Fulbeck until that morning. It was no insignificant event. The Master of the Chapel was a loved and revered member of the royal household and the Queen insisted on paying her personal respects to him. Since she only returned from Greenwich Palace on Saturday evening, the obsequies could not take place until the following day.

It was a moving ceremony, conducted with due solemnity by the Bishop of London and held in the Chapel which Fulbeck had served with such exceptional dedication. The choir were in fine voice as they bade farewell to their mentor and Philip Robinson was allowed the privilege of a solo. The funeral oration paid tribute to the work and character of the deceased while tactfully omitting any reference to the manner of his death. Silent tears lubricated the whole service, and when the coffin was borne out, even Her Majesty was seen to lift a gloved hand to her cheek.

Yet still the murder remained unsolved. Pressure from above was strong and the official investigation was as thorough as it could be, but little evidence had been unearthed as yet and the Queen let it be known that she was displeased. Now that his body had been laid to rest, Cyril Fulbeck deserved to be avenged in the most prompt way. Additional men were assigned to help with the search for his killer.

Raphael Parsons kept his head bent and his thoughts to himself throughout the funeral. When the burial had taken place, he waited until the congregation left in strict order of precedence before slipping away in the direction of Blackfriars. When he reached the theatre, he was annoyed to see a sturdy figure waiting for him.

'I am glad I have caught you,' said Nicholas Bracewell.

'Pray excuse me, sir. I am too busy to talk.'

'But there is no performance here today.'

'Sadly, no,' said Parsons.

'Even *you* would not expect to stage a play only hours after the funeral of the Master of the Chapel.'

'I most certainly would. Sentiment and commerce must be kept apart. We cannot let the former dictate the latter. I was sorry to see my old friend laid in his grave, but I would not, from choice, let it affect the entertainment here.'

'Is that not like dancing on a man's tomb?'

'Not in my opinion.'

'Do you take no account of your actors?'

'Actors exist to act.'

'They have feelings, Master Parsons,' argued Nicholas. 'Senses, emotions, loyalties. That is especially true of your young company. Their hearts were not hacked from the same flint as your own. I'll wager they did not want to tread the boards today.'

'I'd have *made* them!'

'They would have hated you for it. Westfield's Men did not think twice about performance yesterday. When we discovered the body of Jonas Applegarth, the play cancelled itself. Not a member of the company could have been forced upon that scaffold.'

'I'd have willingly taken their place,' volunteered the manager. 'Applegarth dead! I'd have danced a jig all afternoon to mark the occasion!'

Nicholas smarted. 'Where were you when he was killed?' he said. 'With your friend in Ireland Yard?'

'What is that to you?'

'I wondered if you would use the same lie twice.'

'I never used it once,' retorted the other. 'Yesterday morning, when that blessed hangman was testing Applegarth's weight, I was here at Blackfriars.'

'At dawn?'

'My day starts early.'

'Was any else here with you?'

'Not for an hour or so,' admitted Parsons. 'But then Geoffrey, the porter, arrived. He'll vouch for me.'

'I am only interested in the exact time when Jonas Applegarth was murdered,' said Nicholas. 'You have a story but no witness to its credence. It is so with the death of Cyril Fulbeck. You claim to be in Ireland Yard when that occurred. But nobody there will speak up for you.'

Parsons bridled. 'What do you mean?'

'I have asked them all.'

'The devil take you!'

'Most residents did not even know who Raphael Parsons was.'

'You had the gall to intrude on my privacy?'

'Most certainly.'

'By what right?'

'Simple curiosity,' said Nicholas easily, 'and the urge to catch a foul murderer. Whoever killed Cyril Fulbeck used the same villainy on Jonas Applegarth. If he was not in Ireland Yard when he claims, he may not have been at the Blackfriars Theatre when he alleges. Do you follow my reasoning?'

'Hell and damnation!'

Parsons lashed out a hand to strike Nicholas but the book holder was far too quick. He seized the manager's wrist, twisted his arm behind his back, then pushed him to the ground. Parsons cursed aloud. Rolling over, he got slowly and painfully to his feet, dusting himself off and regarding Nicholas with growling hostility.

'Let us begin again,' said Nicholas. 'Where were you when Cyril Fulbeck was hanged by the neck?'

'In Ireland Yard.'

'That lie will not serve.'

'Ireland Yard!' repeated Parsons through gritted teeth.

'Then why will nobody come forward?'

'Why do you *think,* man?'

'Tell me.'

Parsons looked around furtively to make sure that they were not overheard, then glared at Nicholas. After much agonising, he decided that the only way to get rid of his visitor was to tell him a measure of the truth.

'My dear friend in Ireland Yard is not in a position to acknowledge my friendship,' he said.

'Why not?'

'She is married.'

'Oh.'

'Do not ask me to give you her name and address, for that is too great a betrayal. Just accept that I was with the lady at the time when Cyril Fulbeck was hanged.' He glanced in the direction of Ireland Yard. 'She would also swear that I was with her at dawn yesterday morning. Her husband is a merchant and travelling to Holland. Do I need to say more?'

Nicholas shook his head. He knew the man was telling the truth now. It absolved him of both murders and took away the one obvious link between Fulbeck and Applegarth. Parsons argued with the one and fulminated against the other. He gave more detail of his relationship with both men.

'That was what we were quarrelling about only hours before he was killed,' he said. 'Cyril found out about her. He read me a sermon on the virtues of marriage and the evils of adultery. Was I a fit person to be put in charge of his choristers when I was committing a dreadful sin? Would not my mere presence corrupt their young minds? Arrant nonsense!'

'What did you say?' asked Nicholas.

'What any man would have said. In round terms, I told him not to meddle in my affairs. What I do between the sheets, when

I do it, and with whom, is my affair. I called him a vestal virgin and stormed out of the theatre.'

'Before going straight to Ireland Yard?'

Parsons grinned. 'I felt in need of consolation.' The rancour returned. 'As for your second accusation, I can rebut that as well. I hated Jonas Applegarth but I did not hang him. I was enjoying other pleasures at the time.'

'Why did you detest him so?' asked Nicholas.

'Ask of him why he detested *me*? For that is how it began. We admired his plays greatly and invited him to write one for the Chapel Children. And what did he do?'

'Reject the offer and rail at you.'

'Then continue that railing in *The Misfortunes of Marriage*. We work hard here in Blackfriars and have problems enough to contend with. Why should that bloated knave be allowed to sneer at everything we did? It was unjust. Applegarth simply had to be put down somehow.'

'With a knife in his back?'

'That was one way,' said the manager calmly. 'I prefer to stab him in the chest with a Prologue.'

Nicholas studied him for a moment with quiet contempt. There was nothing more to be gained from the confrontation, yet he found it difficult to walk away. The manager might have proved that he was not the Laughing Hangman, but Nicholas still felt that the man had some blood on his hands. Had he planned the murders and left a confederate to commit them? His work at Blackfriars was a testimony to his theatrical skills. Could not those same skills be used to stage two hangings?

Parsons taunted him. 'Have you done with me?' he said.

'For the moment.'

'Good. I must prepare for my rehearsal.'

'On the day of the funeral?'

'They've taken the performance from me. I'll not be robbed of a rehearsal as well. The boys are coming here after Evensong.'

'Why are you making them do this?'

'I am not,' said Parsons. 'They requested it. Ask them, if you do not believe me. You are welcome to watch us, for we only rehearse a few scenes. The boys are rightly upset by the funeral. They want to push it out of their minds for a couple of hours.' He peered at Nicholas. 'Have *you* never lost yourself in work to escape your thoughts?'

Evensong filled the whole building with the most beauteous sound, climbing up into the vaulted roof and penetrating every corner of the chancel and the nave before seeping down into the dank crypt to swirl around the ears of the dead. Ambrose Robinson was oblivious to it all. He knew that Anne Hendrik would be in the congregation but he did not even try to catch a glimpse of her, still less attempt to sit beside her. She now belonged to his past.

When he looked at the choir, he did not see the upturned faces of the boys as they offered their praise up to God. What he noted was the absence of his son from his accustomed position in the stalls. Evensong had always been an occasion of great joy to him when Philip Robinson's voice was an essential part of it. Without him, the service had become an ordeal for his father.

Nor did the sermon offer any comfort or inspiration. The meaningless drone of the vicar's voice was a grim reminder of another service at the same place of worship. When Robinson's wife was buried there, the vicar had consoled him with the simple statement that it was the will of God. Philip Robinson's enforced departure to the Chapel Royal was also characterised by the vicar as the will of God, and the butcher was certain that he would describe the loss of Anne Hendrik in the same way.

One bereavement was enough to bear. Three were quite insupportable. Wife, son and potential second wife. He had lost them all and was now left with an existence that was both empty and pointless. The vicar might counsel resignation but Robinson refused to accept that counsel any more. He would not simply lie down and let the stone wheels of Fate roll over him time and again. He would get up and fight.

With the service still in progress, therefore, he rose from his seat and marched up the aisle before the surprised eyes of the other parishioners. A gust of wind blew in as he opened the west door. Robinson did not hear the rustle of complaint that ran up and down the benches and pews. His mind was on more unholy matters than Evensong.

When he reached his shop, he let himself in and stood in front of his bench. He surveyed the weaponry which hung from the ceiling on iron hooks. Knives, skewers, cleavers and axes were kept clean and sharp at all times. It was a matter of pride with him. Everything was in readiness for the morrow, but some butchery was now called for on the Sabbath. Ambrose Robinson selected a cleaver and examined its blade with his thumb. It was honed to perfection.

He set off on the long walk towards redemption.

Nicholas Bracewell decided to avail himself of the chance to watch the evening rehearsal at Blackfriars and he timed his return to the theatre accordingly. He was halfway across the Great Yard before he noticed Caleb Hay. Tucked away in the far corner, the old man was scanning the buildings with a small telescope. Nicholas walked across to him.

'Good-even, good sir!' he called. 'Is your eyesight grown so bad that you need a telescope to see something that is right in front of you?'

'You mistake me,' said Hay with a chuckle. 'What I look at is the distant past. You see only the vestigial remains of Blackfriars. I was trying to map out, in my mind's eye, the full extent of the old monastery. Then I may draw my plan.'

'I would be most interested to see it.'

'In time, sir. All in good time.'

Nicholas remembered something. 'I am glad we have met,'

he said. 'Andrew Mompesson. Was not he your father-in-law?'

'Indeed, he was. A sterling fellow and a bookseller of high repute. He taught me much.' His eyes twinkled. 'And he entrusted me with the best volume on his shelves when he gave me the hand of his daughter.'

Nicholas smiled, but he was not sure that Hay would make such a gallant remark about his wife in the woman's presence. Joan Hay had the look of someone who had been starved of compliments for a considerable time.

'It is an unusual name,' said Nicholas. 'That is why it stuck in my mind. Andrew Mompesson. He was among the signatories on that petition against the opening of a public theatre in Blackfriars.'

'Your memory serves you well. My father-in-law helped to draw up that petition. He allowed me to make a fair copy of it, which is what I was able to show you.'

'Did he live to see the present theatre opened?'

'Mercifully, no,' said Hay. 'It would have broken his heart. The precinct was still unsullied by a playhouse when he died. No sound of drums and trumpets disturbed his peace. No swarming crowds went past his front door seven days a week. No actors mocked the spirit of Blackfriars with their blasphemy and lewd behaviour. He died happy. How many of us will be able to say that?'

'Not many.'

'Not poor Cyril Fulbeck, certainly. God rest his soul!' Head to one side, he looked up at Nicholas. 'Is that what has brought you here once more? The hunt for his murderer?'

'Yes, Master Hay.'

'And are you any closer to catching him?'

'I believe so.'

'That is excellent news.'

'It is only a matter of time now.'

'You deserve great credit for taking this task upon yourself when the Master of the Chapel meant nothing to you.' He heaved a sigh of regret. 'If only *I* had strength enough for it. Cyril Fulbeck was kind to me. I have many reasons to avenge his death but lack the means to do so.'

'But for him, you might still be incarcerated.'

A hollow laugh. 'That is more than possible.'

'Which prison did they lock you in?'

'The Clink.'

The approach of feet deflected their attention to the other side of the yard. Choristers from the Chapel Royal were processing towards the theatre with their heads bowed in reverential silence. Philip Robinson was at the front of the column as it wended its way in through the main door. Caleb Hay was duly horrified.

'There surely cannot be a performance this evening!'

'A short rehearsal only.'

'On the Sabbath? In the wake of a funeral?'

'Raphael Parsons is allowing me to watch them.'

'Then I will take myself away,' said the old man as he put his telescope into his pocket. 'This is no place for me. Choristers making a foul spectacle of themselves upon a stage! Sanctity and sin are one under the instruction of Raphael Parsons. There's your killer, sir. That man will murder the Sabbath itself.'

Hay made a dignified exit from the Great Yard. Nicholas made his way across to the theatre and explained to the porter why he had come. Geoffrey Bless surprised him.

'Then you will have seen Master Ingram,' he said.

'When?'

'A few minutes ago when he left the theatre.'

'He was here?'

'Talking to me even as you are now.'

'I saw no sign of him.'

'You could not have missed him,' said the porter. 'If you came across the Great Yard, you would need to be blind to miss him. I wonder that Master Ingram did not hail you.'

Nicholas was wondering the same thing. He decided that Ingram must have seen him first and concealed himself in one of the angles of the building. It was strange behaviour for a friend. He went swiftly back through the main door and looked around, but Ingram was nowhere to be seen. Nicholas concluded that he might not yet have left the premises. He returned to the ancient porter.

'What was James doing here?'

'He called in to see me, sir,' said Geoffrey. 'To talk over old times when Blackfriars was a happier place to be.'

'How long was he here?'

'Above an hour.'

'Did he know that there was a rehearsal this evening?'

'I told him so.'

'What was his reaction?'

'He thought it wrong, sir. On the day of the funeral.'

The porter's eyes moistened. He was old and tired. Murder in the Blackfriars Theatre had taken all the spirit out of him. Alert and watchful before, Geoffrey Bless was now a broken man. It would not be difficult for someone like James Ingram to slip unnoticed back into the building.

Nicholas went up the staircase and let himself into the theatre as quietly as he could. Raphael Parsons was standing on stage, clapping his hands to summon his actors. Having changed into costume for the rehearsal, they drifted out from the tiring-house. Philip Robinson was the last to come, wearing a dress and pulling on an auburn wig. Nicholas took a seat at the very back of the auditorium. Parsons and his young company seemed unaware of his presence.

'We'll rehearse the Trial Scene,' announced the manager. 'Philip Robinson?'

'Yes, sir?' said the boy.

'You must carry the action here. All depends on you.'

'Yes, sir.'

'Regal bearing, Philip. Remember that. You may be in chains but you are still a queen. Regal bearing even in the face of adversity. Clear the stage. Set the scene.'

Parsons jumped down into the auditorium and caught sight of Nicholas. He gave his visitor a noncommittal nod before turning back to his work. The stagekeeper set a table and benches on stage, then vacated it quickly.

'Begin!' ordered the manager.

Three judges came on stage in procession and took their places behind the table. Two soldiers, wearing armour and holding pikes, stood either side of the commission in order to signal its importance and to enforce its decisions.

'Bring in the prisoner!' called Parsons.

The gaoler dragged in the hapless Queen with a rope. Philip Robinson did his best to suggest wounded dignity. He stood before his accusers without flinching. The charges were read out, then one of the judges addressed the prisoner.

JUDGE: What have you to say?
QUEEN: The charges against me are false.
JUDGE: That is for us to decide.
QUEEN: You have no power over me, sir. I am a queen and answer to a higher authority than any you can muster here. I'll not be subject to this mean court like any common malefactor. Do you dare to sit in judgement on God's anointed? By what perverse and unnatural right do you presume to put the crown of England on trial here?

The speech was long and impassioned. Philip Robinson began slowly but soon hit his stride, delivering the prose with a clear voice that rang around the theatre. Nicholas was impressed. It was more than a mere recitation of the lines. The boy was a true actor. Of the apprentices with Westfield's Men, only Richard Honeydew could have handled the trial speech with equal skill and righteous indignation.

Having cowed his accused with his majesty, the boy flung himself dramatically to the ground before the judicial bench and challenged them to strike off his royal head. Before the judges could reply, a voice roared out from the back of the theatre.

'Philip! What on earth have they *done* to you?'

Ambrose Robinson stood in the open doorway looking with horror at his son. The sight of the dress and the wig ignited him to fever pitch. He went storming towards the stage with his hand stretched out.

'Come away!' he shouted. 'Come with your father. I'm here to rescue you from this vile place. Come home!'

But the boy showed no inclination to return to Bankside. As his father bore down on him, Philip Robinson leapt to his feet and backed away. Snatching his wig off, he cried out in fear:

'I am happy here, Father! Leave me be!'

'Come with me!'

'No,' said the boy. 'I will not!'

He fled into the tiring-house and Robinson tried to clamber upon the stage to pursue him. The manager moved in quickly to restrain the angry parent.

'Stop, sir! There is no place for you here.'

'I want my son.'

'Philip is a lawful member of the Chapel Children. You may not touch him. I am Raphael Parsons and I manage this theatre. I must ask you to leave at—'

'Parsons!'

Robinson turned on the man he saw as the author of his misery. He went berserk. Shrugging Parsons off, he pulled the cleaver from beneath his coat and struck at him with all his force, catching him on the shoulder and opening up a fearful wound that sent blood cascading all over him. The manager fell to the floor in agony and the butcher stood over him to hack him into pieces.

The young actors were too frightened to move, but Nicholas Bracewell was already sprinting down the auditorium. Before the cleaver could strike again, he dived into Robinson with such force that the butcher was knocked flying. As the two of them hit the wooden floor with a thud, the weapon jerked out of Robinson's hand and spun crazily away. He now turned his manic anger upon Nicholas, rolling over to get a grip on his neck and trying to throttle the life out of him.

Rage lent the butcher extra power, but Nicholas was the more experienced fighter, twisting himself free to deliver a relay of punches to the contorted face, then grabbing the man by the hair to dash his head against the floor. As the two of them grappled once more, footsteps came running towards them and James Ingram hurled himself on top of Robinson to help Nicholas to subdue him. The assistance was not needed. The butcher stopped struggling.

Realising where he was and what he had done, Robinson seemed to come out of a trance. He began to wail piteously. The porter came panting into the hall with two constables.

'I tried to stop him,' he said, 'but he pushed past me. I ran for help.' He almost fainted at the sight of Parsons. 'Dear God! What new horror is here!'

Nicholas got to his feet. With Ingram's help, he pulled Robinson upright and handed him over to the constables. As they marched him out of the theatre, the butcher was still crying with remorse. Raphael Parsons lay on the floor in a widening pool of blood. Nicholas turned to the porter.

'Fetch a surgeon!' he ordered.

'I'll go,' volunteered Ingram. 'Faster legs than Geoffrey's are needed for this errand.'

The actor went running off towards the staircase, but his journey would be in vain. Nicholas could see that Parsons was well beyond the reach of medicine. Groaning with pain, the manager lay on his back with half his shoulder severed from his body. Nicholas tried to stem the flow of blood but it was a hopeless task. Parsons revived briefly. He looked up through bleary eyes.

'Who is it?'

'Nicholas Bracewell.'

'I am fading. Beware, sir.'

'Of what?'

'The theatre. A dangerous profession. It killed Cyril Fulbeck and now it sends me after him.' He clutched at Nicholas. 'Will you do me a service?'

'Willingly.'

'Discreetly, too.'

'I understand,' said Nicholas. 'Ireland Yard.'

'Number fourteen. Commend me to the lady. Explain why I am kept away. Do it gently.'

'I will, Master Parsons.'

The manager was suddenly convulsed with pain. Nicholas thought he had passed away, but then life flickered once more. Parsons's lips moved but only the faintest sound emerged. Nicholas put his ear close to the man's mouth.

'One favour . . . deserves another,' murmured Parsons.

'Speak on.'

'I did not . . . hang . . . Applegarth.'

'I know that now,' said Nicholas.

'But I . . . tried to . . . tried to . . .'

'Yes?'

'Tried to . . . kill . . .'

His breathing stopped and his mouth fell slack. Raphael Parsons took leave of the world with confession on his lips. One mystery was solved. He was the man who threw the dagger at Jonas Applegarth's unprotected back. The playwright had not been stalked that day by a discontented actor with a grudge against him but by a furious theatre manager with an injured pride.

Nicholas could never bring himself to like Raphael Parsons. The man was too malignant and devious. As he looked down at the corpse, however, he felt compassion for him. There was a crude symmetry about his death. Having attempted to commit murder, he had himself been cut down in the most brutal way. On the very day that he bade farewell to the Master of the Chapel, he was sent off in pursuit of him. While rehearsing a trial scene with a favoured son, he was arraigned by a father who appointed himself judge, jury and executioner.

By the time Ingram arrived with a surgeon, Nicholas had taken charge with cool efficiency. The dead body had been covered with a cloak, the weeping porter had been led away, and the actors had been taken to the tiring-house to be comforted. Nicholas did not forget his promise to call on a house in Ireland Yard, but sad tidings had first to be broken to someone else. He took Philip Robinson to a quiet corner backstage where they might speak alone.

'You must be brave, Philip,' he said.

'Who are you, sir?'

'Nicholas Bracewell. A friend of Mistress Hendrik.'

'She was kind to me when my mother died.'

'I know,' said Nicholas. 'But it is about your father that I must now talk, I fear.'

'What happened, sir? I heard a fearful yell.'

'He attacked Master Parsons with a meat-cleaver.'

The boy burst into tears and it took some time to soothe him. Nicholas gave him a brief account of what had taken place. He did not conceal the truth from him.

'Your father will have to pay for his crime.'

'I know, sir. I know.'

'One death may be answered by another.'

'And the two can be laid at *my* door!'

'No, Philip.'

'I killed them both! If I had not been here, Master Parsons would still be alive and my father would not soon be facing the public hangman.'

'You were not to blame,' insisted Nicholas. 'You are the victim and not the cause of this crime.' He held the boy until his sobbing gradually eased off. 'You like it here in the theatre, do you not?'

'I do, sir.'

'You were happy out on that stage.'

'Very happy.'

'So you did not write to your father to say how much you hated Blackfriars?'

'I did not write at all.'

'Would you rather be in the Chapel Royal or at home?'

'In the Chapel!' affirmed the boy. 'Anywhere but home.'

'Why is that?'

The boy felt the pull of family loyalties. Unhappy with his father, he did not want to divulge the full details of that unhappiness. Ambrose Robinson would soon be tried for murder and removed for ever from his son's life. The boy wanted to cling to a positive memory.

'My father loved me, I am sure,' he said.

'No question of that.'

'But it was not the same after my mother died. He told me I was all that he had. It made him watch me every moment of the day. That came to weigh down on me, sir.'

Nicholas understood. Philip Robinson was oppressed at home. The Chapel Royal had been his sanctuary. The boy looked around him in despair.

'What will happen to me?' he wondered.

'You will remain where you are.'

'But will they still want me after this, sir? I am the son of a murderer. They will expel me straight.'

'I think not.'

'Master Fulbeck was my friend. He looked after me. Who will do that now that he has gone?' His face was pale and haunted. 'What will happen to the theatre with Master Parsons dead? Chapel and theatre were my life.'

'They may still be so again.'

'It will never be the same.'

Philip Robinson was right. Cyril Fulbeck had been a father to him, and notwithstanding his strictness, Raphael Parsons had been an excellent tutor. Having lost both along with his own father, the boy was truly floundering.

'Which did you prefer, Philip?' asked Nicholas.

'Prefer?'

'Singing in the Chapel Royal or acting at Blackfriars?'

'Acting, sir, without a doubt.'

'Why is that?'

'Because I may get better at that in time,' he said. 'In the Chapel, I can only sing. On the stage, I can sing, dance, declaim the finest verse ever written and move all who watch to tears or laughter. I long to be an actor. But how can I do that without a theatre?'

Nicholas thought of the broken voice of John Tallis.

'Let me see if I can find you one,' he said.

# [ CHAPTER TWELVE ]

The day of rest was the least restful day of the week for Margery Firethorn. Tolled out of bed by the sonorous bells of Shoreditch, she had to rouse the remainder of the household, see them washed and dressed, lead them off to Matins at the parish church of St Leonard's, and smack them awake again when any of them dozed off during the service. Apart from the four apprentices and the two servants, she had three actors staying at the house until they could find a more suitable lodging. Thirteen mouths, including the ever-open ones of her children, had thus to be fed throughout the day. Since the servants tended to bungle some of the chores and burn all the food, Margery ended up doing more cleaning and cooking than was good for her temper.

When she got back from Evensong with her flock in tow, she was vexed by the irreligious thought that the Sabbath had been invented as a punishment for anyone foolish enough to embrace marriage and succumb to motherhood. Margery looked ahead grimly to an evening laden with even more tasks and groaned inwardly. It was not the most auspicious time to call on her.

Edmund Hoode felt the full force of rumbling dissatisfaction.

'Avaunt! Begone! Take your leprous visage away!'

'I have come on an errand of mercy.'

'Take mercy on me and go as fast as you may!'

'This is no kind of welcome, Margery.'

'It is the warmest you will get, sir,' she said. 'Have you so soon forgot your last visit here when you sewed such discord between man and wife that Lawrence and I have barely exchanged a civil word since?'

'That is one reason I came.'

'To part us asunder even more! Saints in Heaven! You will depopulate the city at this rate. Who can engage in the lawful business of procreation with you standing outside their bedchamber? What woman will submit to her husband's pleasure if she sees your ghoulish face staring at her over his naked shoulder?'

'I am here to beg your apology,' he said.

'Do so from a further distance, sir. Stand off a mile or more and I'll let you grovel all you wish.'

She tried to close the front door but he stopped her.

'Please do not turn me away!'

'Be grateful I do not set the dogs on you!'

'I am desperate, Margery.'

'Shift your desperation to another place, for we'll have none of it. Though it be the Sabbath, I'll use some darker language to send you on your way, if you dare to linger.'

'I must come in!'

'Go ruin another marriage instead.'

'I implore you!'

'You do so in vain,' she said. 'Lawrence is not within. Since you made converse with his wife impossible, he has taken himself off with his fellows.'

'But it is *you* I wish to see.'

'Wait till I fetch a broom and you will see me at my best. For I can beat a man black and blue within a minute.'

Seizing his cue, Hoode flung himself to the ground in an attitude of contrition.

'Beat me all you wish!' he invited. 'I deserve it, I need it, I invite it. Belabour me at will.'

Margery was taken aback. She looked at him properly for the first time and saw the haggard face and the hollow eyes. Hoode was suffering. She bent down to help him up from her doorstep.

'What is wrong with you, man?'

'Admit me and I'll tell all.'

'Have you stared at yourself in a mirror today?'

'I dare not, Margery.'

'Plague victims look healthier.'

'Their symptoms are mild compared to mine.'

Concern pushed belligerence aside as Margery brought him into the house and closed the front door. He was shivering all over. She took him into the kitchen and sat him down.

'What has happened, Edmund?'

'Armageddon.'

'Where?'

'In a lady's chamber.'

'Did she reject you?'

'Worse. She accepted me. Time and again.'

A series of uncontrollable grunts came from outside the door as if a frog with a sense of humour were eavesdropping. Margery darted out to find John Tallis bent double with mirth. She clipped his ear, kicked him on his way, then closed the door firmly behind her. Edmund Hoode's anguish needed the balm of privacy. A sniggering apprentice would only intensify the playwright's already unbearable pain.

She sat on the bench beside him and enfolded him in a maternal arm. This was no bold interloper, pounding on the door of her bedchamber. It was the old Edmund Hoode.

'This tale is for your ears only,' he insisted.

'Then it must be worth the hearing.'

'Lawrence would only mock me cruelly.'

'He will learn nothing from me. Speak on.'

Hoode needed a minute to summon up his strength before he could embark on his narrative. He was honest. He held nothing back. Margery was attentive and sympathetic. She realised that instant help was needed.

'When must you see the lady again?' she asked.

'This evening at the Unicorn.'

'Do not go.'

'That would be ungentlemanly,' he said. 'I must go. I owe her that. But I will not submit to another night of seductive exhaustion. My flesh and blood cannot stand it.'

'Explain that to her.'

'She would not listen. I know what she would say.'

'What?'

'Again!' he moaned. 'Again, Edmund, again, again! As if my manhood is a water-wheel that turns and turns with the flow of her passion. Save me, Margery! I drown!'

'There is only one sure means of rescue, Edmund.'

'What is that?'

She smiled benignly. 'You will see.'

'You have still not told me what took you to Blackfriars.'

'My own folly.'

'Folly?'

'Yes, Nick,' said James Ingram. 'I thought I knew best. I was convinced that Raphael Parsons was our Laughing Hangman and sought to spy on him. While you were watching the rehearsal, I was hiding up in the gallery.'

'You sneaked back into the building?'

'Geoffrey has grown careless. He did not see me.'

Nicholas Bracewell was relieved to learn that Ingram's presence at Blackfriars had no darker significance. His doubts about his friend were groundless. While Nicholas had a personal reason for hunting the killer of Jonas Applegarth, the actor had a personal reason for catching the man who hanged Cyril Fulbeck. From differing motives, both were searching for the same man.

'Parsons will no longer bother us,' said Ingram.

'True.'

'Nor will the Chapel Children.'

'Do not be so sure, James.'

'Why not?'

'One manager may have died, but another will soon come to take his place. A private playhouse with a resident company which can stage its work for twelve months of the year. What temptation! It will not be long before a new Raphael Parsons is installed there.'

'Competing for our audience.'

'We must take our chances there,' said Nicholas. 'We have rivals enough without the children's companies, but we cannot stop them. Westfield's Men must find new and more cunning ways to outwit these young thespians.'

They were walking briskly across London Bridge together. Having given sworn statements regarding the killing of Raphael Parsons, the two men were free to leave. They plunged into Bankside and picked their way through its labyrinthine streets. Nicholas stopped outside a house.

'Whom do we visit here?' asked Ingram.

'You go on to another port of call.'

'Do I?'

'Yes, James. The Clink.'

'You are sending me to prison?'

'Only to make an enquiry.'

'The place is full of debtors and brothel-owners.'

'Not entirely. The man in whom I am interested is neither. Do you have money about you?'

'Sufficient. Why?'

'You'll need to bribe the prison serjeant.'

After arranging to meet him back in Gracechurch Street, Nicholas gave Ingram his instructions, then sent him on his way.

The book holder then tapped on door of the house. When the servant showed him into the parlour, Anne Hendrik got up from her chair with alacrity and embraced him.

'I prayed that you might come, Nick!' she said.

'Why?'

'It has been such a trying time since we parted.'

'In what way?'

'Ambrose Robinson has been here.'

She took him through the events of the previous day and admitted how frightened she had been of the butcher. Nicholas was deeply upset that he had not been there to protect her.

'Did he bother you at all today?' he asked.

'No. The only time I saw him was at Evensong, and that was not for long. Ambrose got up in the middle of the service and stalked out with his face aflame. It was as if he suddenly had an irresistible urge to go somewhere.'

'He did, Anne.'

'Where?'

'To Blackfriars. I was there when he arrived.'

'At the theatre?'

'He came looking for his son.'

'I feared that might happen. Was there a tussle?'

'Yes,' said Nicholas, 'but not with the boy. He ran away from his father. It was Raphael Parsons who tussled with your neighbour and who came off worst. The butcher had armed himself with a meat-cleaver.'

'Oh, no!' said Anne in horror. 'Murder?'

'One blow was all it took.'

'What then?'

'We overpowered him and constables led him away. Master Parsons did not survive for long.'

'What of Philip? It must have been a terrible experience for him. Such humiliation! His own father!'

'Fortunately, he did not witness the killing. I made a point of talking at length with him to explain precisely what had happened and to prepare him for what was to come.'

'Poor child! He has lost everything!'

'There are gains as well as losses here.'

'Ambrose is like to be tried and hanged.'

'Most certainly.'

'Philip will have to bear that stain.'

'He has already foreseen that.'

'Will there be a place in the Chapel Royal for him after this?' she asked anxiously. 'Where will he go if they turn him out? This could blight his young life.'

'There may be salvation yet for him,' said Nicholas, touching her arm. 'But I may not tarry. I came simply to give you the tidings before you heard them from a less well-informed source.'

'I am deeply grateful, Nick. And relieved.'

'Ambrose Robinson will never pester you again.'

'Thank heaven!' she said. 'And yet, it did not seem like that at first. He helped me. I must not forget that.' She glanced towards the adjoining premises. 'Without his loan, I would have struggled to keep the business afloat. That was an act of friendship, whatever else he hoped to gain by it. Was he a good man with a streak of evil in him? Or an evil man with a vein of goodness?' She shook her head. 'Had his dear wife lived, we would not even be asking that question.'

'Too true.' He moved to the door. 'But I must go.'

'Nick . . .'

'Yes?'

'Now that you have remembered where I live, do not pass my house again without calling.'

'We play at The Rose next week.'

She smiled. 'Then I will expect you.'

Alexander Marwood surveyed the yard of the Queen's Head with mixed feelings. Instinct told him to sever all connections with Westfield's Men and thereby liberate himself from the recurring crises which beset the company and the ever present threat of assault upon his nubile daughter by one of the lustful actors. Commonsense whispered a different message in his hairy ear. The troupe paid him a rent and brought in custom. Westfield's Men also gave his inn a status in the capital which was important to him, and, more decisively, to his wife. The Queen's Head was recognised as the home of one of the most celebrated theatre companies in London.

Commonsense was still wrestling with instinct when Lawrence Firethorn and Owen Elias sidled up to him. They beamed with delight at a man whom they found unrelievedly loathsome.

'We need a decision from you,' said Firethorn.

Marwood grunted, 'I am thinking, I am thinking.'

'Is there any way we may aid your thought?'

'By leaving me alone, Master Firethorn.'

'You must not delay the verdict any longer. Too much rests on it. Do we play here tomorrow or not?'

'I do not know, sir.'

'The company is waiting to be told,' said Elias. 'We have lost one performance and would hate to lose another. That would empty your yard for two afternoons next week.'

'Two?'

'Yes,' explained Firethorn. 'We play at The Rose on Wednesday. There'll be no crowds thirsting for your ale.'

'And no ruffians pissing in my stables,' said the landlord. 'No lechers ogling my daughter.'

They could see that he was weakening. Firethorn felt that he could handle the negotiations more easily on his own and nudged Elias accordingly. The Welshman moved away and was in time to welcome Nicholas Bracewell as the latter came in through the archway.

'Nick!' he called. 'Where have you been?'

'I'll tell you anon,' said Nicholas, looking across at Marwood. 'Has our landlord relented yet?'

'Lawrence is slowly bringing him round.'

'He must not be rushed. That's the trick of it.'

'I tried to help but was shooed away.'

'Then I'll borrow you for a weightier purpose.'

'And what might that be?'

'I need to hang you, Owen.'

'Hang me!'

Nicholas laughed at his expression. 'Come. You'll find me a gentle executioner.'

He led the way to the storeroom where the dead body had been discovered the previous morning. The noose had been taken away as evidence by the constables, but Nicholas quickly fashioned another out of a length of rope. Elias watched his deft fingers at work.

'You have done this before, I see.'

'What you see is a sailor's hands at work. If you spent as much time at sea as I have, you learn to tie knots of all kinds in a rope.' He pointed to the floor. 'Now, Owen. Lie there.'

'Why?'

'To please my fancy.'

'What is this all about?' grumbled Elias, lowering himself to the floor. 'Am I the dupe in this little game?'

'It is no game,' said Nicholas, placing the noose around his neck. 'How heavy are you? Half the weight of Jonas?'

'A third at least. I carried that man home and he was like a ton of iron. A triple Owen Elias.'

'I'll make allowances for that. Put your hands inside the rope to stop it cutting into your flesh.' He flung one end of the rope over the central beam. 'Are you ready!'

'*Iesu Mawr!* He really means to hang me!'

'Hold on.'

Nicholas pulled on the rope until it tightened around the hands and neck of his friend. He applied what he judged to be the correct pressure but could not move the body from the floor. Even when he wound the rope around his waist to give himself a stronger purchase on it, he could not lift the supine Elias.

'Thanks, Owen. You may get up now.'

'Good,' said the other, tugging at the noose.

'No, leave that on,' ordered Nicholas. 'I want to find another way to kill you.'

'You've tortured me long enough.'

'One more minute. That's all it will take.'

'Be quick about it then.'

'Stand there and do not move.'

Owen Elias was in the middle of the room. Nicholas moved the workbench until it almost brushed his jerkin. Picking up the mallet from the floor, he mimed a blow to the back of the Welshman's head, then grabbed him by the collar.

'Fall gently back.'

'Are you mad?'

'Go on. The table will catch you.'

Elias did as he was told and Nicholas guided him so that his back was across the workbench. When he tested the other end of the rope this time, he got more response. By applying some real pressure, he lifted the body into a sitting position. Hands inside the noose, Owen Elias gave a dramatic gurgle and pretended to be choking. Nicholas tossed the rope back over the beam. He then brushed the grains of sawdust from his friend's buff jerkin.

'Am I dead?' asked Elias, removing the noose.

'Completely. And now I know how he did it.'

'Who?'

'The Laughing Hangman.'

'Do you mind if we get out of here, Nick? I'm starting to feel like his next victim.'

They returned to the yard and found Firethorn talking volubly to James Ingram. The actor-manager preened himself as the others approached.

'I have done it, sirs! We play here tomorrow.'

A concerted cheer went up from the others.

'Marwood was like wax in my hands. Soft and smelly.'

'But you moulded him into shape,' said Owen.

They congratulated him profusely. Firethorn wanted to take them all to the taproom to celebrate, but Nicholas was more interested to hear the news from Ingram.

'Did you find out what I asked?' he said.

'I did, Nick. At a price.'

'A prison sergeant will do nothing without garnish.'

'I paid up, then came straight back here.' He turned to Firethorn. 'Please give my deepest apologies to your wife.'

'You've been to a prison and seen my *wife*?'

'No,' said Ingram. 'It was on my way back. I did not recognise her until it was too late. She must have thought it rude of me to ignore her. Explain that I was in such a rush to get back here.'

Firethorn was perplexed. 'Margery is in Shoreditch.'

'Not this evening.'

'Where else can she be?'

'Five minutes away at another inn.'

'An inn? Here in the city?'

Elias cackled. 'I spy merriment here.'

'You must have been mistaken, James,' said Firethorn.

'When I passed as close to her as I am to you? It was her. I'd swear that on the Bible.'

'I'm sure that there is a simple explanation,' said Nicholas with easy tact. 'Perhaps she is visiting a friend.'

'What kind of friend?' nudged Elias.

'And why did she make no mention of this to me?' added Firethorn as his suspicions grew. 'Was she alone, James?'

'She was.'

'And how was she attired?'

'In her finest apparel.'

'What was the name of the inn?'

'I did not mean to put you to choler in this way.'

'What was the name?'

'I assumed that you knew Margery was there.'

'The *name*!' demanded Firethorn.

'It was the Unicorn.'

Cecily Gilbourne did not waste much time on the formalities. Romantic dalliance was cast ruthlessly aside in favour of more tangible pleasure. As soon as Edmund Hoode was conducted in to her, she gave him a kiss on the cheek and took him through into the next chamber. He looked down at the bed on which they spent their torrid night together and he blenched. There was no resemblance to the Garden of Eden now. It reminded him of the gruesome rack which he had once beheld in the house of Richard Topcliffe, the master torturer. The bed was an instrument of pain.

'Have you written that sonnet yet?' she asked.

'It is still forming in my mind, Cecily.'

'But you promised to quote it to me.'

'Did I?' He saw a way to delay her ardour. 'Step back into the next chamber and I'll try a line or two for you.'

'In *here*,' she insisted. 'You swore that you would stroke my body with your poetry.'

'Did I?' gulped Hoode.

'Have you so soon forgotten?'

She pushed him into a sitting position on the bed. He was terrified. Cecily Gilbourne's appetite was too great for him to satisfy. Making love to her had turned into an ordeal. The thought that he would have to quote a sonnet to her in the middle of the exercise made it even more unappealing. Hoode looked around for escape but she was already unhooking his doublet.

'Why make such haste?' he said, panic-stricken.

She forced him back. 'Do you need to ask?'

'Will you not take refreshment beforehand, Cecily?'

'*This* is my refreshment!'

She writhed about on top of him until she was panting, then she began to pluck at her clothing. He had no idea that a dress could be removed so easily. When Cecily switched her attentions to his hose, his panic gave way to hysteria.

'I feel the first line of my sonnet coming!'

'Hold still while I take these off.'

' "O hot Sicilian Cecily . . ." Stay your hand. Please!'

'I am in too hot and Sicilian a mood!'

'Cecily!' he protested.

'Edmund!' she purred. 'My rhyming couplet!'

And before he could move, she flung herself full upon him and fixed her lips ineluctably on his. Hoode felt the waters closing over his head. He was just about to abandon all hope and submit when he heard a thumping noise on the door. The maidservant called out the warning.

'Mistress! Mistress! Beware!'

'What is it?' snarled Cecily in mid-rhyme.

'Master Hoode's wife is without.'

'His *wife*!'

'Yes!'

'But he does not have a wife.'

'I do, I do,' said Hoode gratefully. 'Can she be here?'

'Asking to come in,' said the maidservant.

*'Demanding!'* thundered a voice on the other side of the door. 'Edmund! Are you there?'

'No, my dear.'

'Stand aside, girl,' ordered the unexpected visitor.

The maidservant gave a little scream, the door burst open and the redoubtable figure of Margery Firethorn came through it at speed. She bristled at the sight of betrayal. Cecily Gilbourne retreated to a corner of the room, snatching up a sheet to cover herself and trying to show what dignity she could muster. Hoode threshed about helplessly on the bed. Margery did not stand on ceremony. Bestowing a glare of contempt on Cecily, she grabbed Hoode by the arm, hauled him off the bed and dragged him behind her like a sack of grain.

Hoode gladly withstood the discomfort of his departure.

Bouncing down the stairs of the Unicorn was infinitely preferable to being eaten alive by a rampant lover with only one word in her sexual vocabulary—"Again!" Margery played her part to the hilt. It was only when she had brought him out into the street that she relaxed and permitted herself a chuckle. Hoode was so thankful that he threw his arms impulsively around her and gave her a resounding kiss.

Lawrence Firethorn chose that moment to steal upon them.

Nicholas Bracewell knew where to find him. When the man was not at home, there was only one place he could be. It did not take the book holder long to walk to the precinct. He made his way across the Great Yard and into the theatre. Geoffrey Bless, the old watchdog, was slumped in his chair fast asleep, his eyes closed to shut out the fearful sight he had seen at Blackfriars that evening. The porter did not even stir when Nicholas took the key ring gently from his gnarled hand.

Creeping quietly up the staircase, Nicholas came to the door of the theatre and searched for the key to unlock it. He stepped into the auditorium to find it in darkness, the shutters now firmly closed to block out the last of the day. The place seemed deserted but Nicholas was certain that he was not alone. As he felt his way along, one hand held his dagger at the ready. He halted close to the stage.

'Come forth, sir,' he said. 'I know that you are here.'

There was a long pause before flickering light slowly appeared. A branched candelabra was carried on stage and set on the table, which had been used during the brief rehearsal. A figure lowered himself onto the bench behind the table and set out some rolls of parchment before him. He seemed as confident and relaxed as if sitting in his own study.

'I expected you,' said Caleb Hay with a smile.

'Did you?'

'Sooner or later.'

'Then you will know why I have come.'

'Put that dagger away, sir. I am not armed. I will not talk to a man who threatens me with a weapon.'

'It is for my defence.'

'Against what? An old man with a pile of documents?'

Nicholas nodded and sheathed his dagger. Candlelight now illumined the area immediately in front of the stage. He looked across to the place where Raphael Parsons had fallen. The body had been removed but the floor was still covered by a dark stain. Caleb Hay glanced down at it.

'Master Parsons held one rehearsal too many in here.'

'Was he your next victim?'

'Do not look to me. He was killed by a disgruntled father.'

'And spared a more lingering death at the end of a rope,' said Nicholas. 'Is that why you were lurking in the precinct this evening? Until you could come upon him alone here in the theatre? Until you could let yourself in with Master Fulbeck's keys and take him unawares?'

'Why should I wish to murder Raphael Parsons?'

'For the same reason that you murdered Cyril Fulbeck and Jonas Applegarth.'

'The Master of the Chapel was my trusted friend. As for your fat playwright, how could a weak fellow like myself hoist such a weight upon the gallows?'

'With the aid of a workbench,' said Nicholas. 'It was easier to lever him up from that. You used another lever to bring Jonas to the Queen's Head in the first place. That letter, purporting to be from Lawrence Firethorn. An able scrivener would have had no trouble in writing that.'

'Able scriveners are quiet, sedentary souls like me.'

'You are not as weak and harmless as you appear. That was the mistake that Cyril Fulbeck made. Thinking you safe, he let you close enough to strike.'

'He let me close enough a hundred times, yet lived.'

'The case was altered the last time you met.'

'Pray tell me why,' challenged Hay. 'Here I sit at a judicial bench and yet I am accused of unspeakable crimes. A friend whom I cherished. A playwright whom I never met. What flight of folly makes you link my name with their fate?'

'Religion!' said Nicholas.

'Indeed?'

'The old religion.'

'All three of us were Dominican friars? Is that your argument?'

'No, sir,' returned Nicholas. 'I thought at first the theatre was the common bond between them. Cyril Fulbeck was involved with the Chapel Children and Jonas Applegarth was engaged by Westfield's Men. One here at Blackfriars and the other at the Queen's Head, both places of antiquity in their different ways and therefore fit subjects of study for a historian of London. Only someone who knew each room, cellar and passageway at the Queen's Head could have evaded me.'

'I hear no sound of the old religion in all this.'

'The Clink.'

'What of it?'

'You spent a day imprisoned there.'

'Yes,' said Hay. 'I made no secret of that.'

'It is a place where religious dissidents are held,' said Nicholas. 'Even a short stay there is recorded by the prison serjeant in his ledger. I found a way to peep into its pages. Master Caleb Hay was taken to the Clink but three months ago, his name and offence duly entered in the ledger.' He took a step forward. 'Documents favouring the old religion were found in your possession. You were held there as a Roman Catholic dissident.'

'Held but soon discharged.'

'On the word of the Master of the Chapel.'

'Yes!' said Hay, rising to his feet. 'I am a historian. Those documents were at my house so that I might copy them. They are a legitimate part of my work. Go search my study. You will find papers relating to John Wycliffe and others touching on the

Jewish settlements in London. Does that mean I am a Lollard or a member of the Chosen People?'

'Cyril Fulbeck was deceived.'

'And so are you, sir.'

'He later came to see that deception.'

'Wild surmise!'

'Blackfriars,' said Nicholas calmly. 'The wheel has come full circle, Master Hay. This is where it started and must perforce end. Blackfriars was a symbol of the old religion to you. I recall how lovingly you talked of its past. Your father-in-law, Andrew Mompesson, only fought to keep a public playhouse out of the precinct because its noise would offend his ears. You had a deeper objection still. To turn a monastery into a theatre was sacrilege to you!'

'It was!' admitted Hay, stung into honesty.

'Vulgar plays on consecrated ground.'

'Anathema!'

'The Children of the Chapel mocking the Pope.'

'I could never forgive Cyril for that!'

'And then came Jonas Applegarth,' continued Nicholas. 'The scourge of Rome. A man whose wit lacerated the old religion in every play.'

'I saw them all,' said Hay, bitterly. 'Each one more full of venom and blasphemy. I thought *Friar Francis* was his worst abomination until you staged *The Misfortunes of Marriage*. What a piece of desecration was that! He stabbed away at everything I hold dear.'

'You made him pay a terrible price for his impudence.'

'It was downright wickedness!'

Caleb Hay took a few moments to compose himself. When he looked down at Nicholas again, he gave an amused chuckle.

'You have done your research well.'

'It was needful.'

'You would make an astute historian.'

'My study was the life of Caleb Hay.'

'How will that story be written?'

'With sadness, sir.'

'But my whole existence has been a joy!'

'It was not a joy you shared with your wife,' reminded Nicholas. 'She knew nothing of your inner life. You kept her on the outer fringes as your drudge. It was she who first made me wonder about the genius to whom she was married.'

'Why was that?'

'The fear in her eyes. The terror with which she climbed those stairs to call you. What kind of man locks out his wife from his room? What does he keep hidden from her behind that bolted door?'

'You have divined the answer, Nicholas Bracewell.'

'I think that I was not the only one to do so.'

'No,' confessed Hay. 'Cyril Fulbeck got there before you. That is why he had to die. Not only because of this abomination in which we stand. He threatened to denounce me, and my bones are far too old for a bed at the Clink.'

He picked up the candelabra and held it high to light up a wider area of the stage. He shook his head ruefully.

'Centuries of worship wiped uncaringly away!' he mused. 'A religious house turned into a seat of devilry. Innocent children schooled in corruption. A heritage ruinously scorned.'

The elegiac mood faded as he began to chuckle quietly to himself. His mirth increased until he was almost shaking. Then it burst forth in a full-throated laugh that Nicholas recognised at once. He had heard it at Blackfriars before and also at the Queen's Head. The difference was that it now lacked a note of celebration. As the laughter built and raced around the whole theatre, it had a kind of valedictory joy as if it were some kind of manic farewell.

Nicholas was thrown off his guard. There was a calculation in Caleb Hay's mirth. The laughter came to a sudden end, the flames were blown out, and the candelabra was hurled at the book holder by a strong arm. It came out of the gloom to strike him in the chest and knock him backwards. Nicholas recovered and pulled out his dagger. He felt for the edge of the stage and vaulted up onto it. All that he could pick out in the darkness were vague shapes. When he tried to move forward, he collided with a bench.

He was convinced that Hay would try to make his escape through the rear exit and groped his way towards the tiring-house. A sound from above made him stop. Light feet were tapping on the rungs of a ladder. Hay was climbing high above the stage. When Nicholas tried to follow him, a missile came hurtling down to miss him by inches. It was a heavy iron weight which was used to counterbalance one of the ropes on the pulleys. Nicholas moved to safety and considered his choices.

As long as he was trapped in the dark, he was at a severe disadvantage. Caleb Hay knew where to hide and how to defend himself. With no means of igniting the candles, Nicholas sought the one alternative source of light. He felt his way downstage, jumped into the auditorium and made for the nearest casement. Sliding back the bolt, he flung back the shutters to admit the last dying rays of a summer evening. One window enabled him to see the others more clearly and he ran down one side of the theatre to open all the shutters. When he turned back, he could see the stage quite clearly. He approached it with his dagger still drawn.

'There is no way out, Master Hay!' he called.

The familiar chuckle could be heard high above him.

'Come down, sir.'

'I'll be with you directly,' said Hay.

'It is all over now.'

'I know it well.'

'Come down!'

'I do, sir. Adieu, Nicholas Bracewell!'

Caleb Hay tightened the noose and jumped into space. The long drop had been measured with care. The rope arrested his descent with such vicious force that there was an awesome crack as his neck snapped. Six feet above the stage that he despised, he spun lifelessly until Nicholas stood on the table to cut him down.

The Laughing Hangman had chosen his own gallows.

I regard this as a noble act of self-sacrifice, Edmund.'

'It was the least I could do to assuage my guilt.'

'Guilt?'

'Yes, Lawrence. I was too envious of Jonas.'

'That is not crime.'

'I sought to oust his work from our repertoire.'

'Only because we gave him precedence over you.'

'That rankled with me.'

'The fault was mine for riding roughshod over you.'

'All faults are mended this afternoon.'

'Amen!'

Lawrence Firethorn and Edmund Hoode were putting on their costumes in the tiring-house at The Rose. In view of the circumstances, Hoode had insisted that the privilege of performance at a proper theatre should go to *The Misfortunes of Marriage.* It would act as a fitting epitaph to the rumbustious talent of Jonas Applegarth and meet the upsurge of interest in the play which the murder of its author had created. The Bankside playhouse was packed to capacity for the occasion. Hoode was the first to concede that *The Faithful Shepherd* would not have provoked the same curiosity.

Barnaby Gill bounced across to them in a teasing mood.

'Is all well between you now?' he asked.

'Why should it not be?' said Firethorn.

'Rumours, Lawrence. Scandalous rumours.'

'Ignore them.'

'They are far too delicious for that.'

'Edmund and I are the best of friends,' said Firethorn with an arm around Hoode's shoulder. 'We have too much in common to fall out.'

'Too much indeed. Including your dear wife, Margery.'

'That is slander, sir!'

'A hideous misunderstanding,' said Hoode.

'They speak otherwise at the Unicorn,' prodded Gill. 'There they talk of the bigamous Margery Firethorn. One woman with two husbands. So much for the misfortunes of marriage! I give thanks that I never dwindled into matrimony.'

'It is only because the Chapel Children rejected your proposal,' rejoined Firethorn. 'You'd be bigamously married to every boy's bum in the choir if you could!'

Gill flew into a rage and Firethorn threw fresh taunts at him. Hoode found himself back in his customary role as the peacemaker between the two. He was home again.

Nicholas Bracewell gave the warning and the company readied themselves for the start of the performance. Its actor-manager had a last whispered exchange with Hoode.

'Turn to me when you are next in that predicament.'

'To you, Lawrence?'

'I have a remedy even better than Margery's.'

'And what is that?'

'Why, man, to take a woman off your hands and into mine. If this Cecily Gilbourne was too hot for your unskilled fingers to hold, you should have given her to me. My palms are proof against the fires of Hell.'

'Margery's was the eftest way.'

'I would have been a sprightly unicorn to the lady.'

'Then why did she not choose you in the first place?' said Hoode. 'No, Lawrence. The matter is ended and my debt is paid off to you both.'

'What debt?'

'I inadvertently disturbed *your* nuptial pleasure. By way of reprisal, Margery pulled me from the delights of the bedchamber. An eye for an eye.'

'A testicle for a testicle!'

Firethorn's chortle was masked by the sound of the music as Peter Digby and the consort brought the play to life once more. Westfield's Men soared to the occasion.

*The Misfortunes of Marriage* blossomed at The Rose. Its plot was firmer, its characters enriched and its satire more biting and hilarious. The company took full advantage of the superior facilities at the theatre to make their play a more exciting experience. Many dazzling new effects were incorporated by Nicholas Bracewell into the action, including one he had borrowed from Raphael Parsons and adapted for their own purposes. Trapdoors allowed sudden appearances. Flying equipment permitted the dramatic descent of actors and scenic devices. With the book holder in control behind the scenes, the pace of the play never faltered and its thrusts never missed their targets.

The acclaim which greeted the cast as they were led out to take their bow by Firethorn was so loud and so sustained that they could have played the final scene through again before its last echoes died. When the actors plunged back into the tiring-house, they were inebriated with their success. Barnaby Gill was dancing, Richard Honeydew was singing, Edmund Hoode was quoting his favourite speech from the play and John Tallis was croaking happily. Firethorn himself went around hugging each member of the troupe in tearful gratitude.

Even James Ingram was infected by the mood of celebration. He confided his feelings to the book holder.

'It is a better play than I gave it credit, Nick.'

'The play is unchanged,' said Nicholas. 'What has altered is your perception of it.'

'True. It is so much easier to appreciate when its author is not here to obstruct my view of its virtues.'

'Jonas *was* here this afternoon.'

'In spirit, if not in body.'

'That was his voice I heard out there on the stage. Even your mimicry could not reproduce that sound. It was a distinctive voice, James. Too harsh for some, maybe. You have been among them. But impossible to ignore.'

'Westfield's Men have done him proud.'

'No playwright could ask for more,' said Hoode, joining them as he pulled off his costume. 'Jonas Applegarth was a true poet. He died for his art. It is a tragedy that we only have this one play of his to act as his headstone.'

'We may yet have a second,' suggested Nicholas.

'Has he bequeathed us another?'

'No, Edmund. But you could provide it.'

'I could never write with that surging brilliance. Only Jonas could pen a Jonas Applegarth play.'

'Work with him as your co-author.'

'How can he, Nick?' said Ingram. 'Jonas is dead.'

'Yes,' added Hoode with a touch of envy. 'He outshines me there as well. Not only did he live with more of a flourish, he died in a way that made all London sit up and say his name. Edmund Hoode will just fade away, unsung, in some mean lodging. That is what I admire most about Jonas Applegarth. His own life was his most vivid and unforgettable drama.'

'Then there is your theme,' urged Nicholas.

'Theme?'

'Put him back up on the stage in full view.'

'Jonas?'

'Why not?' said Ingram, warming to the idea. 'Change his name, if you wish. But retain his character. Keep that humour. Keep that wit. Keep that belligerence. If ever a man belonged on the boards with a mouth-filling oath, it is Jonas Applegarth.'

'His death will certainly give me my final scene.'

'The play foments in your mind already, Edmund,' said Nicholas with a smile. 'Write it as an act of appreciation. Let him know that Westfield's Men cherish his memory. We loved him but did not have time to tell him so before he left us.'

* * *

It took Anne Hendrik a long time to make a comparatively short journey. The audience at The Rose was too large and too inclined to linger for her to make a swift exit from the theatre. She and Preben van Loew were forced to wait until the earnest discussions of the play gradually subsided and the press of bodies thinned out. The Dutchman escorted her home before going on to his own house in Bankside.

There was no hurry. Nicholas would be delayed even longer than she had been. First of the company to arrive, he would be the last to leave, having supervised the removal of their scenery and costumes, the cleaning of the tiring-house and the collection of the money from the gatherers. There would be a dozen other chores before he could begin to think of slipping away.

When Anne caught herself calculating the earliest possible time of his arrival, she tried to pull herself together and put him from her mind. There was no guarantee that Nicholas would come. When Westfield's Men had last played at The Rose, she had no visit from its book holder afterwards. Why should this time be different? They had no obligations towards each other. Ambrose Robinson may have eased them back together but his arrest would just as effectively push them apart. She soon persuaded herself that Nicholas would be too busy carousing with his fellows to remember her invitation. She sank into a chair with resignation.

It was an hour before she got out of it. The tap on the door made her leap up and rush to answer it, waving away the servant who came out from the kitchen. Adjusting her dress and modifying her broad grin to a smile, she opened the door to find Nicholas standing there. She dismissed his apology for being so late and took him into the parlour.

'Did you enjoy the play?' he asked.

'As much as anything I have seen in years.'

'It is a remarkable piece of theatre.'

'A little too remarkable for Preben, I fear.'

'Oh?'

'He laughed at its jests but shied at its irreverence.'

'It is strong meat for a timid palate.'

They talked at length about the play until they felt sufficiently relaxed with each other to move away from it. Nicholas had some news for her.

'I spoke with Master Firethorn today,' he said, 'and put the name of Philip Robinson in his ear.'

'Why?'

'We need a new apprentice.'

'And you would consider Philip?'

'He recommends himself.'

'He may,' she said cautiously, 'but his situation does not. Did you tell Master Firethorn the full facts?'

'Each and every one.'

'The boy carries a stigma. Did he not baulk at that?'

'The only stigma that Lawrence Firethorn recognises is bad acting. Show him a willing lad with a wealth of talent and he'll take him into Westfield's Men, though his mother be a witch and his father have cloven hooves and a tail.'

'Then Philip is apprenticed?'

'If the Chapel Royal agree to release him.'

'They'll embrace the opportunity, Nick. Thank you!'

'For what?'

'Your kindness and consideration.'

'Philip will be an asset to us. I am only being kind and considerate to Westfield's Men, believe me.'

'I fretted over him,' she said. 'My mind is put at rest by this news. It is a relief to know that some good has come out of all of this upset. I am still wracked with guilt about it.'

'Why?'

'I caused you so much unnecessary trouble. But for me, you would never have met Ambrose Robinson.'

'But for him, I might never have met Anne Hendrik again.'

He grinned at her. 'I call that a fair exchange.'

'Then I am content.'

They fell silent. Nicholas feasted his eyes on her and basked in the luxury of her company. He had not been able to enjoy it to the full before. The obstacles between them had now vanished and he could appraise her properly for the first time. Anne wallowed in his curiosity before being prompted by her own.

'Do you live alone?' she said.

'No. The house is full of people.'

'I was talking about your room,' she said, probing quietly. 'I wondered if you . . . shared it with anybody.'

'I am never there long enough to notice.'

'Still married to Westfield's Men?'

'With all its misfortunes.' They laughed together. 'But what of you, Anne? Alone here still?'

'Not for much longer.'

'Why?'

'That passage with Ambrose taught me much. I felt the lack of a man around the house. I will take another lodger.'

'I see,' he said with obvious disappointment.

'I do it for my own protection, Nick,' she argued. 'He would not need to be here night and day. His scent would be enough. It would keep danger away.'

'What sort of lodger would you seek?'

'One that suited me.'

'In what way?'

Her eyes searched his. Nicholas was the first to smile.

'Where do you live?' she asked, moving closer.

'In Thames Street.'

'How much do you pay your landlord?'

'Too much.'

He took her in his arms for a long and loving kiss.

'I am thinking of moving,' he said.